JIM MORGAN

and

THE KING
OF THIEVES

BY

JAMES MATLACK RANEY

ISBN: 0985835907
ISBN 13: 9780985835903

Contents

Beware all ye who enter here, Dangerous magic lies within...

JIM MORGAN

and

THE KING OF THIEVES

ONE

JAMES FRANCIS MORGAN

Once there lived a boy named James Francis Morgan who was born in a mansion (that was in truth very nearly a castle) on the southern coast of England not far from the town of Rye. Now these were the days when explorers and naval officers, and even pirates who sailed the high seas, were the greatest of all heroes, especially to young boys like James, whose father, the Lord Lindsay Morgan, happened to be one of the most famous of all of the captains in His Majesty's navy. So famous was he that it was even rumored the King of England was a personal friend.

Now, when he was very young, James was a wild sort of boy who used to run down to the beach with his little wooden boat and a little wooden sword and wage imaginary battles with pirates and scalawags so epic that they could only exist in a young boy's mind. All day long he ran up and down the dunes in his bare feet until the salty smell of the sea dwelt in his skin and the ocean wind lived in every curl of hair on his head.

When Jim was still too young to fully remember those spectacular adventures, his father left to sail the seas on a mysterious voyage. Though far-fetched rumors swirled about all of England, no one knew quite where the valiant captain sailed or why. Lord Morgan said he would return in five years – no more and no less. During this time he left young James in the care his Great Aunt, Margarita Morgan - or as she insisted on being called, Dame Margarita Morgan.

Now Dame Morgan, who was as round and pale as the full moon itself and wore an enormous wig with platinum blonde curls to cover her gray, hated the ocean and anything to do with it. The day James's father left on his long voyage, Dame Margarita forbade James to continue his wild behavior and kept him bottled up in the house instead. She replaced his wooden ships with Latin lessons, his wooden swords with harpsichord practice, and his bare feet and wild hair with the best-dressed fashions for growing lords from the finest tailors in Paris, France. She never let him out to play with boys his own age, but kept him up all hours eating chocolates with her and listening to the latest gossip from London, teaching him who was worth talking to and who was not.

In short, she fashioned him into a little version of herself ... which happened to be a spoiled and rotten brat.

"Keep up, will you?" James Morgan snapped at the string of servants following him down the hill to the Morgan Manor Stables. "It simply won't do to have me looking tousle-haired, malnourished, and dressed in the dilapidated rags of a pauper when my father arrives, will it?"

"Of course not, Master James," replied Molly the housemaid breathlessly, nearly tumbling down the hill as she attempted to walk and brush James's curls simultaneously.

"Almost finished, sire," mumbled Melvin the tailor, needles clasped in his pursed lips and scurrying on all fours like an overly-plump squirrel, desperately adjusting the tails on James's new riding coat as he went.

This of course left poor George, the cook (the last of the original house cooks still on staff – the other four having been sacked by James and Aunt Margarita for one offense or another) who deigned not to answer – or even to breathe really – as he precariously spooned custard into James's mouth without spilling a drop on the young master's new riding jacket.

James often marched about the manor grounds with just such an entourage in tow from morning till night. However this morning was a special morning – the morning when the Lord Morgan himself was set to arrive home from his long journey across the sea – and James had something special planned for the occasion.

The moment he reached the stable doors, James's need for his train evaporated and he smacked Molly's brush-wielding hand aside, snatched his hat from Melvin - fitting it dashingly upon his head, and knocked the last spoonful of George's custard away from his mouth.

"That will be all," James sighed, as though such a walk had been exhausting for an eleven year-old boy. "You three may go back to help the others prepare for my father's return party – except for you." James turned and narrowed his eyes on George, the custard meant for James's mouth dripping down the poor cook's face. "That custard was not nearly up to snuff – I believe I shall have you sacked. Good day." Then James turned, a rather nasty smile stretched over his face, and strode through the stable doors, leaving the dismayed George in tears and Molly and Melvin shaking their heads in consolation.

"Jeremiah, prepare Destroyer for me!" James announced as he strutted into the stables. Jeremiah was the Morgan's lanky horse master and stable caretaker, and Destroyer was James's steed. Actually, to call Destroyer a steed was perhaps a bit of stretch. In fact, to even call her a horse was bending the truth. Destroyer was a pony who was even a bit small as far as ponies go and was the most docile creature in the stables, preferring a good nibble of oats and a roll in the grass over any raiding or galloping. But from the time that Aunt Margarita had let him have the pony James had called her Destroyer, his war charger, and envisioned himself riding into glorious battle on her back.

"Sorry, Master James," Jeremiah said, ambling out of one of the stalls. "But the horses are to be kep' 'n the stable this afternoon for the welcomin' and all. Phineus's orders."

"Well, Phineus isn't the Lord Morgan, is he?" said James, putting his hands on his hips.

"Beggin' the young master's pard'n," replied Jeremiah with a smile. "But you're not the Lord Morgan either. He's set to arrive in just short order, which is why, once more beggin' the young master's pard'n, the horses are to be left 'n the stables."

Now James was feeling very put off, but he knew there would be no point arguing directly with Jeremiah. Horses were horses no matter who sat on their backs, and Jeremiah knew more about horses than anyone in coastal England, which made his job sack-proof, even from Aunt Margarita. "Well, we'll just see about that won't we?" James stomped his foot and stormed back to the stable doorway.

"Phineus!" James shouted at the top of his lungs toward the house. "Phineus! Phineus! Phineus!" He stomped a foot on each repetition of the old tutor's name until he was red in the face and the poor old man finally hobbled out of the house and slowly made his way down to the stables.

Phineus was the bushy-browed Morgan family tutor, and had been for three generations. While none of the Morgan children could ever have been accused of being angels, it was whispered among the house staff that only James had pushed the poor old man so close to the brink of senility (a fact of which James was obscenely proud.)

"What is it, Master James?" The old teacher sighed. "Your father is almost here; you've ignored your lessons for the day, per usual, frightened poor Yves half to death - he's still trying to wash the stains out of his clothes by the way - and apparently had another chef sacked.

What more inspirational deeds of chivalry could you possibly wish to accomplish today?"

"I want to be sitting atop Destroyer when Father arrives. I'll be taller than everyone else and he'll see what kind of man I've become in his absence."

James heard a choking sound that was a little too akin to laughter behind him and he shot a glare over his shoulder at Jeremiah, who hid his face behind a horse's rear end and kept right on brushing.

"Destroyer? Your pony?" Phineus screwed up his face.

"I've told you not to call her that! She's a charger!"

"But Master James, we've already worked out where everyone will be standing and it's all been arranged -"

"Well then rearrange it, Master Tooter!"

"Master James, I don't think -"

"And you should keep right on not thinking and GET – MY - HORSE!" James stomped his feet again. "Or I'll call for Auntie Margarita ... and where do you think that will get you, Master Tooter?"

A resigned sigh wheezed through Phineus's wrinkled lips. He shook his gray head and called toward the barn: "Jeremiah, get the bloody pony."

"SHE'S A CHARGER!"

After a few moments James found his pony saddled and ready for him outside the stable doors. He rubbed his hands together in anticipation and leapt into the saddle – only to find himself eye to eye with Phineus and Jeremiah, who once again fell into a sudden fit of coughs into his hands.

"I recall myself being a bit taller ..." James said to himself, looking back and forth between Phineus and Jeremiah.

"You are taller, Master James," Phineus said with a groan, cracking his back as though he hadn't sat down in ages.

"Oh, this won't do at all!" James raged and slapped his thigh in frustration. "I don't want to be *as* tall as everyone else, I need to be tall*er*! Jeremiah! Bring me Thunderbold!"

Jeremiah stopped coughing into his hand immediately and his natural smile fell into a dark frown. "Now sir," he said with a firm shake of his head, "there're funny ideas and then there're just plain stupid'ns, and that's a stupid'n! Whether you're on your pony or on the ground, I'm sure your father'll be pleased to see you. But if he rides up to find you 'n a casket, I'll be quick 'n joinin' you 'n one beside it."

"Are you saying I'm stupid?" James demanded.

"No, I'm sayin' your idea is stupid," Jeremiah said matter-of-factly.

James felt his face grow hotter by the moment. But he knew he would get nowhere with Jeremiah. Instead, he turned his eyes on Phineus. "Phineus … make Jeremiah get me Thunderbold!"

"Phineus," Jeremiah said with a warning in his voice, "Thunderbold really is a charger. I c'n barely hold her to the reins meself. That's a bad accident waitin' to happen!"

Phineus held his head as though it was about to explode, his old hands trembling almost violently. "Master James, you heard what Jeremiah just said. This is a bad accident–" Phineus halted in mid-sentence and stared out into nowhere for a long moment. Then a little shaky smile quivered onto his wrinkly face. "Jeremiah," he said, his voice noticeably more warbly. "Get Thunderbold."

TWO

THUNDERBOLD

P hineus, did you hear what I just said?" Jeremiah asked.

"Oh, yes, Jeremiah! I most certainly did!" Phineus's eyes were opened as wide as they could go and his little grin had grown into a full-fledged, crooked smile.

"Glad to see you have finally come to your senses, old man," James said and swung himself off Destroyer.

"Be it on your head!" Jeremiah growled angrily and stormed into the stables, shaking his head furiously.

Now James could hardly contain his excitement as Jeremiah led the enormous steed out of the stable. If this didn't get his father's attention, nothing would.

Thunderbold was James's father's old war-horse that he rode to all of the most formal military events. She had belonged to an army major

7

who had given her to Lord Lindsay as a gift and Jeremiah had always said that she had never lost the thirst for the thrill of battle. The bottom of her blood-red flanks stood taller than James's head, and her snorts and the sharp stomps of her feet rumbled deep and fierce.

"I need some help up!" James demanded, snatching a riding whip off the stable wall. Phineus rushed to James's side, waving Jeremiah over.

"Oh, yes!" Phineus said, and James thought the old man sounded more gleeful than he had ever been in his entire life. "Come on Jeremiah, don't be a prune, help me lift the boy up onto his steed!" Phineus actually giggled and Jeremiah begrudgingly helped James onto the huge horse.

As soon as James was in the saddle he knew this is what he needed. He was hands taller than Jeremiah and Phineus (who was looking oddly deranged at the moment) and felt like he could see for miles from atop Thunderbold. James puffed his chest out and tried to fix his face into the hard, chiseled look of a lord.

"I shall ride about the grounds, gentlemen, until my father arrives." Then James raised the riding whip high above his head, ready to lash Thunderbold's side as he always had to do with lazy Destroyer.

"No!" Jeremiah shouted, seeing what was about to happen, but it was too late. James cracked the whip into Thunderbold's flank as hard as he could. And Thunderbold didn't like that, not one bit.

The mighty war-horse reared up on her powerful hind legs, neighing with the force of a storm's gale. Jeremiah's eyes flew wide and Phineus snapped out of the sleepwalking madness that had temporarily possessed him as Thunderbold's sanguine forelegs churned in the air and James cried out with a shriek that would have done an Irish banshee proud.

"Thunderbold, no!" Jeremiah cried, but it was too late. It seemed the horse felt it had been insulted by an inferior and was not going to stand for the cheek. Thunderbold bucked and kicked as James howled like a siren atop her back. Jeremiah leapt over the fence into the riding circle and landed face-first in a pile of mud and horse mess while

Phineus reeled backward from the thrashing mare until he fell into a water-filled trough. James though, however terrified and shrill he was at that very moment, did somehow manage to hang on to the wild charger (a fact he would later recall with a bit of pride, mostly to make up for the distinctly unpleasant memories of his girlish screams.)

Thunderbold stopped bucking after a particularly marvelous spin maneuver and, seemingly realizing that her rider had yet to surrender, decided to give him the ride of his life. She tore off toward the house with pounding hooves like rapid-fire cannon shots while James harmonized to the staccato beat with his most elegant falsetto scream.

The next five minutes were something of a blur to James, though he had a reoccurring nightmare about the incident, which seem to put the one-horse stampede in the following order:

First, Thunderbold blasted over the hill between the stables and the gardens. James didn't recall too many specifics, but he was positive that he heard Yves the gardener scream about ten really awful curse words in one breath so they came out sounding a bit like a startled, foul-mouthed goose. The horrified gardener dove aside in his freshly pressed party clothes into a pile of fresh mulch as Thunderbold tore past him, tromping over his just-watered rose bush and daffodil presentation, leaving only churned dirt like a tilled field in her wake.

Second, Thunderbold careened around the corner of the manor toward the front entrance where Dame Morgan herself was making her way out to check on the progress of the decorations. Upon seeing James hurtling toward her on Thunderbold like a terrified, weeping centaur, her face screwed into a squished-up cross between a mad bull and a pufferfish. James thought she didn't so much dive out of the way as fall over to the side, rolling and bouncing down the grassy hill in her new party dress.

That was when James and his steed – or, rather, Thunderbold and her tagalong - came to the decorations for the homecoming. The massive banner that read "Welcome Home Lord Morgan" was stretched between two tall poles and the tables on the lawn were covered in the best linens and the servants were busy topping them with trays of delicious hors d'oeuvres. The galloping duo quickly blasted through and, in the aftermath, the banner was wrapped around the servants who were topped in the food beside the overturned tables that covered the grass-stained linens.

Finally, Thunderbold tore away from the house toward the thick forest that surrounded the manor grounds. Jeremiah had always told James the most frightening ghost stories of wicked nymphs, wild dryads, and magical gypsies that made the forest their home. As James barreled toward the tree line he imagined that if the large tree branches he was about to smash into didn't kill him, the ghosts and goblins would probably finish the job. James gripped his legs to Thunderbold's flanks, squeezed the reins in his hands, shut his eyes tight, and waited for his short life to flash before his eyes, as he had heard it would.

Then, just before the moment of impact, a commanding voice called out from James's left - deep and forceful. James wouldn't even describe it as a loud voice necessarily, though he heard it distinctly above the thundering hooves. But it was a heavy voice, as though the words it spoke could push one down or lift one up all by themselves. "Whoa, Thunderbold, hold, hold!" the voice called.

James felt a hand grip the reins over his small fist. The hand gripped tight, so tight that James bit his upper lip quite hard and his nose stung and tears leaked onto his cheeks. The strong hand must have belonged to a powerful man James knew, for it pulled back hard on the reins and Thunderbold obeyed. The ballistic mare snorted and neighed and came to a subdued trot.

"Easy girl, easy," said the voice.

James's wild ride slowed to a complete stop. The sound of pounding hooves against the ground quieted, but a steady thumping still thudded in James's ears. It was the beat of his slamming heart. James peeked open one bleary eye. The dark, twisted trunks of the forest at the edge of the grounds stood not one horse-length before him, and beyond the tree line lay only shadow and silence. The big hand still held tight over James's own, gripping the reins firmly. James followed the hand to the arm it belonged to, up to the shoulder, and then to the face of the man who had saved his life.

The man sat on a horse as black as coal and wore a gray great cloak and a simple, dark blue waistcoat and breeches beneath it. A plain, tricorn hat that had seen a great deal too much sun and rain in its life sat atop his head. Salt and pepper stubble framed the man's sun-darkened, steady jaw. He wore no powdered wig of a gentleman but let his dark hair hang in a ponytail over his collar. Not one mark of a socially acceptable nobleman could be found on the man's entire person James noted, save for flashing blue eyes that gleamed in the light. But James knew this man was noble indeed. This was the Lord Lindsay Morgan. This was his father.

"F – f – father," James breathed, his head growing light and his cheeks flushing pink.

Lord Lindsay looked James up and down. Neither a smile nor a frown belied his thought, But the Lord Morgan's fierce eyes bored into James's face so intently that James was forced to look away.

"It ... it was this stupid horse," James stammered, realizing he was not making the impression he had originally sought. "I'm a brilliant rider, I am, really!" James felt his cheeks go hot and sudden fury at the dumb beast beneath him raged inside him. "It was this stupid horse's fault!" James cried and raised the whip to take out his anger on Thunderbold.

But his father's strong hand again caught James's and he wrenched the whip roughly from his son's grasp. "That is enough of that," Lord Morgan said, a hard edge on his tone. He took the whip in both hands and with one swift jerk snapped it in two. "I never begrudge a man for his mistakes, son, only his excuses." Lord Morgan turned from James and tugged on the reins. Father and son rode together back down to the tattered welcome party in awful silence.

The ride back was a solemn and unbearable one for James, whose heart still slammed and tears still threatened. He only glanced twice over at the Lord Morgan. The first time, his father was still as grim faced as he had been just after saving James's life. But the second time, as the pair crested the hill that ran down from the forest to the manor and the destruction once meant to be Lord Morgan's party came into view, a small smile crossed Lord Morgan's serious face. Another man, dressed very much like Lord Morgan, though twice as rough and weathered, waited for them on his large steed, looking out over the catastrophe below.

"Looks like the party already started, milord," the other man said in an unmistakable Highland burr.

"It would seem so, Hudson," James's father said.

"'Minds me a bit o' the party the former mayor of Shelltown threw for you years back, jus' wit'out the harpies," the man named Hudson said with a laugh.

Almost by instinct James nearly told the man, who was without doubt a commoner, to mind who he joked about and with whom and to demand exactly what he meant by harpies (obviously not real harpies, James knew), but he was interrupted by a most surprising and jolly outburst. James's father tried to cough to control his laughter, but it seemed he found himself unable and he and the man Hudson laughed themselves all the way down the hill, without even bothering to include James in on what was so funny.

How rude, James thought.

The flummoxed, flustered, and humiliated servants did their best to hold their heads up as their lord approached the debacle that was to be his party, but to James's continued confusion Lord Morgan appeared not only undisturbed by the destruction around him, but he actually looked each of his servants in the eye with thanks and remembered their names, greeting them as old friends.

"Hello, Molly, how's Wilifred? Still arthritic? Too bad, I'll send the surgeon on Tuesday." Molly grabbed Lord Lindsay's hand and began to cry and James nearly fell off his horse when his father actually shook it back. "Where on earth is Mildred, Molly?" James's father asked, but Molly's face pinked around the cheeks and she just shook her head. James swore he thought he saw her flick her eyes in his direction. The nerve! As though that woman's sacking had been anything but her own fault!

"Greetings, Tom! And how is England's deftest sword master? Why on earth are you limping, Tom?"

Tom looked down at his foot and tried to smile it off, but the slightest glance in James's direction gave the answer away. "I see," said Lord Morgan. James reminded himself to stab the old git in the other foot on their next lesson.

"Hello, Yves. Good lord, man, what on earth is all over you? Taking a more natural approach to gardening these days? Ah, of course." James saw his father nod again after a sly look from that traitorous Yves.

"Phineus, Jeremiah — well, in God's name gentlemen, what happened? Or need I ask?" James felt a small stab in his heart when his father added the last part wryly, but that brief embarrassment faded away into cold hate as the two wretched servants betrayed him again to his father.

"And where is George, the cook? He always made the best custard, and I've been looking forward to — ah, of course." James's chin sunk a little lower and he tried to hide his reddened face beneath his hat, all the while plotting revenge on these dreadful, common traitors who were painting him out to be the villain – him, indeed!

But then, finally, Aunt Margarita strutted up, or as much as one could hope to strut when wearing a tattered gown splotched in green grass stains from top to bottom. But, fortunately for Margarita, she was a practiced snoot and still managed to keep her nose in the air in spite of the current predicament. James admired her sense of place, but he saw the smile on his father's face fade immediately upon seeing her.

"Margarita," he said, noticeably leaving off the "Dame."

"Greetings, Lindsay," Margarita managed, her face growing suddenly a purplish shade of crimson. "We are grateful beyond measure for your safe return. We had planned a party for you–"

"No matter," Lord Morgan cut her off. "I too am grateful, Margarita." James's father's voice was deep and cheerless. "For the care and ... culture you have given my son."

13

Margarita said nothing, but her eyes narrowed and a crimson flush in her cheeks darkened with hateful rage. But Lord Lindsay Morgan had already turned his back on her to address the house staff once more.

"It's good to be home. Take your time with the decorations ..."

Even some of the servants laughed at this. Who did they think they were all of the sudden, James wondered crossly to himself.

"Jeremiah and Phineus, please help Hudson with the horses. I need to have a word with my son."

James felt a huge dose of dread like the first drop of a terrible rainstorm splash over his soul. He refused to look at anyone as he slunk off Thunderbold and followed his father's footsteps down the trail toward the beach not far from their home.

THREE

LORD LINDSAY MORGAN

It was an awful walk for James as he followed his father down the grassy hill and onto the beach. James saw his small footprints beside his father's large ones in the sand as they came to a stop not far from where the ocean waves lapped against the shore. They stood there quietly for what seemed like an eternity to James. The sound of the small waves in the distance began to feel like a slowly ticking clock inside James's anxious mind as he waited for the forthcoming tongue-lashing.

"I've been away for so long," James's father finally said and James about jumped out of his skin when he heard it. But his father's hands were clasped behind his back, his face pointed toward the dusky horizon, out over the ocean that went on forever. His words were soft and quiet. "I sometimes think I should not have left you."

"You were doing your duty weren't you, father?" James said, trying hard to sound like an adult and hide the shaking fear he felt inside. "I'm sure you had no choice."

James's father laughed bitterly and the sound of it scared James more than a little. "No choice ... no choice," he said again, still looking nowhere but the ocean. "There's always a choice. Only cowards say there's no choice. Perhaps that's what I've been all along ..."

"Don't say that father!" James chided a little too forcefully. "You're a hero. Everyone says so! Why just last week one of Dame Margarita's friends was saying–"

"Quiet James, and speak not of that which you do not understand!" his father suddenly barked, and so forcefully that James sucked in a quick breath and shut his mouth with a clap of his teeth. "And believe me when I tell you there is much you do not understand."

Still James's father would not look at him, but he now took one hand and began playing with a necklace that hung just over the collar of his shirt. It was a metal seashell, and Lord Morgan held it as delicately as a freshly plucked flower in his rough fingers.

"I have thought so many nights of how difficult it has been, these last few years, for me ... and for you. There's so much, so much you don't know about yourself and why I left and where I went ..."

"Were you killing pirates father? Dame Margarita said you must have gathered the most amazing hordes of–"

"Can you not keep silent and listen even for five minutes, boy?" lord Lindsay shouted again. James once more shut his mouth, but a hot, prickling bristle of anger bloomed in his chest this time.

"As I said," James's father continued. "There is much you do not understand about our family, my son, or about the world in which we live. There are dangers out there, James, and wonders, monsters and beauties, pirates and heroes, even magic, and treasures beyond your wildest dreams ..."

"Treasures?" James asked quickly, shutting his mouth again the moment the words left his tongue.

"Yes, treasures." His father did not reprimand him this time, and James breathed a sigh of relief, thinking about all the glittering piles of treasure his father must have seen and collected over the years. "And you might think that I would say that those aren't what's the most important of all those marvels in the world, that it is duty and honor and all of that that drives us, but there you would be wrong. It is the treasures, James. For where your treasure is, there will your heart be also. Remember that always, James, for it is as true as any truth in the universe."

"Of course father, I'll remember." James was about to explain just how excellent his memory was and how he could remember every bit of gossip about every person Margarita ever talked about, but his father, who had just scolded him for interrupting, cut him off! James again felt the bristle of anger rub his insides.

"Before I speak of where I've been these last five years, tell me something, James." And finally James's father looked at him, blue eyes tunneling deep into James's face. "Do you still come down to the beach every day and play with your boats and your swords and fight your imaginary battles? Do you still run up and down on the dunes and flap your arms like a gull and splash into the water without a care for what waits for you in the waves?" The question seemed deeply important to Lord Morgan, as though the outcome of a great battle pended on the answer. But James knew his father would be impressed with him now.

"Oh, heavens no, father!" James tried to laugh like a grownup. "You'll be so pleased with how much I've grown up since you've been gone. Dame Margarita has taught me well and I don't waste my time with such childish pursuits any longer." James smiled brightly, but just when he thought his father would smile in return, finally proud of how his son had come along, his father's face dropped like a falling star and his eyes grew distant and cold as though James had stabbed him in the stomach with a knife of ice.

"I see," James' father said, tucking the necklace back under his shirt and clasping his hands again behind his back.

17

After a long moment of silence, Lord Morgan turned his head back toward the ocean and the two of them stood there in uncomfortable silence again for what seemed to James like another bit of forever. His father's disappointment and constant yelling had put James in a sour mood indeed, and just when he thought things couldn't get worse, they did.

"I want you to go to your room until dark."

"You want me to do what?" Now James was truly taken aback. "No one's sent me to my room in four years! I do what I want. I'm practically an adult!"

"Well, my son," Lord Lindsay growled, "things change. You will go to your room and think about the havoc you wreaked today and the trouble you put the staff through. After that, I will tell you of my travels."

"Trouble?" James scoffed, too angry to think about the words spilling from his angry mouth. "Father, it's no trouble for servants to clean up our messes ... that's why they're called servants!"

Lord Lindsay's hand crossed James' cheek with enough sting to shoot a sharp pinch into his nose and tears into his eyes. James gasped and looked with shock into his father's cold, blue eyes. "You will stay in your room until 8 o'clock when you will come to my study. You have much to learn, boy."

"How - how dare you strike me!" James's voice was not quite as defiant as his words. His lips and his chin quivered. "Dame Margarita never—"

"Dame Margarita no longer presides over this house," James's father said. "I do. She will be gone by morning. I never should have left you in her care. I have much to undo and little time in which to undo it. Now get up to your room. And do it without the cheek this time, if you please."

James was too stunned to argue. He turned in a daze and trudged back to the house, only looking back once, when he was up the hill and nearly to the door. His father still stood like a statue facing the darkening horizon, toward the edge of world where the ocean met the sky.

FOUR

A Conversation in the Kitchen

James stormed into his room and slammed his door behind him. He'd whined and whimpered to himself for most of the way up the stairs and down the hall, but the farther he'd gone the less scared and shocked and the more furious and enraged he had become. Who did this man think he was? James fumed to himself. No father should treat a son that way. James was, after all, the future Lord Morgan. To be treated in this manner was an outrage.

James made sure to stomp as loud as he could as he paced his room in anger. He kicked every piece of furniture (except his mirror, of course; he was angry, but there were limits to a gentleman's wrath, after all) and threw all of his clothes (sparing the good ones) all about the floor.

But after some time (for no one came to rescue him from his rage, as they always used to do when Aunt Margarita was running the show) James realized that all of his fuming had made him hungry, and he further realized that his father had made no provision for his supper. The inhumanity of it all! There should be an inquisition, James raged inside his head. This was downright abusive! But there was no hope of something like that at this hour and James decided to take matters into his own hands, as any clear-thinking, future Lord Morgan would. No one told James Francis Morgan how to live his life.

Mustering up a snide grin he snuck out of his room and down to the kitchen, where he quietly tiptoed into the pantry and began helping himself to Aunt Margarita's chocolates. She always shared them with him anyway, he told himself, so it wasn't like he was stealing. James was a noble for heaven's sake and he would never, ever, ever sink so low as to become a thief. He would rather starve!

James was deep into his second handful of chocolate-covered cherry candies when a door slammed and raised voices barged into the kitchen accompanied by heavy footsteps. James nearly choked on his cordial syrup and froze like a statue in the pantry. Luckily for him, though, the door to the pantry remained closed and no one caught him red (or sticky) handed.

"This, this is an outrage!" The unmistakably manly voice of Dame Margarita shook shrilly with anger just beyond the pantry door. James inched closer to get a better listen.

"Your journeys across the sea have turned you into a paranoid mess, Lindsay! Who has fabricated these lies about me?"

"They aren't lies, Rita."

"DON'T CALL ME RITA!"

James imagined Aunt Margarita's bulging eyes and reddening face as she screamed and raged.

"It's DAME Margarita, now."

Now James smiled a chocolaty and syrupy smile as he imagined Aunt Margarita setting his bully father straight. But his smile lasted only as long as that one sentence.

"Oh, shut up, Rita," James's father said, dismissing her as though she were a common maid. "You're no more a dame than that old weasel you've been meeting in secret is a count."

"Lies, Lindsay, all lies!" Margarita insisted, but she didn't sound quite as authoritative as James was used to.

"They aren't lies! You've been meeting with Cromier every morning for months now. He's a scoundrel and a bully and as dirty and slimy as a worm in the mud."

"*Count* Cromier is an old friend of this family, Lindsay! He was your friend once, if you don't recall! He is a great man with great ideas, and his son Bartholomew is now a captain in his majesty's navy. You may not think it, but he will be a man of great power one day, Lindsay. It is not wise to stand in the way of such men."

"I have stood in the way of such men my whole life. And he has not been my friend ever, Rita. And neither, it seems, have you."

"Well," Aunt Margarita sucked up the word as though she were about to huff and puff and blow Lord Lindsay's house down. "If it is rumors that we shall believe, perhaps I'll fancy a few of the darker about you, Lindsay Morgan!" James could practically see his Aunt's rather plump finger pointing right into his father's face and his ears perked up a bit. Dame Margarita had mentioned several juicy bits of gossip concerning his father's mysterious journey – but none of them had been called dark.

"Most of the nobles believe you sailed once more for the crown, Lindsay," Margarita continued. "As I'm sure you would have them believe. But one evening, after a bit much champagne, Lord Carlisle let slip that you resigned your commission to the king five years ago! Some say that you went in search of your old enemy, the pirate king, Dread Steele. Some say that you even became a pirate yourself! But the most wild rumor, the most vile of them all, Lindsay, was that you were hording a secret treasure, one more valuable than all your others. A treasure to rival that of the King's entire kingdom!"

If James's ears perked up before, now they simply trembled on the side of his head for more. A treasure to rival the very crown of

England? James pictured the mounds and piles of gold and silver, his mouth watering. He could buy anything in the world with a treasure like that.

"But the real question, Lindsay," Aunt Margarita raged. "Is not why you would hide such a treasure from the rest of the world, but why you would hide such a treasure from your own son? From your own flesh and blood!"

That was a good question, thought James, and anger toward his father flared up in chest once more.

"As if you care for James at all," said Lord Morgan. "Your real question is why I would keep such a treasure from you, you and *my old friend, Count Cromier*. Had you ever asked me Margarita, you could have had all the gold I own. But that was never your way, was it? Your way is to sneak and to scheme, as it has always been. And as that is the case, I will not have plotters under my roof. Take your things and leave my home immediately!"

Now James almost spat out the same cordial upon which he nearly choked a moment ago. Who did his father think he was? Lord of the manor? That was family he was tossing out like a common servant!

James heard Margarita's ominous silence in the dark of the pantry, until she finally spoke. It wasn't the same angry tone she'd used with the servants. It trembled and boiled, a bitter cruelty lurking beneath her words.

"You'll regret this, Lindsay. Mark my words. You've been an arrogant rebel your whole life and the time has come for your comeuppance! Count Cromier has told me many things you have tried to keep hidden ... dark secrets. I'll find out the truth of this treasure– I swear I will! And mark my words, you'll wish you'd never crossed me!"

"I already do, Rita," Lord Lindsay said, and if James hadn't been so furious with his father he would have heard the true sadness in his voice.

After the two had left the kitchen, James snuck back up to his room to wait until the dreaded strike of eight. The conversation in the kitchen had rattled Jim's mind to say the least. A great treasure? The

Morgans were one of the richest families in England. What could this great treasure be? Where had his father hidden it? And why? And who was this Count Cromier? Aunt Margarita had never mentioned him in her gossip. But if she said he was a great man that was word enough for James. But now his father had gone and kicked Aunt Margarita out of the house. Everything in James's world had been perfect until this day, and in merely one afternoon his long-gone father had smashed it beneath his foot.

Well, James though to himself, this just couldn't stand. At eight o'clock he was going to march down to his father's study and sort this entire mess out.

FIVE

THE STORM

A peal of thunder rumbled in the distance as the clock in James's room finally chimed eight times. James burst out of his room, boldly strutting through the manor's long hallways to his father's study, his chin and shoulders set. He had decided he wasn't going to apologize for his behavior. In fact, he had thought to himself during his afternoon long imprisonment to his room (an unjust act that he meant to remind himself about which to pen a letter to the local magistrate for an investigation) it was his father, not he, who owed the apology. James was almost glad that the weather was turning ugly outside. It would match the storm that was about rage within the house.

Oh, James had practiced his proud little speech in his room until it was perfect. In his mind he imagined growing so loud during the giving of it that nobles from all around heard and came and applauded his good sense and impeccable logic. But the closer and closer James drew to the large oak doors at the end of the hall that led to where his father waited, his strut became slightly less bold and his set chin and shoulders drooped ever so lower. James suddenly wondered how good his sense really was and how impeccable his logic. He could no longer see the lords and ladies clapping for him. His stomach churned and did a somersault. In his mind, all James could see were his father's deep and penetrating eyes staring straight into his own.

The hardwood floor creaked beneath James's feet and he shivered with a sudden chill. The house was so quiet tonight, and dark - darker and quieter than usual. James realized for the first time that besides the groaning of the floor as he walked and the gathering storm outside, there were no other sounds, and besides the light peeking out from the cracks around the study door, there was no other light in the hall. This was very odd indeed. Where were all of the servants?

When James reached the door, however, all other thoughts but the image of his father's stern eyes fled his mind.

"Just rush in and say it," he told himself, taking a deep breath and grasping the door handle. "You're not sorry, you're not. Just say it. He's the one who should be sorry." James was sweating now from nerves, but he could wait no longer. With gritted teeth he flung open the door and rushed inside.

"Father!" he cried, his voice warbling and squeaking out about four pitches higher than normal. But there was no stopping now and he pushed the words out of his mouth in a falsetto mishmash that sounded not too unlike yodeling. "I'm-not-sorry-about-anything-I-said-earlier-and-I-think-you're-dead-wrong-about-Aunt-Margarita-and-you're-holding-me-back-from-who-I-truly-am-as-a-noble-and-in-the-end-you're-the-one-who-will-be -"

Then James saw him. His father sat rigid as stone at his desk. A lone candle flickered its light over his father's sweat-glistened features. He gripped the side of his desk with one hand, and in his other he held a trembling quill. Before him on the desk rested a peculiar wooden box, and off to the corner sat a shining, silver goblet, still half full of blood-red wine. Every muscle in Lord Morgan's body strained taut against some invisible agony.

"–sorry." The final word of James's diatribe escaped as nothing but a whisper. "Father?" James stepped within an arm's reach of the frozen man.

Lindsay Morgan's eyes flicked to his son. James gasped a startled breath and his heart nearly exploded at his father's raspy, choked words.

"James." Lord Morgan forced each painful word out. "Poisoned."

"Poisoned?" James said with a gasp. His head began to spin.

Lindsay released the desk and pointed a violently quaking finger at the goblet upon the desk.

"Poison! Oh, father no!" Panic flooded James's chest and he called out for the one person he always ran to in times of trouble. "Aunt Margarita! Aunt Margarita, come quick!"

"No!" His father's face twisted into a snarl of pain and rage and his pointing hand shot out and grasped James's shoulder tightly.

"Hudson ... Hudson."

James's stomach was no longer churning: It was frozen solid, along with his throat and heart. But he did as his father said. "Hudson!" James called and ran out into the hall. "Hudson! Hudson! Hudson! Help!"

From around the corner Hudson appeared, still dressed with his cane in one hand and a rack of burning candles in the other. "Aye young master, I'm here. What do ya' want? And where are all the bloody servants?"

"Hudson ... it's Father ... he ..." James stammered, but he had no need to finish the sentence. Hudson's eyes grew wide and alert with fear and he dashed past James, down the hall and into the study.

James ran as fast as he could behind Hudson, catching up just as he came to stand at James's father's side. James's father looked Hudson in the eye. Sweat covered his whole face now and his entire body shook.

"Margarita–" he said. His voice was a terrible growl and his teeth clenched tightly. "Protect James, Hudson - the treasure!"

"I understand, milord ..." Hudson's own voice was husky and quavering. He held his master's hand and fell to one knee at his side. But Lindsay Morgan shifted his eyes over to James. Sorrow and pain filled his face. James wanted to look away - he could hardly stand the weight of his father's stare upon him - but he lacked the strength to pull his eyes from his father's face.

"My son – be – my son," Lord Morgan said. Then he spoke no more. The shaking ceased and he breathed one more breath. He slumped onto his desk and did not move again.

"Milord?" Hudson shook him once, but not again.

"Father ..." James's lips trembled. He stared wide-eyed at his father's still form until his eyes filled with water. He and Hudson remained quiet and unmoving for what seemed like hours. Only the whispering of the burning candles filled the room.

Finally, Hudson stood and removed the note, written on an old and yellowed piece of parchment, from beneath his Lord's hand. Then Hudson reverently unclasped the chain with the shell on the end from around Lord Morgan's neck. The old valet stared for a long time at the two objects now in his hands. He stared at them, and then he glanced at James – his eyes full of fear.

Hudson took the objects and carefully placed them in the small wooden box from the desk. With a shaking hand and watering eyes he closed the lid with a soft tap.

"Your father knew what was happenin' soon as he tasted the wine," Hudson said thickly. "There are things, young master, things he never told you. But he's written a letter explainin' everythin' and stamped it with your family's seal." Hudson's eyes were now red and tears wet his wrinkled cheeks. "We should go to your father's house in London now. I don't think it will be safe here for long. The King was an admirer of your father and perhaps he will give us aide."

"What's happening, Hudson?" James asked, his own hands starting to tremble.

"I donno' have time to explain it all, but in this box, young master, is the secret to a great treasure. Your father kept it safe for so long. And now, it passes to you." He held out the box with his shaking hand to James. "You are the Lord Morgan now, James."

James shook his head, tears springing from nowhere to fall hot from his eyes onto his cheeks. He had dreamed so many times of being the lord, of having everything his father had and more, but now those dreams tasted bitter and he felt like he was going to vomit them up. He never wanted to remember those dreams again. "No!" he cried and ran to his father's side, shaking him. "We just need a doctor! He's going to be all right! Get up, Father, get up!"

Hudson grabbed the sobbing boy and turned him around. "A doctor canno' help now, son. He's gone."

"Gone?" a deep voice asked from the study's doorway. "Who has gone?"

James turned toward the voice and Hudson jumped to his feet. It was Aunt Margarita, still dressed in her finest dress and corset, pulled as tightly as possible about her plump frame, her head topped with cascading ringlets of a platinum blonde wig.

"You know good 'n well who has gone and why, witch!" Hudson seethed.

"Watch your tone, *man*. I am the Dame Margarita Morgan."

"Aunt Margarita." James's mind whirled and without thinking he staggered toward his aunt. She was his friend, he thought. She was the one who had taught him about the world and the people in it. She had shared her chocolates with him and given him his mirror and all of his clothes. She could not have possibly done this evil deed. "It's Father —"

"Do no' go near her, James!" Hudson ordered, but all of James's memories refused to let him believe that his aunt would do this to his father, to him.

"Why wouldn't he come near me, Hudson?" Margarita said sweetly. "I'm his best friend ... his only friend."

James reached his aunt and she touched his face, lightly pinching his cheek. "Aren't I James? Aren't we the best of friends? And we can be still, if you want. We don't have to let such things as this come between us."

A cold shiver shook James out of his stupor. "Such things as this ...? But, how could you know unless ..." James's eyes went wide, but it was too late. Dame Margarita seized James by the wrist and held him tight.

"Unless ... I killed Lord Lindsay Morgan?" All the false sweetness bled out of Margarita's face and voice, and James suddenly saw her for who she was.

"You're goin' to pay for this!" Hudson raged. "You're goin' to pay for wha' you've done!"

"What I've done?" Margarita stared icily into Hudson's face. "You mean, what *we've* done."

The doorway to the study suddenly filled with light and shadows as four men stepped into the room. Two were red-coated soldiers with torches, the firelight glinting off the steel bayonets that tipped their muskets. The third was an old man in a black velvet coat. He wore the long wig of a true noble, parted at the top and flowing down both sides of his head, barely concealing a purple scar lining the curve of his face. But instead of the traditional white, his curls ran deep scarlet.

But James's eyes were drawn to the fourth man. His face was a younger version of the man in the red curls, though he wore no wig. His hair was black as coal and his face pale as a mist. His eyes were blue and cold. He wore the uniform of ship's captain and his fingers drummed on the hilt of the captain's sword at his side. Of the four men that now stood before him, the last was the most terrifying by far, and the small smile that played on his pale lips frightened James to his very core.

James writhed and twisted to free himself from his aunt's grasp, but she would not release him. "You! You traitor!" James screamed at her. "I'll — I'll have you all arrested!"

The four men and Aunt Margarita laughed at James, and his aunt squeezed his wrists even tighter. James struggled to turn and find Hudson for help, but the valet's face was now drained of color, staring at the men before them.

"You?" Hudson said to the old man. "You did this?"

The old man smiled and stepped forward, looking around the study as though he'd been there before.

"I'm glad you still remember me, Hudson. I was afraid that after the last time we were all together you and Lindsay might have forgotten me. It was most unpleasant, wasn't it?" The older man said, smiling a mirthlessly while tracing his scar with a finger. "But it looks like neither of you could quite let go of the past."

The red-wigged man looked to a picture hanging above the study fireplace. Four men stood proudly in the painting. One of them was James's father. James had no idea who the other two were, but the fourth, he now knew for certain, was the old man standing in the study now, leaning in close to read the inscription on the picture's frame.

"A man's heart, a man's mind, and man's hands are the keys to every locked door in all the seas and all the lands." The old man laughed and straightened back up. He shook his head and turned back to Hudson with a cruel smile. "Somewhat treacherous, don't you think, for the kingdom's most famed pirate hunter to have such pirate texts so openly displayed?"

"But you would know all about treachery, wouldn' ya'?" Hudson seethed. "Why now? Why?"

"Well, I thought that would be obvious, Hudson. We're here to finish what we started so long ago. We're here for the treasure."

"Over my dead body."

"That's the idea, old chum." The old man snapped his fingers and the two guards leapt to attention. "Let's tie up loose ends, shall we?"

"And the boy?" Aunt Margarita asked.

"I said ends, not end, didn't I?"

James looked to Aunt Margarita. Surely, he thought, surely she wouldn't let this happen, not to him, not to her James. But, with a shake of her blonde curls she shrugged and let James's wrist go as the two guards surrounded him.

James felt suddenly cold and alone, completely lost and without hope. The guards behind him seized him by the shoulders and forced him to his knees.

The black-haired man sauntered forth and looked James right in the face with the calm smile still curled up on his pale lips. "You know, boy," the pale captain said in a voice as icy as his blue eyes. "I often dreamt of doing this to your father. To repay my father's scar. Alas, I suppose I shall have to settle for you." He drew his sword from its scabbard in one flick of his arm.

But just then, as he had for James's father so long ago, faithful Hudson now did for James. Almost forgotten, with the guards and the black-haired captain's attention on James, Hudson leapt into the middle of them, bowling the two soldiers holding James onto the floor. Then, in one fluid arc, Hudson pulled the top half of his cane apart from the bottom to reveal the hidden blade of a sword and swung it toward the raven-haired captain. The young captain evaded the blow but was forced to back away. Hudson picked James up by the shirt and thrust him toward the hallway.

"Run, James, run!" Hudson cried as he backed the captain and the guards away once more with another slash of his blade. "Be your Father's son! You are the Lord Morgan now!"

"But what about you, Hudson?" James shrieked. He knew nothing of combat, but even he could see that there were too many for Hudson to handle on his own.

"RUN!" Hudson yelled again, and finally James obeyed. He dodged the outstretched hands of Aunt Margarita, who had tried to sneak up and catch him again, and raced toward the stables. He heard the clashing of blades and shouting behind him, but it only lasted for a moment.

SIX

FLIGHT THROUGH THE FOREST

James found Destroyer still saddled from earlier in the day, waiting for him by the stables. He wasted no time and leapt upon the pony's back. "Yah!" he cried, and Destroyer kicked out toward the road.

The first drops of rain fell from the darkened sky and pelted James with large, gloppy splashes. He wiped the water away from his eyes and steered Destroyer in the darkness toward the main road that ran along the coast toward the nearby town of Rye. But the frightening thud of pounding hoof beats behind him quickly shattered that idea.

The two soldiers from the study now thundered toward James on powerful stallions. However faithful to James was Destroyer, the pony was no match for those horses on the open road. James veered sharply toward the hill. It was the same hill Thunderbold had charged up earlier that day and James could still make out the dark imprints of the war-horse's powerful hooves in the grass. The tracks led to the haunted forest and all the dark things that dwelt within its shadows.

James's heart beat harder and harder as he neared the trees. He heard the throaty breaths of the stallions amongst their hoof beats – almost on top of him now. James's fear of the soldiers was greater than his fear of the ghosts and with one last surge Destroyer cleared the trees and James plunged into greater darkness.

The rain came harder. It flew down through the branches and stung James's skin on his hands and face. Sharp twigs and prickly pine needles scraped his arms and his cheeks. Lightning flashed, and in the momentary brightness James saw the soldiers still close behind him working their way through the forest.

The thunder crashed and suddenly another spark of lightning lit up the way before James. He had wandered into the open space of a large meadow, devoid of any trees to slow the pursuing soldiers. James dug his heels into Destroyer's sides. The pony neighed and pushed forward toward the cover of more trees on the far side of the clearing.

The soldiers on their war-horses hit the clearing a moment later and drove their chargers across at a breakneck pace. Their steeds' hooves sloshed against the muddy earth and the horses coughed and gasped for air. They drew close enough for James to hear the riders' grunts and the metal and leather harnesses creaking and groaning under the strain of the chase.

Then James saw them out of the corner of his eyes. They were already at his sides. A leather-gloved hand reached out over James's shoulder, grabbing for him.

"Come on Destroyer!" James called, and though his little pony had almost nothing left, she leapt forward once more into the protection of the trees.

The thick forest once more gave James space, but the tumultuous rumble of raging water ahead made his heart sink. A river, driven mad by the torrential downpour of rain, ran through the forest and cut off James's escape.

James ran Destroyer along the banks, hoping against hope to find a stretch shallow enough to cross, but the rainstorm had turned the river into an impassable wall of water.

Snapping branches and neighing horses sounded at James's back. The soldiers were on top of him again. He pushed Destroyer forward as fast as the little pony could manage. Tears of hopelessness were about to fall from James's eyes when a lightning bolt blazed white hot through the air and struck a tree before him. A crack and boom accompanied the sudden orange glow of fire. Destroyer reared up and threw James as a branch from the falling tree swung down on the pony and rider, striking James on the side of his head. The last thing James felt were the cold hands of the river catching him as he fell, just as all went dark.

SEVEN

EYES IN THE NIGHT

James choked up water and gasped for air as he finally came to rest on the river's muddy banks. He crawled on his hands and knees out of the water, collapsing into slimy muck. The right side of his head throbbed and even in the midst of all the water and mud he felt the warmth of blood on his forehead and cheek. He had no idea exactly how he had survived his fall into river. He remembered the lightning and the tree; he remembered all going dark; and, just before passing out, he recalled grasping the very same tree branch that had struck his head. He awoke a few moments later, his mouth full of water and his hand still on the branch as the fast current swept his body downstream.

After gathering his senses, James sat up. The rest of his body hurt as badly as his head, he found, but there was nothing to be done. There

37

were no servants to summon to help him, not even his aunt. Aunt Margarita. James's insides turned to cold water again. He had been so afraid while the soldiers had chased him, so terrified of losing his life that he had thought of nothing but escape. Now, sitting on the dark banks of a river, in a deep forest in the black of night, James was alone with his brief memories of what had just happened.

His own aunt had betrayed him. She had looked right into his face while men had suggested killing him, and then she'd let them try. James wasn't entirely sure who those other two men were, but they had known Hudson and his father. And the one, the dark-haired man who had been so eager to finish James off, was a captain in his majesty's navy. James knew the uniform and the rank. He must have been that Bartholomew Cromier his aunt had mentioned to his father. His eyes had been so terrifying and cold. James had seen how fast he'd pulled his sword from his scabbard, like the wind.

Then James thought about Hudson. The old valet had hardly known James, but he had been willing to sacrifice himself so that James could escape. James had seen the way Hudson had looked at his father; there had been tears in the old man's eyes. James's father. Now James's thoughts turned solely on his father and the last words James had ever spoken to him: "You're the one who should be sorry."

James could bear it no longer and wept furiously. All by himself in the dark he cried and sobbed aloud, never caring if anyone heard or what they thought even if they did. For a long time James sat there, until finally he fell over, exhausted from weeping. As he fell, something hard stuck his side and the pinch of pain snapped him out of his misery.

It was the little wooden box in his pocket. James pulled it out and opened it. A few drops had seeped in through the cracks, but the letter on the ancient-looking parchment and the necklace were mostly undamaged. James stared at the letter. His father's last words and the story of his great secret. James couldn't understand why, but he was afraid of the letter - so afraid that he refused to touch either of the items inside the box and slammed the lid shut. When James closed the box he noticed for the first time the intricately carved decoration on the top. Even in the dark, between his eyes and the touch of his fingers he made out the bizarre image. It was some sort of scepter, James thought, or perhaps a spear of some kind, with three points at the tip instead of one. And behind the strange spear was a pearl resting in an open shell.

James stared at the strange image for a long time. He had never seen this symbol before but it looked to him like a family crest of some sort, though certainly not one with which he was familiar.

James sighed and put the box back in his pocket. He felt like his whole world was spinning out of control and nothing made any sense anymore. The only things he knew were that his box held a secret – the secret of a vast treasure, and that the last thing Hudson had told him was that they were going to London to keep it safe … that it was James's duty to keep it safe. He was the Lord Morgan now. So that is what James decided to do.

James stood and looked around. The rain had stopped and the moon and the stars peeked out from behind the clouds. James was surprised at how well he could see after his eyes adjusted to the dim light. But the further and further he waded into the dark forest the more even the moonlight struggled to squeeze between the canopy of branches and leaves.

As James walked beneath a small opening in the trees above him and looked up to the rapidly clearing sky, he suddenly had the brilliant idea to navigate using the stars. But, alas, he had ignored all those astronomy lessons from old Phineus, so that idea was dashed. Then James remembered Jeremiah offering to take him out into the woods to teach him how to build fires and survive in the elements.

"Why should I learn that?" James had scoffed. "I have you to do it for me!" He had laughed then, but he wasn't laughing now. Right then and there James made a promise to himself to never turn down the chance to learn anything new from anyone in the future, no matter how silly it seemed at the time.

So without the aid of the stars by which he had absolutely no clue how to navigate, and without the light of a fire, which he hadn't the slightest idea how to build, James picked a direction and set off down the bank of the river. He seemed to recall some lesson or other (to which he had paid half-attention at one point) that suggested that people gathered near water for some reason or another and he just might be lucky enough to meet someone who could help. Unfortunately, luck was not on James's side.

More than once he slipped in the mud and nearly rolled back into the river. He was soon covered in slime and, not being used to walking around a filthy mess, grew steadily more and more miserable. But worse, he soon began to suspect fouler things than mud dwelt in the forest shadows. Strange noises echoed amongst the trees. Sometimes James saw floating pairs of green orbs in the dark, but they disappeared as soon as he caught them in the edges of his vision. They were eyes, he imagined, but eyes that belonged to what?

There were stories, James knew. Stories that Jeremiah used to tell about creatures in the forest; fauns and nymphs and dryads, creatures of the woods that tricked little children into following them deeper into the forests. They sang songs and offered treats and then captured their prey and held them captive for years and years … or worse. Once or twice James thought he heard the soft notes of a faun's panpipes in the dark, and his heart hammered against his chest.

Then he heard a rumble.

James stopped dead in his tracks. Fear froze him cold from his fingertips to his toes. He heard it again. It was a soft growling and it sounded like it came from all around him. He took a few steps forward.

A branch snapped loudly behind him and James whirled around and froze.

Two green orbs stared at him from only a few yards away. But these neither disappeared nor flitted away. They remained locked on James. For a moment, the orbs and James stood completely still, staring at each other without blinking.

"Hello, Mr. Faun or Ms. Nymph," James finally offered, shakily. "My name is James Morgan. Just looking for London, that's all. No harm being done. Perhaps you've been there a time or two? Lovely place really - there's some terrific gardens and parks you might like."

The orbs remained in place. James backed up a step, then another. The orbs were perfectly still.

"Anyway, just wanted to let you know that I won't be following you into the woods to be your late-night snack this evening, but I hope you find some other children to chase later. Happy hunting, cheers."

James thought he might be in the clear as he backed up one step farther, but then the orbs advanced upon him. They bobbed in the dark until finally the form that carried them passed into the pale light of the moon. It was no faun or nymph. Bristling fur covered its lean, grey body. Lips on a long snout peeled back over a row of white fangs, glistening in the starlight. For the first time in his life James looked into the eyes of a wolf.

Fear crawled out from James's chest and turned his whole body to stone. He stood petrified as the wolf stepped closer and closer. It sniffed at him, licking its chops with a long red tongue, but still James stood frozen to his spot. Only when the wolf barked hungrily did the spell of stone suddenly release James with a hot flash.

The pain in James's feet scorched his every step, but he never ran so fast in his entire life. With dread, however, he realized it was still not fast enough. The wolf nipped at James's heels then broke off to his side. In the shafts of moonlight the beast glided through the trees alongside James before streaking on ahead. James hoped for only a moment that it had given up for some other prey – until the feral creature burst into the clearing before James, skidding to a stop.

James gasped for breath. There was no strength in his body to run again. The wolf stalked forward, wet slobber dripping from its jowls. James closed his eyes. The images of his life flashed like the leafing pages of a picture book. Aunt Margarita, Phineus, Jeremiah, the manor, his pony, Hudson, and finally his father. He wondered what it would feel like when the wolf bit him. He cracked his eyes open just as the wolf crouched to spring.

But in that instant, as James stepped back, he felt an unseen hand snatch his ankle and heard two snaps like whips. The wolf yelped like a pup and James's legs whipped out from beneath him, his head smacking the ground. James suddenly found himself hanging upside down and for the second time that night everything went completely black.

James woke with a throbbing head. The world was upside down - everything that was, but the wolf, which hung suspended in midair as James did. A biting pain dug into James's ankle. He looked up to find a coil of rough rope tied to his leg, hanging him from the top branches of a tree. The cord had worn through his socks and now cut into the soft skin of his leg. James tried to pull himself up to reach the knot and loosen himself, but he was too weak for the task. He let his head fall back down and found an upside-down man's face staring into his own.

James screamed and thrashed in the air until the man's hand shot out and gripped him roughly by the throat. James's scream squeaked instantly into silence.

"Silence," the man said in a thick accent that was not of James's country. "If you are qviet, I vill cut you down. If not … I vill cut your throat."

"That seems fair enough," James said in a choking rasp, and the man released him with a small shove that sent James swaying back and forth in the air like a piñata. After a moment of swinging the tension in the rope went slack and James tumbled to the ground in a miserable heap.

"Ouch!" he said with a yelp. "You could have done that …"

The man let his long knife gleam in the moonlight.

"… softer," James whispered.

The man ignored James and went to the wolf. He didn't offer the animal the same deal as James and after he had killed the beast, he let it down and slung its body over his shoulder, walking to the edge of the little clearing.

"Hey wait!" James shouted to the man. "Don't leave me here!"

The man said nothing and kept walking. So James clambered to his feet and rushed to follow, limping badly from his blistered heels, tired soles, and ragged ankle.

"You could slow down a bit, there!" Once again James's words came back unanswered and the pitiless man refused to slow his pace even a little. James studied the hunter as well as he could in the dark. He was swarthy and short, dark curls poured out from beneath a red rag tied over his head, and a dark mustache and beard lined his thick mouth. He was obviously strong. The weight of the wolf seemed not to bother him in the least nor hinder the speed of his gait.

This was unfortunate for James, for as well as having even shorter legs than the squat man he followed, his body ached and his head still swam from being hunted, struck twice, nearly drowned, almost eaten by a wolf, and hung upside down for a good portion of the night.

After what felt like miles to James, with sweat pouring down his face, the pain burning like a fever, he could go no farther. "Now look," he gasped through ragged breaths. "This is most inhumane, my good man. We really should take a break." The man still gave no answer. "Can't you see that I'm hurt?" James demanded to the man's back. "I'm bleeding, you cur! I can't go on!" And with that, James collapsed in a heap on the forest floor.

At this the man finally stopped and turned to look at James.

"Finally come to your senses, you brute?" James snapped.

But the man just smiled and shrugged and then kept right on walking. James was incredulous. How could this man be so cruel? Couldn't he see that James was hurt?

"Are you daft!" James called after him. "Don't leave me here like this!" But the man acted as though he heard not a word. With no choice left to him, Jim finally got up once more and staggered after the man, whimpering and limping the entire way.

At some point James stopped thinking about the cruel foreigner he followed and even about the pain that clawed at his feet with every step. His tears dried into a stiff mess under his eyes and on his cheeks and his mind wandered through myriad bizarre memories and thoughts. He remembered his aunt pinching his cheek, but in his mind she pinched it so hard that it bled. He remembered old Phineus shaking his head and the nurse getting sacked, but for what he could not recall. He remembered Hudson leaping forward to defend him.

But of his father, the memory was distorted. Lord Lindsay sat at his desk in the study, his whole body taut and face slicked with sweat. He held out the box to James, but James refused to touch it.

"My son," James's father strained to say the words. "Keep it safe!"

The visions played over and over in James's mind until finally he realized he had stopped walking. He was in another clearing, but this one lit by a roaring fire, the salty-sweet smell of cooking meat filling the air. Many more men and women of the same dark hair and skin as the wolf hunter sat about the fires. They wore bright silks of red and blue and they sang songs in words James had never heard and danced dances that were not of this land.

"Oh ..." James said aloud. "Gypsies. How nice." Then he collapsed and all went dark.

EIGHT

THE GYPSY'S MAGIC

James woke with a start in the dark, kicking about wildly until he heard the creak and groan of wooden wheels on a rough road and felt the rough wooden floor tilting and jostling beneath him. A light rain pattered the canvas above James's head and everything about him smelled deeply of steamed cabbage. He was in the back of a covered gypsy wagon.

James shook his head to clear the cobwebs. He had been dreaming he was back in his father's study. In the nightmare, his father had been reaching out to him, trying to tell him something important, something about a treasure and the letter in his little box. But Aunt Margarita and the horrible man with ink-black hair were suddenly chasing him, all the while Hudson was shouting, "Run, Jim! Run!"

Now James was awake, but the dream still haunted his mind and his feet still throbbed from the night before. Looking down, James found his shoes removed and his feet wrapped in cloth. He pulled back on one of the bandages, but the blisters and sores were freshly scabbed and burned like fire when he tried to remove the cloth. Tears of pain rose up behind James's eyes. To keep from crying, he forced himself to look around and focus on where he was and what he would do next.

It was as dark as night beneath the canvas covering, but James's eyes slowly adjusted. All manner of bizarre artifacts and seemingly worthless junk filled the wagon: piles of rags and sticks beside skeins of silk, broken lanterns and rounds of candle wax, strange stringed instruments and pipes, tambourines, and drums, and, hanging to the side, even a monkey in a cage. James inched closer to the monkey, who appeared to be enjoying a small nap on his perch. James tapped on the side of the cage.

"Hello little monkey," he whispered. "I imagine you do some tricks or something." He tapped a little harder but the monkey slept like a rock. James felt like he deserved a little entertainment in light of all the horrors he'd been through and in a jolt of frustration slapped the cage and barked "Wake up!"

The monkey flew awake and immediately launched itself against the side of the cage with a screeching howl, clawing and biting at James's fingertips. James cried out in surprise, falling back against the side of the wagon into the pile of rags and sticks with a clatter. Only, the sticks weren't sticks at all. They were bones, and the rags were the skins of wolves, their yellow-white skulls staring into James's face with empty eye sockets. James screamed again, scrambling to the middle of the wagon floor, the screeching monkey on one side and the pile of bones and skins on the other.

A slow cackle, dry as sand, rattled from the front of the wagon. James sucked in a startled breath. The front of the wagon was darker than even where he sat, and he saw no shape or form the shadows. "Who's there?" James said with a whimper. "Show yourself!"

"I vas here the entire time, young sir," said the dry, laughing voice. "'Twas not I who failed to show myself, but you who failed to see me."

"I didn't fail anything!" James pouted. "You were spying on me!"

"I vas vatching you, young sir," the voice said again. "As I vas all night."

James looked back down at his bandaged feet. "You did this?" he asked.

"I did."

James peered into the darkness. He could now barely discern the outline of the figure hunkered in the corner. "I still can hardly see you."

"So be it," the voice said with a sigh, and the sound of a match striking against the wooden floor accompanied a bright orange flame that lit the face of an ancient crone. She looked as old as the mountains, her nose was large and hooked like a sharp cliff and her skin was dark and craggy from a life lived in the open air. A few wild and brittle gray hairs poked out from beneath the edges of an old, faded red scarf tied about her head. The skin on her long fingers and frail arms clung directly to her old bones. She laughed in her gravelly voice again. "Have you never before seen an old voman, young sir?"

"Of course I have!" James said indignantly, trying to hide the shock on his face.

"How your feet feel?"

"They hurt!" James snapped. "How do you think they feel? Your friend last night, a right brute he was by the way, tromped me through the forest like a bloodhound with not one rest or stop! And that was after he dropped me from his wolf trap nearly twenty feet in the air right on my head! I'm lucky I didn't break my neck!"

The old woman said nothing and just stared at James for a long moment. James sniffed. If she was expecting any thanks from him she would find herself waiting for a long time. Saving his life was the least any self-respecting person could have done, and she had done a pitiful job on his feet, he thought unhappily.

"You dream last night?" the old woman said, changing the subject.

"No," James lied, and the old gypsy laughed.

"You are a liar, for I heard your dreams. You call for father. He gave to you a secret, yes? A secret in a box? You would know the secret, but the voman chased you avay before you learn, the voman, and the cold man vith the hair like a crow's wings."

"I ... I said all that aloud?" James stared at the old crone with his eyes wide open, for that had truly been what he had seen in his dream.

"Not all ... I heard your dreams. I heard them, and I saw them." The woman smiled a crooked smile and pulled something from behind the folds of her wrinkled and tattered dress. She held the spherical glass on the tips of her claw-like fingers. It glimmered in the candle-light, casting rainbow droplets on the canvas and the floor and on James's face and in his eyes.

"Is that ... is that a crystal ball?" James asked, staring into its perfectly clear surface. He had heard the maids and the groundskeepers talk about such things before, but Aunt Margarita had always told them to stop speaking about such rubbish. "Does it ... does it show you the future?"

"It shows me ... things," the gypsy said, waving her hand over the ball. "Some things vithin, some vithout, some that have come and gone, and some that no man has yet known."

"There's no such thing as magic," James said as defiantly as possible, but his eyes were fixed on the glass orb.

The gypsy cackled again, this time as loudly and gleefully as if James had just told a dirty joke. "This comes from the boy who did not see an old voman right in front of his own face? There are many hidden things in this vorld ... treasures that none but those with free hearts might find. Your father knew this vell."

"My father? How do you know about my father?"

"From your dreams, young sir," she said, and her voice trailed into a whisper and then spoke in words that James had never heard. The clear surface of the crystal ball suddenly grew cloudy, and light flashed from within like lightning in a storm.

48

"What are you doing?" James demanded, suddenly quite as frightened of the old woman as he had been of the dark-haired man.

"Silence!" the old woman commanded, her eyes fixed on the glow of the crystal ball. James wanted to say something smart to the old hag just then, but the aura emitting from the crystal ball lit up the entire wagon with pulsating blue light and it was all James could do to keep from turning his back and covering his head in fear.

"The first steps of a journey lie before you now, Son of the Earth and Son of the Sea!" the gypsy rasped in a far-away voice. Her eyes sparkled with the blue light of the crystal ball. "The treasure you must find – but the vay is fraught with peril and death! To have any hope of unlocking the treasure, you must first unlock your heart. The chains are heavy and they are strong. But this you must do and fail not!"

"Son of who?" James said. "Have you gone completely mad?"

"Son of Earth and Son of Sea, the treasure you must seek! For more than you know hinges upon the treasure's fate!" the gypsy cried out in a loud voice that turned James's insides to prickly crawlers. "Bevare the others that seek it and hold fast to those that come to your aid in the darkest hours ... for the hope of your journey is balanced as a feather on its point!"

With those words the orb's light went dark, and the old gypsy slumped against the side of wagon, as though her vision had sapped the last of her frail strength.

James sat in silence. The wagon fell into an even deeper black and the candle that had seemed so bright a moment before was dim compared to the brilliant blue that had been but was now gone. Son of Earth and Sea? Who was that? And what was all that about heavy chains and his heart? As far as James Morgan was concerned there was not one thing wrong with his heart at all – it was everyone else who could use a point in the right direction.

"Would you mind going over all of that again?" James finally asked. "Or at least the important part? Do you see what exactly the treasure is and how I might find it?"

The old gypsy crone said nothing, but sat as still as though she were fast asleep. "Hey!" James shouted, but still the old woman did not stir. "I'm talking to you! You can't just ignore me like that now! I have questions for you! Look, do you know who I am?"

The crone's eyes flew open in furious rage and James fell back against the back wall of the wagon. "I know who you are meant to be!" she shrieked, pointing a long, bony finger right at James's face. "But you are not yet vorthy! You do not deserve the secret you have been given!" From behind the folds of her clothes the gypsy produced another object, but this one James recognized immediately.

"That's my box!" James shouted, exchanging his fear for indignation at seeing his only current possession in a witch's grasp. "Thief!"

"Qvite wrong, young sir!" the gypsy hag cackled again. "I vill keep that vich resides in your precious box more safe than any chain or lock!" She waved her hand over the box and spoke more words in the language James had never heard before this day. "This box vill not open now until proper time and place intended by fate … until you are ready for that vich lies vithin!" The small flame on the candle sparked and burned bright blue as the gypsy woman pronounced her curse.

"Give me back my box, you witch!" James demanded.

"Here, take it," the old woman said tiredly, tossing the box into James's hands. James tugged at the lid. He pulled and pulled until his fingers hurt. Then he slammed it against the floorboards, and even tried to beat it open with his fists (which only cut his tender little hands) but still the box would not open nor would it break.

The tears James had been fighting since he woke from his dream spilled hot and angry onto his cheeks. "Make it open! Please! It's all I have left!"

"I cannot," the old woman said flatly. "The curse is more powerful than even she who casts it. The box vill only open at the time it is meant … ven you are ready to use that vich is vithin."

James had no idea what to think or do. He put his hands over his face and wept loudly.

"Fear not, young sir," the gypsy woman said, this time with some pity in her voice. "Dark days do not last forever. One bright day the morning vill bring the light. Sleep now, you need your rest. The adventure is only just begun."

Then she waved her hand again, this time toward James's tear-stained face, and James felt suddenly heavy and his eyes closed. This time he slept without dreaming.

NINE

LONDON

The thick pelt flap over the back of the wagon pulled back and white light streamed over James's face, startling him awake. He sucked in a quick breath and with a humming heart went from dead-sleep to wide-awake in an instant. He blinked his eyes in the harsh light and when they were finally adjusted he found the gypsy hunter staring at him with his dark eyes.

"London," he said with a jerk of his head. "Is this not vere you vished to go?"

"Yes," James said hesitantly. "Did the old woman tell you that?" James turned his head to the front of the covered wagon expecting to see the old crone still watching him, but he and the hunter were alone.

"Old voman?" the gypsy said with a scowl.

"Yes, the old *v*oman," James retorted. "Big nose, craggy skin, creepy voice, likes to look in crystal balls and all that? Where's she gone off to? Probably out scaring the wits out of some more unsuspecting children if I've read her right."

Though James was quite unsure it was possible, the hunter managed to scowl even deeper, his dark eyebrows closing in low over his black eyes as he bored holes into James's face with his stare. "An old voman you say? Vith a crooked nose and hair like lifeless straw? And a face as old as the stars in the sky?"

"Yeah that sounds like her, all right, except you forgot ugly as a toad and mean as a snake."

A strange smile split the man's swarthy face with the yellowish white of his crooked teeth. "You've been meeting vith Baba Yaga! Leave it to me to vander these foreign lands and have brought the old vitch of my country along in my vagon and not have known it all these years."

"Baba who?"

"Baba Yaga is a vitch vith strange powers. She lives in a house that valks about on chicken legs and flies through the sky in a teacup. Sometimes she is friend, sometimes she is trickster, but if she has traveled all this vay to talk to you of that vich is yet to come, then I vould suggest you take it close to heart and do not forget vat she has said!"

James looked at the gypsy hunter for a long moment. "So, she lives in a house that walks on chicken legs ... and flies ... in a tea cup?"

The gypsy hunter nodded happily.

"Look, I don't know what exactly your lot drinks around your camp fires, but you should consider quitting it ... immediately."

The hunter just laughed and helped James down from the wagon. Then the train of gypsies pulled on down the road, leaving James once again by himself.

"Baba Yaga ... what rot," James said to himself, not quite sure if his memories from the night before had been real or a dream. But he pulled his box out of his tattered pocket and tried to open the lid. It was held on as tightly as a steel locker. James looked after the wagons as they crawled on into the city and, just for a moment, thought he saw an old woman stick her head out of the back of one of the wagons and laugh.

It never before occurred to James just how enormous London was nor how vast the number of people the city contained. Usually he and Aunt Margarita only passed through the streets in a carriage, Dame Margarita hardly even glancing out the windows she found the sight of commoners so annoying.

However, now that James walked the streets toward his father's London home with the comfort of his fine carriage replaced by the breaking soles of the shoes on his aching feet, the simple streets of London filled with her simple people seemed anything but ordinary. The sheer number was enough to overwhelm him and the variety was unbelievable. He passed by a number of shops simply bubbling over with activity.

"Turnovers!" shouted a plump, old pastry maker, red in the face and sweating profusely as he called to the passersby. "Hot fresh apple turnovers and cakes!"

James wanted desperately to buy one - the smell was nearly more than he could resist - but with sudden disappointment he remembered he had no money. James couldn't remember a time when he wasn't able to get what he wanted, especially not something so trivial as a piece of bread. The sensation was entirely unfamiliar ... and decidedly unpleasant.

Unfortunately for James, the farther he walked from the center of town and the bustling market the more unpleasant his feelings became.

"A coin, boy?" said a haggard old beggar, clawing at James's arm with filthy fingers. The beggar's face was sunken and his eyes hollow, the greasy gray hair atop his head hung like mop threads about his head and his skin was as dry as cracked earth. "Just a coin for a crust of bread ... please!"

James yanked his arm away from the wretched beggar. "I don't have anything!" he shouted, running for the next few steps. After that,

James walked by a house that was really no more than a shack, the boards so flimsily put together that James could see right through the cracks. An entire flock of children sat on the steps leading up to a door that barely hung onto its frame by a single hinge. They were the most sullen children that James had ever seen, circles lining their eyes and their cheeks utterly colorless. James stared at them. He wanted to look away, but couldn't. He'd never seen children like that before.

James was suddenly not so curious about these people. He wanted this nightmare to end. As soon as he got to his London manor he would put on some of his good clothes and send a letter to the king. Hudson said the King might help him, and surely, James thought, the King would know someone who could open his box - no matter what that stupid gypsy hag had blabbered on about fate and chains around his heart and all that other rubbish.

It was early evening when James finally reached his family's London house. The sun was dipping back behind the buildings of London and while half the street still bathed in warming streams of sunlight, long shadows slowly unfurled over much of the city. James trudged up the walk toward his family home, his tired feet screaming for rest. James was positive they were bleeding again and his aching body longed for the comfort of his spacious bed. James had no key but he imagined that the house would be completely empty and he could sneak in through a window or down through the cellar to get inside.

He was almost to the door when a lamp in one of the windows flicked to life. James's exhaustion momentarily fled, his eyes went wide, and his heart pounded.

Aunt Margarita appeared in the light of the lamp, as carefree and at ease as if she had just come from the country on a shopping trip to London.

James clenched his fists and gritted his teeth. The traitorous woman must have gotten here ahead of him by carriage. He was just about to launch himself right through the window and let the treacherous witch have it when, to her side, stepped the old man in the red wig and the pale captain with the jet-black hair. James's anger spun immediately into fear and instead of leaping through the window he dove beneath the bushes under the sill to hide.

James crouched in the dirt, breathing as shallowly as possible and praying his hammering heart did not sound nearly as loud as it felt. When he was finally sure he had escaped being seen, James crawled under the cover of bushes to the side of the house and around the corner. It was sweaty and prickly work, and a thorn from a rose bush left a nice, long scratch down the side of James's face, but eventually he made it beneath an open window. Judging from the smells wafting out, James figured it was an open window to the kitchen. He breathed in the warm scent of fresh-baked bread and oil-basted chicken and his belly rumbled again.

When he could stand the tempting, delicious smells no longer, James risked a quick peek through the window. But just as soon as his view had crested the sill he suppressed a surprised gasp and threw himself back down into the dirt. James had seen old Phineus and Molly the housemaid settling down at a servant's table for dinner. Fortunately for James, though, they had been looking at each other and not out the window and he had gone unseen yet again.

James sat amongst the bushes for a long moment. He half wanted to leap up and demand that Phineus give him some blasted dinner before he absolutely starved to death, but he had no idea if Phineus and the others had been in on Aunt Margarita's traitorous plans. So instead he listened very carefully as they began to speak.

"It's all so horrible I don't even want to talk about it anymore!" said Molly, her voice as thick and warbly as though she had just finished sobbing.

"I must admit," Phineus said, sounding more tired and aged than ever before. "This has all left me rather shaken. Lord Morgan was a great student as a boy when I taught him so long ago. He was an even better man."

Molly sniffled and choked back more tears. "He was always so kind to me and Mildred, especially about the holidays! Always makin' sure there was money for gifts and food. And now, for that witch, Margarita

Morgan, to have the Cromiers over so soon, as if nothing had ever happened at all! They were in league, I tell you!" Molly whispered a little too loudly. "Her and the old Count and his son, Bartholomew, that pale creature. Have you ever seen a man look so close to death and still be walking and breathing? The most deadly man in his majesty's navy, they say, and the most merciless!"

Bartholomew Cromier. James pictured the dark-haired man with his terrible sword in hand, cold, blue eyes fixed on James as he came to take his life.

"Hush, Molly!" Phineus snapped, and James envisioned the old man peering out from beneath his bushy eyebrows for listening ears.

"You can't hush the truth, Phineus! I couldn't stand her or her little tyrant, God rest him."

"Molly! Don't speak ill of the dead. No matter what else he may have been, he was still just a boy."

So they thought he was dead, James realized. Well they were all in for a surprise weren't they?

"He was old enough to know how to behave!" Molly's biting tone pricked the fresh wounds on James's insides. "I have two boys of my own and they are as kind and sweet as the saints and angels! But that one, ooh, if I weren't a Christian woman I would swear that that little monster never saw the pearly gates and took a nose dive straight down to you know where!"

"Molly!" Phineus said, gasping. A pit formed in James's stomach and a knot in constricted his throat at the same time. Did they really hate him so much? Why did they love his father so and hate him with such fury?

"While I don't share your vituperative spirit, Molly, I must admit, the boy hadn't been nearly the flower of honor that his father had been," Phineus said with a sigh. "No discipline, no motivation, no desire for the greater deeds in life.

"You know, there were rumors," Phineus said, his voice growing distant. "That the Lord Morgan had found a great treasure at sea. I was never sure whether or not to believe them, of course. But I knew that whatever his secrets, Lord Morgan had hoped to pass them on to his son one day. And while he didn't say as much, the look in Lord Lindsay's eyes when he saw what his son had become made me almost sure that such hopes were forever dashed, and that James was the greatest disappointment his father ever had. Perhaps it was a blessing that they both died before that spoiled boy turned into an even worse man."

The words turned James's insides to ice. He sat there, frozen in place on the ground. Every word that Phineus spoke stung, but none so much as to hear that his father, the great lord and famous captain, had thought that his own son was his deepest shame.

Finally the servants went quiet and all James heard was the sound of silverware clinking on dishes.

James sat there in the dirt. His own father, he thought, along with everyone else he had ever known, hated his guts and thought him unworthy to inherit neither title nor treasure. Worse, the only person who had seemed to like James, his Aunt Margarita, was the very one who would have let him die. James's throat felt suddenly tight and his nose stung.

For a moment, James thought of leaping up and revealing himself to those treacherous commoners – and how would they feel then having said all that rubbish about him? But with the Cromiers lurking about, just waiting to get their hands on him, James gritted his teeth and instead crawled back toward the street.

No matter what anyone else said, James still had his box, and that meant he still had hope of getting his life back into some sort of order, even if everyone in the world hated him. He would come back, he thought angrily. He would find his father's treasure and march up the street triumphantly with his own private army in tow. He would laugh as they locked Aunt Margarita and her cohorts in irons. Only then he would he think about forgiving the servants for their beastly words ... perhaps.

James crawled toward the corner of the house and was about to make a sprint for the far side of the street when he ducked back behind the bushes. A man had stepped out of the shadows and into the setting sun's reach. He was obviously a man of the sea and wore the long great cloak of a ship's captain, weathered and cracked like a worn-out saddle and as black as pitch. His upturned collar was buckled to the front and his dark, tricorn hat was pulled low, hiding his face. All the more strange and unnerving to James, a black raven sat perched upon the man's shoulder.

A breeze blew up the street and tugged at the man's coat. From beneath the flapping lapel James caught the glint of a cutlass handle at the man's side. The man stood still as a statue, staring at the Morgan house as though he could burn it down with his eyes. James wasn't sure why, but the mere sight of the man terrified him. It terrified him like the thoughts of Bartholomew Cromier coming to get him.

James forgot all about his painful feet and his desire for his warm bed. He crawled back the other way and headed toward the street on the backside of his house. The moment his feet touched the cobble-stone road he ran as far and as fast as he could. Night was coming. It was obvious to James that no place his family owned was safe and his only hope was to make it to the palace on his own and find the king. The king would make things right. Perhaps he could even find a way to open the magically locked box. Then James could find the treasure. Then he could get revenge.

TEN

BIG RED

James ran just a few blocks from the house before what little strength he had failed him, then he all but sleepwalked the rest of the way toward the palace. The servants' condemning words still rang in his ears, anger burned in his heart, and a thick knot lodged itself once more in James's throat. James harrumphed and hocked as best he could to dislodge it, but it refused to budge. Fortunately for James the palace appeared around the next corner and the need to create a plan distracted him for a few blessed minutes.

It had suddenly occurred to James that the King of England had never met him in person (though James had often imagined him doing so and at his greatest pleasure no less) nor had anyone in the king's court ever seen James's face. This would be a problem, James imagined, considering the fact that he practically looked (and smelled) like

61

a gypsy and it was doubtful that anyone would simply take his word that he was the Lord Morgan's dead son come back to life – and could he please have an appointment with the king, if you'd be so kind? Westminster Palace wasn't exactly a barbershop after all, it did have guards who carried particularly sharp swords and rather real muskets.

James was cursing his bad luck once more for Phineus's failure to teach him strategy (though in his heart he knew it was he who'd ignored the old man) as he came to stand before Westminster Palace, within a stones throw of the entranceway. James pulled the box out of his pocket and tried to put together the first words he would say to the guard at the gate ... then to the king.

While James pondered all of this he lost track of where he was walking (as people who ponder and walk at the same time often do) and unfortunately (or fortunately, as what happened next affected the entire course of James's adventure) ran smack into the back of a burly boy and a couple of his lunkish friends.

"Oy!" the burly boy exclaimed, whirling on James. He was big for his age, freckles running wild over his cheeks and nose and a home-spun cap atop his head. Out from underneath the hat's edges sprouted the curly puffs of the brightest red hair James had ever seen. "Watch where you're walkin', mate!"

"Maybe you should watch where you're standing!" James snapped back with apparent agitation. He was very busy thinking of how best to approach the palace gates and he really had no time for stupid red-headed street ruffians. However, James immediately regretted his quick temper, for these young men were hardly James's frightened house servants, and quite disinclined to quail before James's sharp tongue. The red-haired tough's mates surrounded James, firm jaws and the set looks of boys who had been in enough fights to always be ready for the next one.

"Well, well, well chums," the red-haired boy, who was obviously the leader of the pack, crowed to his friends. He looked James over, and unimpressed smirk on his lips. "What sort of strange bird do we have here? By his plumes and his cheeks I'd say he was as dandy as

Gentle Jack, but from the smell of him by gawd I'd say he was a jumpin' gypsy!"

The other boys, who were apparently Red's yes men, chimed in one at a time.

"Sure has some pretty locks — a dandy, all right, a dandy!"

"Apply some fresh powder to your hands this morning, darling? Plumes and cheeks, plumes and cheeks, look at 'im!"

"Ho'ever — smells like cabbage ... could be a gypsy."

Big Red snapped his fingers and his yes men shut their traps, but they continued to leer at James. Their confidence soared along with James' ever-whitening cheeks. It must be understood that James had never really been forced to stand up for himself. Some servant or another had always been about whenever James had been in London before, and he'd never thought twice about his snide comments made from the safety of Aunt Margarita's carriage. But now, facing four boys far more well put together for a row and far more eager for one than James himself, and having nothing but his clothes and the cool London air between himself and them, the world suddenly felt a mite bit more unpredictable.

"Well, fellows." James felt it wise to turn to his vast knowledge of their "street talk" than to tell them what he really thought. "I think there's hardly call for a tussle over a bit of a bump ... wouldn't you say?"

"No, I wouldn't ... fellow." Big Red's lips curled his sneer one more tick up in the direction of wicked, as though he smelled a hint of fear just over the nearly overwhelming scent of cabbage lingering all over James.

"No, we don't know, do we?"

"Do we fellow? Do we? Fell-o-o-w?

"Fellow, fellow, fell-OW"

Red snapped his fingers again and again his boys stopped yakking, mustering the biggest, dumbest grins they could. But to James, and to all other young boys who have been a bit on the smallish side, such big dumb smiles looked nothing but. Rather they appeared to James as cruel and bloodthirsty. Red, on the other hand, wasn't smiling. He was staring - staring hard at the box in James's hands. The look crossing his face was one that James should have recognized: the face of a little boy who suddenly wanted something that wasn't his.

"So, fell-ow." Red walked in a close circle around James, puffing out his chest and voice dripping with disrespect. "I'm thinkin' you're right about not needin' any sort of tussle or nothin' for such a lil' bump."

"You are?" James wasn't so sure about that. "That's quite civil of you, thank you."

"Oh, you'll find I'm all about civilness, my good fell-ow." Red's gang giggled.

"Ah, of course," James said. "That would be 'civil-ity,' but I appreciate it nonetheless."

Red's friend's giggled even harder now.

"I think we can get over all of this with a simple tradin' of goods." Red stopped circling and came face to face with James, arms crossed over his chest. "You gimme that box, and I'll let you off the old hook and call us square."

James may have been selfish and naïve, but stupid he was not. He saw what was coming and his grip tightened on his precious box. Whatever happened, he wouldn't lose it – he couldn't lose it. The box held all that was left of who James was and his only way of getting it all back again. James once more regretted tossing down the swords of his fencing lessons and shrugging at the old master's attempts to teach him a few tricks of wrestling. Those lapses in attention, it seemed, were about to cost him.

"It's mine," James said as hotly as he could. Sweat slicked his palms and flickering fear twinged in his stomach.

"A tussle it is then!" Red smiled with glee and snapped his fingers. The gang of yes men seized James by his arms while Red grabbed the box.

James did his best. He could not be faulted for lack of effort. He kicked and squirmed, twisted and thrashed in the bigger boys' grip (he may have even bitten an arm or hand or two and certainly exercised his knowledge of foul words), but it was no use because something happened that all the old servants predicted would happen to James for a long, long time.

Big Red hauled back and planted his fist right into James's face.

James fell back through the gang of boys and landed flat on his seat with a thud. His face lit up with pain like a candle and his eyes flew wide as tea saucers. He gingerly raised his hand to his lip. The flesh was already tender and swollen and when James pulled his hand away red blood ran down his fingertips. "You ... you s-s-truck me," James said, eyes watering and chin quivering.

"I ... I ... s-s-ure ... did," Red mocked, his band of lunks joining in.

"How ... how ... did it f-f-feel?"

"Is b-b-aby gonna c-c-ry?"

"Can't even fend for himself ... he's a dandy all right, an absolute dandy!"

James sat there, throat tightening and face flashing with heat. No one came and picked him up. No one stood up for him or came to mete out justice. No one reminded the boys that he was a lord and they were commoners and no one came and reminded them that stealing was wrong. Instead, the thieves heaped derision on poor James - and he just sat there and took it because he had no idea what else to do.

"Thanks for the trade, my good fell-ow!" Red said. He snapped his fingers again and he and his little band strutted off down the street.

James sat there silently for a moment, and then he did the last thing that any self-respecting boy would do in the middle of the street: he balled his eyes out. It was hard to blame him really, after all he'd been through, but the crying wasn't solving any of his growing list of problems.

"Tears won' get your treasure back, m'boy," a beggar who had sat by and watched the entire awful incident advised. "I know, I've cried a river full meself and still my tin cup stays as empty as me belly."

James stared incredulously at the beggar and wanted to ask why he bloody well hadn't spoke up before now. But the man was right after all. So James jumped up and chased after the hoodlum gang.

Fortunately, Big Red was just that: big and sporting hair bright as a firework, so finding him was hardly the issue - what to do after the fact was a bit more prickly. James had nothing even resembling a plan, but he was so desperate to retrieve his box that he pursued the boys down the crowded streets of London, through alleys and over bridges, until the streets grew unrecognizable and the light in the air approached true night.

James finally caught up with them and, lacking any better ideas, closed his eyes, lowered his shoulder, and ploughed headlong into Red's back. He had hoped to knock the big lug over, but having never rammed anyone before, James lacked the momentum to weight ratio and suddenly found himself in the exact same situation as only a few minutes before.

"Oy!" Red whirled about. "Watch where you're — you?" This was certainly a surprise to Red, and his band echoed his sentiment.

"You?"

"You?"

"Cabbage — it's him all right."

"I need that box back," James said, this time without the snide tone or dismissive gaze. All he had were tears and bloody lips. But Red wasn't a forgiving sort of boy (he'd also had a rough childhood, you see, with a missing father and poor mother and all that), so once more he snapped his fingers and again the gang seized James in their arms. Red pulled back for another doozy of a haymaker.

James shut his eyes tight, anticipating the blow. But just before it came he blurted out his desperate reason for his desperate need: "I have to have it back! I have to take it to the king!"

James waited for the punch, hoping it wouldn't land on his nose (that would hurt a lot, he imagined), so he angled his forehead toward Red's fist, thinking it might be the least painful spot on his face to take a beating. And so James waited, looking completely ridiculous, with his scrunched-up face and forehead poked forward like a charging rhinoceros ... but the beating never came.

James peeked one eye open. Red's fist hung suspended in mid-air, his mouth gaping on his stupefied, lunkish face. James opened the other eye and found the same stunned looks on the faces of Red's acquiescing compatriots.

"Did you just say you ... you were taking this to the king?" Red asked, holding the box up with his other, un-fisted hand.

"The king?"

"The king?"

"Shouldn't see the king smellin' like cabbage —"

"Shut up!" Red shouted instead of the usual finger snap. This was apparently serious. "So?" he asked James again, raising his fist back to remind James how serious the question was.

"Yes," James said with a nod, still trying to angle his forehead toward the potential blow. He was completely confused, but supposed the truth couldn't hurt now.

"What's in it?" Red demanded.

"Nothing ... a letter on a bit of parchment and a necklace," James managed.

"A necklace?" Red arched one eyebrow and then slowly lowered his fist and stood to his full height. "Let's 'ave a look-see, shall we?" he said and tugged once on the lid. Then he tugged again. Then he bent over the box and pulled so hard that his face turned as red as his hair and his freckles nearly disappeared. He growled in anger and yanked James toward him by the front of his shirt.

"How d'ya got it locked up so tight?"

"I ... I ..." James tried to think of a clever lie, but the bizarre truth tumbled out instead. "I didn't lock it ... a gypsy, a gypsy witch did it with magic!" He spewed and half expected the boys to beat him senseless on the spot for even suggesting something that ridiculous. But the gang just stood there, mouths open, staring back and forth at one another, dumbstruck.

Red looked as if he wasn't sure what to do. After a moment, Red's friends, who looked just like Red now, sporting the same clueless faces they'd worn since James first saw them, collectively had an idea. They looked at one another, then at Red, then one of them spoke up.

"Well, if that lil' box is for the king ... hadn't we be'er be takin' him to see the king?"

James would have thought they were mocking him again if it weren't for their serious expressions. And he didn't want to tell them that the box wasn't actually *for* the king as that seemed to be the only reason they weren't beating him like a rug that very moment.

"You know the king?" James asked skeptically.

"Know him?" Red said with a growl. "WE — my good fell-ow - happen to be in the king's employ, if you know what I mean. And if you can keep your dandy mouth shut for a minute, WE might find the civilness to take you to see him."

"You will?" James nearly collapsed in disbelief. The thieves who had just robbed him seemed entirely certain that they not only worked for the king, but that they should take James to see him. Any relief that James felt, however, slipped away as Red leaned in close, looking him eye to eye, his lips curled into that horrible sneer.

"But if the king says he don't know you, and I find you made all this hog slop up ..." Red clucked his tongue, his eyes smiling in cruel delight. "Me and my chums here are gonna redecorate your pre'ty visage, go' it?"

"Got it ..." James said, nodding vigorously. And without further ado the quartet of ruffians turned and bustled quickly down the street, with James, having anything but another option, hurrying after them.

ELEVEN

THE KING OF THIEVES

The final, curved edge of the sun disappeared beneath the horizon as James followed the four boys who, just a few minutes ago, had been ready to pound him into little boy pulp. Though the farther they went the more and more James wanted to turn and run, box or no box. James had never walked these streets nor even ridden down them in a carriage. This was the dark side of the city - dark as though a permanent cloud stretched over top of it just to keep out the light.

The buildings here stood shabby and gray, rundown windows and faded doors like sad little faces all in a row, eyes turned down toward the ground. Every once in a while James glimpsed a candle-lit figure in a window or doorway. But the moment their eyes met, doors slammed, drapes snapped shut, or quick breaths snuffed out the light.

The people on the streets looked no happier than the houses around them: filthy from head to toe, soot imbedded in the creases of the frowns lining their greasy faces. They scurried down the streets with their heads down, or huddled in twos and threes on the street corners, whispering amongst themselves.

"Is it much farther?" James asked, shivering as the cool night swept away the last warm traces of the day.

"Not far," the closest lug said over his shoulder. "Good thing, too. We don't wanna to be late for court!"

James had no doubt that this gang of thugs were liars as well as thieves, but the sure tone in their voices and the swift pace of their gait had James just hoping against hope that they were telling the truth. Those things and the fact that they could have easily pummeled James into the cracks of the cobblestones had they desired, but they had not. Such was their respect for the king.

Finally, after walking for miles along streets as bleak and cheerless as James had ever seen, the four boys led James down an alleyway that seemed to drop straight into the earth itself. They tread slowly down the steep hill where, at the bottom, they came to an ancient church (abandoned, though still guarded by hideous gargoyles,) backed at an awkward angle into an empty warehouse and a crumbling stack of mortar and stones overtop a city sewer. The boys fell to their knees and without hesitation crawled through a broken drain.

"The king is … down there?" James asked, just as the last boy was about to crawl into the hole. The tunnel was black as ink and the three toughs that had gone before had completely disappeared.

The boy nodded "yes" and without a word vanished himself into the dark. But a moment later James heard his voice echo back down the drain. "You'd be'ter hurry! Court's nearly started!"

James stared into the solid blackness, his knees and hands trembling nervously. A nightlight had lit James's bedroom every night of his life from his first crib to the four-post bed he now missed so much, and the dark frightened him to the point of petrifaction. But James's options were more than a little limited. So, drawing in a trembling breath and shaking the nervousness from his hands and feet, James mustered up the last of his courage and threw himself down the pipe.

The wet, slimy ground stuck and slurped beneath James's hands and feet and scuttling bug feet and buzzing insect wings clicked in the dark. "I hate bugs," James whimpered to himself. "I hate rats, I hate worms and snakes, and I hate red-headed thieves, and all of bloody London!" He would have continued listing the numerous objects of his disaffection, but the tunnel wasn't that long and a spot of light appeared before James's eyes. As he neared the light, the sound of a great many voices echoed down the drain. Perhaps this was a secret passage into court after all, James wondered, and hope flared up once again in his chest for a brief moment. But when he finally reached the pipe's end and stood up on the other side, he saw a sight he'd never imagined in a thousand dreams.

Children were everywhere, hundreds of them. The space between the back of the church, the warehouse, and the sewer wall formed a courtyard indeed, but instead of nobles and ladies and consorts gossiping and paying homage to the king (which is what Aunt Margarita had explained what court was really all about) street urchins no less filthy and rough than the redhead and his gang filled the entire space. They sat on walls and perched in knocked-out warehouse windows, screaming and shouting at one another across the yard. They rolled dice and spun tops and hung from the gargoyles, sticking their tongues out at the hideous stone creatures.

And the clothes they wore! Not one of them had a single piece that matched another. Breeches of gray wool matched with brown canvas jackets, and red knit hats with blue stitched scarves, or a black shoe with a gold buckle on one foot and a brown shoe with silver on the other. It was as though a single piece of clothing had been lifted from every clothesline behind every house in London and passed out one at a time at random to every member of this kinder court. James stared at it all, dumbstruck. This wasn't the court he'd expected to find, but he had to admit that it was the brightest burst of color he'd seen in the gray streets of this forgotten borough, a dirty stained-glass kaleidoscope of jabbering, hooting, and hollering pandemonium.

Just when James thought the scene could grow no stranger, a young boy appeared from behind a decrepit arch at the back of the empty church and blew a warbling note on a dinged-up, brassy horn that sounded not too unlike a dying goose. The courtyard grew silent in an instant. The games of dice and hopscotch and the running and wrestling ceased immediately and the center of the little gray square emptied out in a flash. The children gathered in groups, lining the walls and staring in anticipation at the boy before the arch.

"Ladies and gents of London! Welcome one and all!" the boy shouted. He wore a scuffed-up silk hat and a dirty cravat about his neck, but he wore them with all the pride and dignity of a circus ringmaster.

"Welcome!" the children shouted back at him, and the boy pranced about before the restless crowd.

"Anover monf has slipped by under the noses of the truant officers!"

"BOO!" the children clambered.

"Out of the grasp of the priests and the nuns!"

"BOO!"

"Behind the back o' our esteemed Constable Butterstreet and his bumblin', tumblin', stumblin' band o' lawmen!"

"DOUBLE BOO!"

"And who do we have to thank for that?"

"The king, the king, the king ..." The chant started slowly and quietly.

"Who keeps us in order and eatin' and sleepin' and playin'?"

"The king, the king, the king!" The volume rose with each successive shout.

"And who fills our pockets up wif more than we ever go' from any stinkin', filthy, lyin', no good grownup any of us ever met?"

"THE KING, THE KING, THE KING!"

"Ladies and Gents!" the boy cried, whipping the throng into a wild frenzy, "I give you the one, the only, untoppable, unstoppable, undroppable ... THE — KING — OF — THIEVES!"

The crowd cheered wildly as out from behind the archway stepped a full-grown man in black breeches and a black split-tail coat; glimmering, shined gold-buckle shoes; and one of the sharpest silk, tricorn hats even James had ever seen. He stood straight up and down from head to toe, as spindly as a spider, twirling a neat cane in his left hand like a rat might twirl its own tail. Behind him, in the shadows and nearly unnoticed by all else in the crowd save James, a squat man crept, with a huge thrummed cap too big for his head. The little man waddled more than walked, but as soon as he had appeared he slunk back into a dark corner to remain unseen as his flashy counterpart took center stage.

The king, as the children of the court hailed him, held his long arms open to the crowd, smiling and soaking in their affection. He then took off his hat to reveal long strands of black hair greased back over his head, and bowed deep and low to the thunderous applause of his miniature court. But while the other children clapped and whistled, James felt his stomach slide down to the bottom of his gut. Whoever this King of Thieves was, he was not the king James needed to see.

"Welcome! Welcome! Welcome!" The king paraded before the mob. "My friends of the streets, my brothers and sisters of the alleys and sewers, I welcome you yet again to my court! Every clan of our kingdom is represented here tonight!"

"The Liversham Lions!" A fierce group of boys roared and growled and James thought they seemed very lionish indeed.

"The Westminster Night Owls!" A rather bookish clan stepped forward, large, stolen glasses that didn't quite fit properly on each of their clever faces.

"The Redbridge Banshees!" An all-girl clan who nearly pierced James's ears with their cry.

"The Sutton Flyers!" Who were indeed a very acrobatic bunch.

"And the Dragons of Kingston!"

One of the dragons leapt out before his clan and blew a ball of fire like a carnival performer, and the entire court, James included, oohed at the bright flash of light. James noticed Big Red clapping and cheering his red head off at the name of this clan. He was a Dragon, James surmised, and for the first time he noticed on Red's sleeves a crude patch of a serpent with a flame for a tongue. The Dragons were the biggest and boldest of all the children, and James noticed how the others shrank back just a little at the sound of the Dragons' cheers.

"Now that we've all been introduced —" the king began again, but was immediately interrupted by a high-pitched squeak from the back.

"What about us?" the voice complained, and children all around the voice split to reveal what must have been the most pathetic excuse for a clan in this entirely bizarre court. There were only four members, and three of them were the shortest, most mousy set of boys James had ever seen. And what was more, he could hardly tell one from the other: they were without doubt three brothers. To add to all of that, the fourth member of the clan was a girl so innocent and sweet looking that James would never believe her capable of stealing a thing.

"How could I forget?" the king said dryly. "The Ratt Brothers." He flipped his hand toward the boys, and though they did their best to clap for themselves and puff out their chests the entire congregation laughed and teased them off, shoving them back to the rear as the court of the King of Thieves returned to business.

"Right!" the king said, plopping his hat back on his head and twirling his cane. "The rest of the world lives by its boneheaded rhyme and reason. Who needs 'em? Out here, we have our own rules. Just two of 'em! What are they?"

"Take what's yours!" was the first. "Share and share alike!" was the second.

"So have you taken what was yours this month?" the king smiled knowingly, the children laughing at cheering at their own guile and cleverness. "Then it looks like it's time for some sharin'."

The king opened his arms and children from every clan rushed in to pile their earnings from a month's worth of picking pockets, shamming vendors, and looting unminded shops at the tall man's feet. When the flock of depositing thieves cleared, they had left a mighty pile of gold necklaces, shiny coins, silver pieces, family heirlooms, and glimmering pieces of jewelry nearly half as tall as James himself.

"An excellent month's work," the king said, nodding with satisfaction. "Before long, we'll have enough to make every one of our dreams come true. You know the promise I made to you: if you put the rich stuff into my hands I'll turn it into your dreams. I'll find us a place, a perfect place, where we can breathe easy and put up our feet for the rest of our lives! You can trust me, friends, I'll put this all away in our secret vault and when the time is right we'll spend it like it was sand on the beach!"

The children roared their approval and chanted "the king!" over and over at the top of their lungs.

"Now," the king said, seemingly eager to wrap things up, "any other business needing tending this evening?"

He was about to assume that there was none, and James also hoped the same, but to the king's disappointment and James's horror, Big Red spoke up.

"'Scuse me, sir," Red said, looking nor sounding nearly as tough as a few hours ago, when his fist had been poised to smash James's nose. He timidly stepped out from the ranks of the Dragons. "There is somethin' ..."

"And what is that?" the king asked, concealing only slightly well the ample hint of irritation in his voice.

"Well, sir," Red said, gulping down his nervousness before pressing on. "This boy over there." Red pointed directly at James. All eyes in the court turned on him and James wished he could disappear into the shadows like a ghost. "We nicked this box from him you see, but he said he was bringin' it to you. We tried to open it, but we couldn't. He says it's because it's been locked up tight by gypsy magic."

James heard a small gasp followed by a trickle of murmurs as the crowd of children grew oddly hushed and excited, craning their necks to gawk at the boy and his magic box. Even the king suddenly seemed quite a bit more interested, more interested than James particularly liked.

"Let me see the box, Red," the king said, patting Red on the head with a kind hand as the street thief handed him the box. "Well done. Bonus future share for the Dragons!" the King proclaimed, and the Dragons cheered loudly, clapping the now-swaggering Red on the shoulders.

The King's eyes turned on James. He studied him intently for what seemed like ages with eyes so dark they seemed black within black - but James refused to look away. He had to recapture his box no matter who he had to go through to get it.

"Well, well," the king said. "We have a haughty one here don't we?" The court of clans mocked James with false oohs and aahs. "Gypsy magic, eh," the King said, smiling. "Let's see what you've got for me."

The King reached with his long spidery fingers for the lid of the box. But no sooner than he did, he stopped cold. The briefest flash of surprise blinked across his face as he stared at the lid of the box. If James had not been quite so distracted by the hundreds of faces staring down at him, he would have recognized that brief glance for what it was with a chill: recognition. Somehow, someway – the King of Thieves knew the symbol carved into James's box. But as soon as that fierce glance flared up it disappeared again. Reaching out with one long arm, the oily smile returned to his face, the king beckoned James closer with a curling, spindly finger.

James abhorred being called like common dog, but he had to get his box back, so he begrudgingly stepped forward. The king eyed him intently and James felt the stares of hundreds of wild thieves on his back.

"What's your name, my friend?" the King asked James with syrupy sweetness.

"James Morgan," James replied, trying to sound unshaken, but the tremble in his voice betraying him.

"Well, Jim," the King said. "Why be so formal? Down here, we're all just friends. After all, Jim Morgan has a bit more of a ring to it, wouldn't you say? Now, tell me, where did you steal this box?"

"I didn't steal it, it's mine," said Jim defiantly (and whether he liked it or not, the name the King of Thieves gave him stuck.) But just as soon as he spoke, Jim wished he hadn't. There was a moment of perplexed silence, and then the entire court, the king included, exploded into uproarious laughter.

All his life Jim had laughed at others, those more common than himself. But now, here he stood surrounded by a mob of children more common than the trees on the hills. Yet it was them, not him, who were doing the laughing now. A thick lump formed in Jim's throat and his nose began to sting yet again.

The king quieted the crowd down with a wave of his hand, and, still smiling his foxy smile, looked Jim and the box over. "I'm sure it is," the King of Thieves said patronizingly. "All of us down here are simply laden with personal possessions. So if the box is yours why don't you just open it for me?"

"I can't." Jim suddenly felt his emotions getting the best of him and his little chin quivered.

"Look!" Big Red pointed his big hand right at Jim's miserable face. "He's gonna blubber like a baby!" The court burst into ridiculing laughter again, and this time the king didn't stop them. He let them laugh and while they did he leaned in on Jim's downcast face, looking at him nose to nose.

"Tell me the truth, boy." All things false went away. The king spoke plainly to Jim while his whole army of feral children laughed their heads off in the background, his voice as flat and cold as the gray bricks beneath their feet. "Where did you steal this box?"

"I didn't steal it," Jim whimpered pitifully. "I just want it back, please."

"Hmmm," the king's eyes were keenly thoughtful. "This is very interesting indeed." Then the king abruptly stood back up and quieted down the raucous crowd. "Silence!" he cried, getting what he asked for instantly. "It seems, my friends, that Jim Morgan and I have a disagreement about who owns this box." The King looked about at his faithful followers, the glimmer of an idea growing in his dark eyes.

"Now as you all know, we have a way of settling such disputes, don't we?"

"YEAH!" the court cried, bubbling over in excitement.

"And what is it?"

"THIEVIN'!" the crowd roared back.

"That's right, lads and lassies!" the king nodded in agreement. "In order to share and share alike, my boy, you must take what's yours first. So here we have Jim Morgan and he must prove he belongs. He must prove that he is one of us! Only then will he earn the right to have his box shared back to him!" The court cheered their approval while Jim's spirits sunk lower than ever before.

"But!" the king held up one bony finger. "Like the rest of you, Jim here needs a clan ... who will take him?"

Jim scanned the crowd and he saw them leer back. The looks on their faces did not escape him. They didn't want him. Not one of these bands of thieving commoners wanted any part of James Francis Morgan ... the most filthy children in all of England wanted nothing to do with him at all.

"We'll take 'em!" a shrill voice piped up from the back and Jim's spirits, if it can be believed, sunk even lower than a moment before. Jim had heard that voice just a few minutes before, as had every other member of the court. Their reaction was not quite so subdued as Jim's.

"The Ratt brothers," the king announced, smiling. "Perfect," he said as the other clans once more burst into uproarious laughter.

"Then the deal is set!" the King of Thieves announced over the cacophony. "The King of Thieves will give Jim Morgan a chance for the gypsy's box! If he can prove he is one of us, he shall gain what he has lost, but if not ... the box is mine forever!" The crowd cheered and once more the King leaned in close to Jim.

"I don't want anything to do with your stupid bet!" Jim protested. "I'm not a thief!"

"Oh you will be, my son." The king smiled a toothy grin. "When your belly starts to ache you'll become one real quick. And you'd better become a good one too, or you'll never see your little box again."

"Why? You can't even get it open!"

"Don't underestimate the King of Thieves, Jim. Gypsy magic is hardly the only sorcery still lurking about old England and certainly not the most powerful. If they were such good wizards, don't you think they could get rid of that wretched smell?" The King laughed along with his court, walking away as his silent partner appeared from the shadows to collect their pile of treasure.

The children of the court also slowly trickled out, still laughing and catcalling to Jim, who slumped down on the cold cobblestone in a miserable heap. At that moment, with the tears threatening and not a friend in sight, he may have been the loneliest boy in all of England.

TWELVE

THE CLAN OF THE RATT

Jim sat there in the deepening dark of the courtyard. All had grown quiet about him and he was sure that the entire audience of children had abandoned him to his own means when a small hand gently patted his shoulder.

"It'll be all right," the voice that belonged to the hand said. Jim was about to wrench the hand off of his shoulder and spout some nastiness when he looked up to find himself staring into the bluest set of eyes he'd ever seen. "I still cry sometimes myself, and I've been here on the streets for weeks now."

She was a girl just a tad bit younger than Jim himself. Her auburn curls hung in a tangled mess about her dirt-smudged face and her big blue eyes were clouded over with pity.

Jim forgot the nasty words he was about to say. But though he was secretly in need of such kind words as hers, he still remembered his pride.

"I wasn't crying," Jim said with a huge sniffle. "I just got a little … upset is all. So you can stop looking at me like that if you please."

Suddenly, the blue eyes on the little girl's face glared quite brightly under a hot scowl. "You absolutely were crying, or just about to, Mr. Jim Morgan, and it's absolutely the stupidest thing in the world to lie about the most obvious things, and it's even more stupid and rude to turn away a kind person when you haven't got a single friend in the whole wide world!" At this she stomped her foot and crossed her arms in front of her.

Well this simply caught Jim completely unprepared and he climbed to his feet, stammering to justify himself before this completely confusing girl. "I — I have friends," he said. "Loads of them!"

"Well some friends they are if they aren't even here to help you when you need them the most. That doesn't sound like friends at all."

"How should you know what a friend is like?"

"Because my mother told me! And she also told me how to *be* a good friend. And besides that, I have three friends while you have none!"

As if on queue, her three comrades, who had been standing there timidly watching the entire time made their presence known. "Hullo, mate!" said the first. Jim glumly recognized the squeaky voice and little mousy faces of the three boys.

"You must be the Ratt Brothers," Jim said, and as he stared at the nearly identical brothers with their small heads buried under oversized hats (held up only by their ears, which stuck out like a mouse's) he suddenly remembered that the fate of his box (and thus his entire future) rested on their slight shoulders. Jim really did want to cry then.

"You betcha!" said the first again, apparently unfazed by Jim's lack of enthusiasm as he proudly introduced himself and his two brothers. "Allow me to introduce the greatest of all the thieves in London! My brothers Peter and Paul, and my name is George. And we are: the Brothers Ratt!" They simultaneously took off their hats and bowed low before Jim, but no sooner had they stood up than Paul angrily slapped his hat back on his head and shoved George hard on the shoulder.

"I thought we agreed that it sounded better to say: My brothers Paul and Peter, George!"

"It does not! That sounds awful. It'd be like saying meat-mince pie. It's all backwards!" Peter retorted. "Besides, I definitely popped out before you did and that definitely puts me next in line, doesn't it? So I should be before you no matter how it sounds!"

"The priest just told you that to make you feel better about being the smallest, Peter! I'm older!"

"A priest wouldn't lie about that, Paul!"

"Both of you cool your socks!"

"Shut up, George!" Peter and Paul turned on their brother, and in a moment they fell upon one another, tumbling to the ground in a pile of punching limbs.

"Really! Not again!" the little girl said, stomping her foot in exasperation. "Are all boys this senseless? Boys! Boys! Stop it this instant!" She then surprised Jim even further, reaching into the rumbling trio and yanking them apart one at a time like a dogcatcher pulling apart a scrapping pile of pups. Jim stared at her with raised eyebrows.

"I had four cousins ... all boys," she said, catching Jim's stare. "And all stupid," she added with a disapproving look in the Ratt Brothers' direction. But, noticing their crestfallen faces at her rebuke, she added with some tenderness: "But as far as boys go, they are at least as good a thieves as they say."

With that compliment, the boys' exuberance returned and they clasped arms around one another's shoulders, smiling with faces formed of black eyes, bloody noses, and swollen lips.

"So, how do I know who's who?" Jim asked.

"Isn't it obvious?" the boys said in perfect unison. "I'm the good-looking one!"

The girl rolled her eyes and quickly instructed Jim on the actual way to tell them apart. "There are two ways. First, George has three freckles going across the bridge of his nose."

"I do not!" George said, immediately putting his hand to his nose as if he could feel whether or not the freckles were actually there.

"Peter really is the smallest."

"What!?" Peter exclaimed, but the girl immediately soothed his concern.

"But only by a little and I'm sure you'll grow out of it. And Paul has the curliest hair."

"And what's the second way?" Jim asked.

"By what they do of course!" the girl said, as though it were obvious. "George picks pockets, Peter picks locks, and Paul —"

"Picks his nose!" Peter said.

"I DO NOT!" Paul raged, and the boys immediately set upon one another once again.

"— and Paul is a natural born con man," the girl finished, and this time she just sighed as the boys tussled until they finally either forgot about what they were fighting over or just plain wore themselves out.

"And what's your name?" Jim finally asked.

"My name is Lacey," she said, and then turned back to the Ratts, who were now dusting one another off and praising each other's fighting skills.

"You have a mean right hook, Peter! An absolute earth shaker!"

"Your chin is like an oak, Paul! Like solid oak!"

"Men should mind their distance about us, that's for certain!"

"Now boys," Lacey said, and they straightened up to listen. "We need to get home and to bed so we can start practicing tomorrow."

"Practicing?" Jim asked. "For what?"

"For thieving, mate," Peter said.

"We'll need to be in tip-top form if we're going to get your box back. The Dragons may be as big and dumb as they look, but they aren't bad crooks, that's for sure."

"You — you're really going to help me?" Jim asked.

"Of course we are, Jim," George said and clapped him on the shoulder. "You're part of our clan now. That makes you our friend, and we always help our friends." Jim didn't know why, but his throat got all lumpy again, but this time, to his surprise, it wasn't an entirely sad lump.

"So," said Peter. "Is that box really yours?"

"Yeah," chimed in Paul. "Must be somethin' important to have you take on the King himself for it."

Jim swallowed hard. As kind as these new friends seemed he was not quite ready to share his secret. "It's just a family heirloom, that's all. From my father."

"Ah, yes," George nodded knowingly. "I have me father's earlobes as well. Always important to keep such things safe." Jim was about to correct him, but George and his brothers seemed quite satisfied with themselves and with no further discussion turned to leave the courtyard.

So, being completely exhausted and with nowhere else to go, Jim followed his new friends out of the court and down the street, hoping against hope that there was even a small chance of getting back his box and setting his life straight once again.

THIRTEEN

CONSTABLE BUTTERSTREET

J im opened his eyes to a gray London morning after tossing and turning through one of the most miserable nights of sleep in the history of sleeping. Of course there was the obvious fact that Jim had just come off one of the most miserable days ever as well, having been robbed, beaten up, mocked, held at the mercy of the King of Thieves, and press-ganged into a troupe of pickpockets called, of all things, the Brothers Ratt.

But the actual act of sleeping had been equally horrendous as the only pillow Jim had been able to find was a hard, flat brick, and his only blanket had been a dingy old coat that one of the Ratts let him borrow. All of this might have been tolerable, but Jim also dreamed a nightmare of his aunt, the horrible captain with black hair and blue eyes, and, just before he awoke, of the shadowy cloaked man, raven perched atop his shoulder. What was worse, Jim knew that by losing the box the night before, had lost his only means of making all of this mess right again.

Jim hobbled to his feet, twisted, and popped his back and neck back into proper position, then took a look around. The Ratts lived in an abandoned cellar beneath a shoe factory with a hole in the wall that acted as the only window and only door to their "house." Although, Jim noted, as far as homes made out of abandoned cellars beneath shoe factories went, this one was only half horrible. Its occupants had managed to steal enough odds and ends to give the place a sense of homeliness.

A wooden coat rack leaned crookedly by the hole, the Ratts' stolen caps and scarves hanging haphazardly from its hooks, and a small set of empty drawers sat nearly collapsed against the far wall. Beside the chest of drawers a rickety shelf barely stood on its wobbly legs beneath a load of stolen books the children couldn't read. On the top shelf sat a row of various soldiers' hats stolen off various soldiers' heads, and even a cracked vase containing a few flowers with broken stalks and only a few petals stood on a small, plain table in the middle of the room. As for bedding, the Ratts had piled bunches of burlap potato sacks in the corners of the room, one for each of the brothers and Lacey – though each of Jim's new friends had been decent enough to loan him one sack from each of their own piles to make him a bed beside the chest of drawers.

"It didn't always look this fantastic, Jim," George said as he popped out of bed, the seemingly everlasting smile stretched across his small face. "Believe you me, before Lacey came along this place was a real dump!"

"I can only imagine," Jim said.

"Yes, sir!" George exclaimed. "She made us sweep up and even got Paul to talk an old florist into lending us that vase with the flowers, if you catch my drift ... don't go back to that corner much anymore though ... he was a fast blighter for a florist. A woman's touch, Jim, that's all the old home front needed, a woman's touch! And now look at it!"

"Home sweet home, eh?" Jim tried to force a smile and turned away before his true feelings about the cellar accidentally escaped, as he needed these Ratts help to retrieve his box.

"Yep," George said. "A man's home is his castle as long as he's the king of it, that's what our Pa always used to say."

"You didn't know our father, George!" Peter said from the pile of sacks that was his bed, stretched and yawning himself awake.

"Or our mother, for that matter," Paul added, wiping away the sleepy goobers from his eyes.

"True," George said with a nod, still smiling. "But that doesn't mean he didn't say it, does it?"

"True enough indeed!" Peter said, and he and Paul jumped merrily out of bed.

Jim said nothing about it, but he was entirely perplexed at the never-ending smiles the Ratt brothers wore on their mousy faces. As far as he could tell, the three of them were disliked by their peers, had never known their own mother or father, had not a penny to their name, and lived in a cellar (however orderly a cellar it may have been). Yet Jim had seen nary a frown on their faces, even when they were beating one another to a pulp.

"How about some breakfast, Jim?" George said. At the mere mention of food, Jim felt his insides rumble and realized it had been quite some time since he'd had his last meal. But the instant image of he and the Ratt Brothers gnawing on old birdseed or rotten tomatoes behind a shack somewhere popped into Jim's head and his appetite grew suddenly dubious.

"What's on the menu?" Jim asked warily.

"Buttered eggs!" Peter shouted, his eyes wide.

"Greasy bacon!" Paul added.

"Warm toast!" George said.

"Apples!"

"Tea!"

"Hot coffee!"

"Pastries!"

Jim's entire mood immediately lifted and he almost did a cart-wheel at the thought of such a magnificent feast. Perhaps being poor and homeless wasn't so bad after all, he thought, and he and the three brothers bolted toward the hole when Lacey's sharp voice caught them from the rear.

"Now boys!" she said, standing on her pile of sacks, arms crossed and foot tapping. "Aren't we forgetting something?

Over the past few days, Jim had been feeling all manner of new sensations and emotions, and now he experienced a bit more of the unpleasantness of guilt. He and the Ratts hadn't even thought about waking Lacey before dashing off. "We were going to bring some back for you, I'm sure," Jim offered with a weak smile.

"That's not what I mean!" Lacey said angrily. "They know why they didn't wake me first."

"Why's that?" Jim asked, noting the three brothers' faces were indeed more guilt-ridden than even his own.

"Oh c'moff it, Lacey!" George said, Peter and Paul immediately taking up his side.

"Do we have to?"

"We're starving! We can do it after breakfast!"

"We absolutely cannot do it after breakfast, Peter!" Lacey said, stomping her foot. "That defeats the entire point."

"Point of what?" Jim asked.

"A bath!" the three brothers said as one, throwing their hands up in the air.

"This i-i-i-s i-i-intolera-a-ble!" Jim tried to say a few moments later through chattering teeth as he stood waste deep in the cold water of the River Thames. He had never taken a bath in open water before and, having been drawn hot baths his whole life, found the experience rather earth shaking and immediately wiped clean from his mind the idea of homelessness being anything less than barbaric.

"O-o-ne of th-these d-days we're gonna to f-f-freeze to d-death!" Paul said, angrily staring at a rock in the water, behind which Lacey bathed herself.

"Stop whining, you whelps!" Jim heard her call without shivering from the other side. "I swear, boys are such wimps!"

"W-w-e are n-n-not!" George said, the cold bringing tears that nearly ran down his cheeks. "I l-l-love b-b-baths! Th-there my f-f-favorite th-th-ing in th-th-the whole w-w-world!"

"Y-y-y-yeah!" Peter tried nodding his head one time but it kept jittering up and down to the point that Jim couldn't tell when he had stopped nodding and was just standing still. Of course, all three boys still kept trying to smile and Jim couldn't help but think that those happy boys - with chattering teeth and little arms wrapped tightly around their skinny white bodies - really did look like three mice holding a squeaky conversation. Then Jim noticed something about himself. He was smiling. For the first time in some days, was smiling. In fact, he was laughing.

"H-h-h-h-h-a-a-a!" Jim's laugh chattered out. And that itself was as funny to the Ratt Brothers as they were to him. Soon all four boys were laughing their heads off and splashing in the water.

"S-s-see!" George exclaimed. "W-w-we do love b-b-baths!"

Fortunately the baths lasted only a few, freezing moments longer and the children clambered out of the water and quickly dressed. They then ran all the way to a nearby market square. The sun peeked out from behind the drab clouds and between the warmer air and the running, all five of them were quite dry by the time they reached the busy market.

The square sat just beyond the shadowy streets where the King of Thieves held court and the people there seemed as much brighter as the city around them. The inns and shops were open and crowds bustled from store to store or sat down at tables on the cobblestone to enjoy some breakfast. The delicious smells of a hundred different foods filled the air, including all the ones the Ratts had mentioned and more. Jim's mouth watered and he rubbed his hands together in anticipation.

"So, where shall we eat?" he asked.

"Behind this building, under that tree," George said, jerking his head toward the shop to his left.

"Meet us back in ten minutes," Peter added, and with that they were off.

"Wait!" Jim cried after them. "I don't have any money!" But it was to no avail: his four new comrades were already out of sight. Jim kicked a rock at his feet and listened to his belly growl again. "Well, that was nice," he said to himself. But he did remember that the Ratts had put a roof over his head and had invited them to join their gang, so perhaps they would spot him a few coins upon their return. He went and sat down under the tree behind the shop and waited – but not for long.

Peter came back first, a small sack in his hands. He sat down and opened the bag to reveal an entire greasy pile of buttered eggs and a whole grilled potato. Paul arrived next, juggling a splendidly long chain of linked sausages while trying not to spill a cup of steaming hot tea. George and Lacey came right behind Paul with a loaf of bread, some pastries, and a handful of crispy bacon.

"Did you already eat all of yours, Jim?" Peter asked through a mouthful of potato.

"That wasn't very polite," Paul said with a sausage in his mouth. "We usually share, except when George is being a pig and doesn't leave me any bacon!"

"I always share with you youngins!" George shot back, nearly spitting some half chewed bread out as he did.

"One year, George! You're only one year older than us!"

"One year is a lifetime with you yahoos!"

The brothers were about to tumble again when Lacey noticed Jim's wide-eyed stare and the bit of hungry drool hanging from his lips.

"Jim, you didn't get anything yet did you?" she said, her blue eyes shining brightly in the sunlight. "We should be ashamed of ourselves! Here, take some of this and this and this!" In the blink of an eye Jim found a nice pile of bread, eggs, bacon, and sausage set before him.

Jim wanted to say thank you but his hands were, at the moment, strictly under his stomach's control and he immediately began shoveling food into his hungry mouth.

"Didn't you see a good opening over there, mate?" George asked.

"Were the King's Men around, you know, the constables?" Paul wondered.

"Yeah, Butterstreet and his crew? Did you see 'em?" Peter asked.

"I don't know what you mean," Jim said with a mouthful of everything, which never tasted better to him in his whole life. "I just didn't have any money."

The three brothers stared at Jim for a long moment, then exploded into laughter, rolling around in the grass and all over each other, food flying in all directions from their mouths, and landing all over their faces and their clothes. "You got me with that one, Jim! That was a winner! That was a winner!"

"He's a master of comedy! A master!"

"A regular court jester!"

"I think he's being serious," Lacey said. "And stop talking with your mouths full of food; it's disgusting!" The three brothers stopped laughing and sat still, staring at Jim.

"None of us have any money, Jim," George said matter-of-factly. "Don't you remember what we do for a living? Remember, last night? King of *Thieves:* tall chap, rather creepy, big pile of treasure? We don't buy things Jim, we steal 'em."

"I've never stolen a thing in my life!" Jim said, indignant.

Now the Ratts didn't just stare, their little mousy jaws fell open and just hung there, agape with stupefaction. "You've never stolen ... anything?" Paul finally asked.

"No," Jim said. "In fact, I'm not sure I would even know how if I wanted to." And then, even though part of him was still stuck with the idea that he was a noble, Jim grew suddenly afraid that the Ratt Brothers were going to kick him out of their clan - and he would lose the only opportunity he had to get his box back, even if it did involve stealing. But, as usual, the three boys smiled as brightly as ever.

"Well, fortunate for you, mate. You've joined the greatest clan of thieves in all of London! A few simple lessons from us, and you'll be as right as Robin thievin' Hood!"

Not a few moments later, after all the food had been gobbled up and the dishes returned (Lacey said it was rude to leave them in the grass and that even though they were forced to be thieves at the moment they could still afford to be polite,) the five children stood in the market across from a stand piled high with neat rows of scrumptious, green apples.

"Right then," said George, rubbing his hands together and nodding toward the cart. "Watch us first, just to get the general idea of it all. Then you'll give it a go, right?"

"Right," Jim agreed, focusing intently on the apple cart. Crowds of people passed back and forth, browsing and buying. Some stopped to look at the apples and inspect them for ripeness. "You can go ahead and start," Jim said, "I'm watching closely and I won't miss —" He turned his head back to George and found he and his two brothers munching on crunchy green apples. Paul had one in each hand and Peter was trying to hold five or six and kept dropping some while he trying to take bites. Jim's mouth hung open in disbelief and his eyes went as wide as saucers.

"That was incredible!" Jim exclaimed. "You are great! That was the fastest thing I've ever seen!"

"We told you!" the three exclaimed together.

"So why don't the other clans want you around?" Jim asked them. "You guys are amazing!"

"Jealousy," Peter said as he spat out an apple seed.

"They're green with envy," Paul said, sticking out his tongue with chewed-up green apple all over it.

"Disgusting, Paul!" Lacey said.

"Well, they are fairly jealous of our tremendous skills," George explained, polishing his filthy nails on his filthy shirt. "But part of it is also our set of rules."

"Rules?" Jim asked.

"Well, guidelines, really," Peter said.

"Sort of our code, like for knights or somethin'," Paul added.

"Exactly, our code!" George nodded vigorously. "We don't steal from children. We only take what we need, and we never take from someone who has less than us."

"Which fortunately leaves us with loads of options!" Paul said cheerfully.

"See, the Dragons took from another kid; you namely," Peter explained. "They do it all the time. They're dirty scoundrels. Rotten to the core. They'll take from anyone, even if it was the last farthing in some bloke's pocket or the last crumb off his table!"

"How unscrupulous," Jim said.

"Exactly what I said!" said George, as though he knew what scruples were and what it was to be without them. "So when we saw that they had nicked your box, we decided it was the right thing to lend you a hand and get back at those lugs!"

"Well, I'm ready," Jim said, and tried to loosen up for the task at hand. Ever since his disastrous trek through the forest, when he realized he had missed out on several good opportunities to learn some rather useful skills, Jim had decided not to turn down such chances again. To learn the art of thieving from the Ratts was as good a time to start as any. "What do I do?"

"Right then," George said, the Ratts gathering close around Jim like three trainers in a boxer's corner. "Here's what you do. Walk up to that cart ... and take one of those apples!"

"Brilliant!"

"Spot on, George! Solid advice!"

"Go get 'em, Jim!" The brothers clapped Jim on the back, excited beyond control for Jim's first action.

"That's it?" Jim asked, puzzled. "Just walk up and take an apple, that's all there is to it?"

"Well, not exactly," George said. "But it's a great start. So go for it! We're right behind you!"

"Just walk up and take an apple?"

"That's it!" the three of them replied together.

Jim took a deep breath and started toward the apple cart. Although it sounded easy, Jim had never been more nervous in his life. He felt hot and itchy all over, his face feeling as though it were all but on fire, and his hands trembled uncontrollably. It seemed to Jim that everyone in the market was staring right at him at that exact moment.

"Look casual, that's the ticket," Jim said to himself. He shoved his shaking hands in his pockets and started to whistle. Then he tried to look absolutely anywhere but at the apple cart. Unfortunately for poor Jim, although he had the right idea, his efforts had a slightly confusing effect. He couldn't walk in a straight line because he wasn't looking. His head was rolling around on his neck from trying to look everywhere but the apple cart and his whistle sounded like a dying bird.

"What's he doin'?" George asked from where they stood watching.

"I think he's pretending to be dimwitted … you know mad or something. Like a charity con, you know?" Peter said.

"He's not a bad actor really," Paul said. "He looks completely feebleminded from here."

Jim found the apple cart when he ran face-first into it. The whole cart trembled violently and Jim held his chin in pain where it had slammed into a wooden corner. That feeling of everyone watching him washed over Jim again, and then he did the worst thing one can do when trying to appear casual. He panicked.

Jim desperately grabbed the first apple he saw and turned to run. But he realized too late that he had seized a fruit that was impossibly wedged into the bottom of the pile. Instead of trying for a different apple, Jim - as people who are panicked often do - made the fatal error of yanking on the one in his hand as hard as he could.

The apple finally popped out, along with every other apple on the entire cart, and they all went spilling onto ground.

"Oh, dear," Lacey said from where she stood by the Ratts.

From behind the quickly shrinking pile of apples the furious red face of the cart owner appeared. His eyes fell directly on Jim, standing by the cart with an apple in his hand, a hundred at his feet, and look of dread horror on his face.

"THIEF!" the cart owner screamed, leveling an accusing finger right at Jim's face.

"Well," George remarked in stunned dryness, "that didn't go very well."

"Oh, run, Jim, run!" Lacey pleaded. But it was no use. Just as he had in the forest, facing the floating green eyes of the wolf, Jim froze in place amongst a sea of rolling apples as the cart owner continued to shriek.

"THIEF!"

Jim probably would have stood there forever, staring at the furious apple seller had Peter, Paul, and George not leapt to his side to drag him away. But just as they reached their new friend's side, the crowds staring at the strange goings on parted to the left and to the right, revealing a sight that paled even the faces of the three Ratts.

There, standing in the parted waves of people, was the biggest man Jim had ever seen. He wore a faded blue tricorn hat, a droopy beard that surrounded his fiercely frowning face, and the badge of the King's Men over his heart. In his left hand he balanced a long, thick staff with expert fingers.

"What in blazes?" Jim exclaimed. "It's a giant!"

"That's no giant," Paul cried. "Worse!"

"Constable Butterstreet!" his brothers cried as the big man covered the distance between he and the young thieves in just two enormous strides. The boys looked to run, but the constable's two deputies suddenly appeared behind them, tapping staffs of their own in their burly hands.

"Well, well, well, if it isn't the Ratt Brothers up to their old tricks," the huge king's man rumbled in the deepest voice imaginable.

"Hullo, Butterstreet ol' chum," George offered with a tug on his cap like a small salute. "Hope the missus is well and that you've recovered from that nasty bit o' pneumonia you came down with last month."

"Oh, I'm doing just fine, George, thank ya' kindly. How nice of you to check on my health after our little incident by the riverside."

"Water under the bridge as far as I'm concerned," George said, but his brothers smacked their foreheads and Butterstreet gripped his staff a little tighter.

"Still workin' for the King, I see," Butterstreet growled.

"Oh, you've got it all wrong," Paul said, flashing a winning grin and winking at the constable. "We were just here to help this poor man pick up all his apples. Clumsy old goof, isn't he?" Paul thumbed over to the cart owner but when he looked at the miserable old seller - who's face was as red as a turnip with fury - his con man's smile dropped right off his mouth.

"I'm sure you are, Paulie," said the constable, almost laughing. "And who is your new friend, here?"

"J-j-im Morgan ... sir," Jim said as the shadow of the constable loomed over the four boys. "And might I add that I too am glad you're over your pneumonia. If it was only a month ago, though, might I suggest a little bit more rest at home by the fire?"

"How thoughtful of you, Jim. But I'll tell you this. Nothing heals my body and soul like the sound of converted thieves singin' in my parish choir and recitin' their lessons day after day." The constable stared down at them from beneath a huge set of bushy eyebrows that drooped just like his beard. "Sorry boys, but this is the end of the road. You had a good run, but —"

Just then, an apple, as if dropped from the sky, bopped the old constable right on the noggin and fell into his hand. He looked at the apple curiously and then up into the air. Then another smacked him on the side of the head.

"Birds!" declared one of the two deputies, neither of which were nearly as clever or devoted as faithful Butterstreet. "Birds are dropping apples out of the sky! Just like in the Bible!"

"Not birds, you imbeciles!" Butterstreet thundered. "It's her!"

"You betcha!" Lacey cried, firing another delicious green projectile at the constable's head. "Come and get me!" She stuck out her tongue and the constable's face turned as red as the cart owners. He whirled about to take one of his massive strides to snatch Lacey up, but the Ratt Brothers didn't miss the golden opportunity.

"Kick!" George shouted to Jim.

"What?" Jim asked, but got the idea as soon as the three brothers kicked the apples around their feet into Butterstreet's path. Jim joined in just in time, kicking a perfectly placed ball of fruit beneath one of Butterstreet's huge feet so that the big man's legs flipped right out from beneath him.

"Scramble!" George cried, and without another word the four boys and Lacey were off like a shot.

The two deputies, more concerned with their fallen chief than the escaping pickpockets, leaned over to pull Butterstreet up, but he was far heavier than they expected. Not to mention that they also stepped on several rolling apples themselves, so that in another moment they too ended up on their backsides beside their captain.

"Not me, you dolts!" Butterstreet roared. "Get them, the thieves!"

The two witless deputies sprang after the fleeing children, leaving Butterstreet sitting with a mess of freshly mashed applesauce all over his britches.

FOURTEEN

CLOSE ESCAPES, ROOFTOPS, AND HIDDEN LAIRS

As Constable Butterstreet picked himself up off the slimy ground, the children ran for their lives from his two comrades. They leapt over bums in the street, scattered pigeons, knocked over street vendors, and upset tables. From a distance, the little gang looked like five small bowling balls rolling down the street destroying everything in their path. The two King's Men followed as closely as they could, dutifully holding their hats on their heads and apologizing to everyone as they went.

"Sorry, sire!"

"'Scuse us, milady!"

"Don't worry, we'll apprehend the little runts!" they declared as they high-stepped over the destruction in the streets.

The Ratt Brothers, who had practically grown up on the run from one authority or the other, were as fast as jackrabbits. And Lacey, while new to the outlaw life, was a natural athlete and had little problem keeping pace. But Jim, who had hardly ever needed to walk down a hallway for his own cup of water, found himself gasping for air after only two blocks. By the fourth block he felt the sudden (and terrifying for the first time) burn of a fierce stitch in his side.

"I can't go on!" he sputtered. "I'm having a heart attack!"

"You're not having a heart attack, nitwit!" Lacey said, barely out of breath. "You're just in horrible shape. Really, didn't you ever run anywhere?"

"No!" Jim gasped.

"All right," George interjected. "Split up. Me and Lacey are the fastest and we'll lead the quicker deputy right. Paul and Peter, take Jim up on the roofs! You know what to do from there!"

"Right!" Paul and Peter said, and the five children broke in opposite directions at the next intersection. Fortunately, George's plan worked, and the faster of the two deputies followed Lacey and George. But they were small and light and knew the streets of the city like an old nursery rhyme and the poor deputy hardly stood a chance.

Paul and Peter, meanwhile, even though slowed down a bit by Jim, had a plan of their own.

"C'mon, Jim!" they shouted to their lagging friend. "We just need to do a little climbing!"

"Climbing?" Jim said, dismayed. "I can barely walk!" he complained, but one look over his shoulder at the steadily gaining deputy changed his tune. "Climbing it is!"

The three boys almost bowled over a sad little old man and old woman hobbling out of a two-story pawnshop where they must have traded the last of some precious family heirlooms for enough money to eat. Jim had never been to a pawnshop before, but Phineus had told him what they were: sad and tragic places. The Ratts didn't lead him inside the pawnshop, however, but rather around to the rear of the place, where thick ivy grew up the back of the brick building.

"Up we go!" Peter shouted, and Jim watched in amazement as the two Ratts scampered up the ivy as nimbly as squirrels. Jim, on the other hand, was not nearly so dexterous. He clumsily put one hand over the other and refused to move his feet until they found an overly sure toehold. While safer, this technique was not nearly fast enough. The deputy, who was now hot, red-faced, and highly agitated, rounded the corner, skidding to a halt at the ivy.

"Oy!" the exhausted deputy cried up at Jim. "I've had just about enough of you lot today! Now c'mon, school's not so bad, or church, or work even! Why not just come down and make it easy on me, eh?"

"Sorry," Jim said. "But I have other things I need to get done! I —" Jim was about to say something smart when he made the dreadful mistake many before have made of looking down while in the middle of a climb. The effect, as it always is, was rather dizzying. Jim was about two thirds the way up the building (which is a fairly long drop for an 11-year-old boy) when he looked down, fear suddenly telling him that two-thirds was as far as he was going to go.

"Come on, Jim!" Peter urged from the ledge of the roof.

"You're almost there, mate!" Paul added.

"I'm stuck!" Jim said, but what he really meant was that his frightened hands and feet no longer possessed the power to move.

"You're not stuck!"

"You can make it!" Jim's friends tried to encourage him, but it was no use, he wasn't climbing another inch.

"Fine then!" the deputy called up. "I was going to go easy on you with Butterstreet, but not if you're going to make me come up there after you!" The deputy leant his staff up against the wall, took a deep breath, and then grabbed onto the ivy and started to make his way up the wall.

"COME ON, JIM!" Peter and Paul were desperate now. They couldn't wait much longer before they would have to run and leave their friend behind or risk being caught themselves. But even though

Jim felt the dreadful tug of the deputy climbing up beneath him, he was frozen in place.

Fortunately though, luck chose a good time to side with Jim. There was a reason that this deputy was the slower of the two: the extra twenty pounds he carried in a belly that hung over his belt. The ivy that easily held the weight of 11-year-old boys was not so reliable under the strain of a full-grown man.

The ivy trembled. Then it groaned. Strands pulled away from the wall. The poor deputy, who was right at Jim's feet, looked up and winced.

"Oh, dear," he said as the vines in his hands tore away just below Jim's shoes.

Jim looked back down. The deputy lay in a giant pile of green leaves and tendrils. The Ratts, thanks to the fact that the ivy was no longer stuck to the wall as much, pulled Jim up by the vines.

"That was close," Peter said as he and Paul strained to pull Jim onto the roof.

Jim's heart beat like a hammer and he sat down gasping for air. "That was horrible!" Jim took steady, deep breaths, trying to calm himself down.

Paul peered back over the ledge, smiling at the flustered deputy, who had had quite enough sport for the day.

"Madness! That's what this is! Madness!" The miserable man stood and, in a daze from his fall, swayed back and forth as he ripped and pulled at the vines that covered him. "I should have been a tailor, or an innkeeper, or even a blacksmith! These kids are animals! Animals! I quit!" he shouted to himself, and still decorated in leafy green, staggered out of the alley and down the street.

"How many is that this year, Peter?" Paul asked. "Five?"

"Six, if you count the one on New Year's," Peter corrected his brother and they slapped their knees and laughed out loud at their own private joke. "Now, come on Jim, we're not home yet."

"How are we going to get down?" Jim asked. "The vines are broken."

"Down?" Paul said with a laugh, pointing. "We don't go down yet. We still have to go *over*!"

"Over?" Jim's face fell as he followed the direction of Paul's pointing finger. There was a path of rooftops leading all the way back to the lightless and drab section of town that was their home. "Are you daft? You can't be serious!" Jim gaped.

"It's easy Jim," Peter assured him. "It's like flying!" And then without hesitation he leapt over the small space between the two roofs. (It was only about five feet mind you, but do remember this was a different time and a different place, and, under normal circumstances, Jim was absolutely right. Jumping across rooftops is a very bad idea.)

"It really is no problem, chum," Paul added as he too sailed over the space between the buildings and landed safely on the other side. "Just don't look down and you'll be right on target!"

Paul meant the advice well, but Jim took it just a bit too literally. Looking straight ahead (or even a little bit up) Jim stiffly stood and took a running start. However, by not looking down at all he failed to notice that his feet were still tangled in the long vines of ivy used to pull him to safety. Just as Jim was about to make his jump, he felt a small tug at his ankles.

"Bloody hell!" Jim exclaimed, and down he went. Now Jim wasn't only looking down, he was flying that way, dropping straight through the air toward the cobblestones beneath him, screaming the entire way. But once more the sticky ivy saved his life. Just as Jim thought he was going to finish his dive face-first into the alley, he came to a jolting stop and hung suspended by the long vine wrapped around his ankle.

"Why does this keep happening to me?" Jim asked the fates as he hung upside-down for the second time in only a week. Now, there's not much one can do while hanging upside-down by the ankle save spin around in a circle and try to keep the blood from rushing to the head by looking up and around. So that's what Jim did, and as he slowly drifted around, gazing anywhere but at the ground, his eyes passed the dingy pawnshop window, and there inside Jim found himself staring at the long-nosed face of the King of Thieves.

FIFTEEN

THE KING'S SECRET

The King of Thieves hunkered his spindly frame over desk in the pawnshop office, squinting one eye around a rather complicated bronze monocle. The King constantly fiddled with the device at his eye, rotating a small gear with his long fingers to shift a number of multicolored lenses through the eyepiece. Through these lenses the King intently analyzed a golden charm dangling at end of a fine chain, all the while comparing the charm to a peculiar drawing in a book on the desk. After a few moments of study the King tossed the necklace over his shoulder with a disgusted snarl and slammed the book shut with a grunt. Jim watched the necklace sail through the air in a glittering arc land on the floor in an astounding pile of hundreds of such treasures, tossed aside as if they were trash.

"You look for a needle in a haystack," Jim heard a voice say from the back of the office. It was the short, dumpy man who had hidden in the shadows in the court, and he looked none too pleased with the situation.

"Yes, but this particular needle is the key to untold treasures, my dear Wyzcark," the King said. "Treasures that will make us as powerful as the kings of both of our countries!"

"So you say," Wyzcark replied with a grunt, and Jim noted that the squat man's accent sounded similar to the gypsy's who had hexed his box, though not nearly as thick. "You also say that it is magical and can unlock many great secrets. But in this age of reason, such things are disappearing and have become nearly impossible to believe in, much less find, in spite of the texts you've shown me."

"Doubting me already, Wyzcark? You've read the ancient manuscript – the details are too rich to be fabricated. But arcane texts or no – I've seen the Amulet with my own eyes. I've seen what it can do." The King took the monocle away from his face, his dark eyes glaring fiercely at his counterpart. "Besides Wyzcark, can we really stop now? In the face of this incredible stroke of luck we've just had?" The King set the monocle down on his workbench – right beside Jim's box.

Jim's heart skipped a beat. There, just beside the King's elbow, sat Jim's box! There was also a crowbar, a chisel, a hammer, and a saw. All of these tools were broken or bent, but the box remained whole, nary a chip on it's stained lid. The gypsy magic held stronger than the King of Thieves thought, Jim realized with some satisfaction.

"Luck is for amateurs," Wyczark said with a sniff. "I grow impatient, and if your little thieves continue to fail us, I will bring in experts from my country. I will have this done properly."

"The moment your 'experts' step foot on English shores the authorities will catch wind of our venture and King's Men will pour in like rain from the heavens to take our prize!" the King of Thieves exclaimed, throwing his hands into the air only to quickly calm himself and make his case. "Wyzcark, my portly friend, trust me. My ways are the best ways: the slow ways, the patient ways, yes, but the quiet ways, the shadow and whisper ways. Soon the amulet will be ours, and perhaps, just perhaps, even more than what we had first hoped." The King kept his eyes on Wyzcark, but his spidery fingers lightly crawled across the box's lid.

"I thought you said that the amulet is our great prize?" Wyzcark asked, one eyebrow arching as he followed the King's hand to the box. "What could you possibly want with the boy's stupid box?"

"The Amulet is a key to a great many treasures, Wyczark," the King said with the noticeably forced patience that all adults are so poor at faking. "But we aren't looking for just any treasure are we? We're looking for *vast* treasures – great and immeasurable treasures men have sought through the ages."

"What could this boy's box possibly have to do with such treasure?"

"Oh, dear Wyzcark," the King said, dryly, drumming his spidery fingers on Jim's box. "Would you only give yourself over to study every once in a while. I have examined the old legends, the arcane and ancient tales and texts. In such texts are many symbols, and this symbol, the simple image engraved on the box's lid is a pirate symbol … the pirate symbol of a legendary treasure thought lost beneath the waves long ago."

Jim's beat-skipping heart began to hammer in his chest. So the symbol of the scepter had a meaning after all! Hudson had told him that the secret to his father's treasure had been *in* the box. Was it written *on* the box as well? Could his father have possibly found this legendary treasure on his last, mysterious voyage?

Jim strained his ears to hear more of the muffled conversation when the sound of another familiar voice chimed in behind him, and unfortunately there was no wall between Jim and this speaker.

"Well, well, well, if it isn't the la'est, grea'est member of the Ratt clan, or does he think he's a monkey swingin' from a vine?" Jim closed his eyes and sighed as a rough hand spun him away from the window and back toward the alley. Big Red stood in the alley, upside down in Jim's eyes, the widest and wickedest smile Jim could imagine splayed across his face. Red's lunks were there too, laughing dumbly beside their chief.

"A monkey! Brilliant!"

"That's what he is all right, a lil' monkey, you said it, Red! Spot on! Spot on!"

"A monkey — a monkey that smells like cabbage!"

All three of the lunks pranced around, hooting like organ grinder's monkeys until Red snapped his fingers (although he did have to snap twice because the third lunk continued hooting and laughing at his own ridiculousness after the first time.)

"So does the monkey want somethin' to eat?" Red taunted. "An apple perhaps? A nice green one?" Red said with a laugh, his three lunks laughing with him. Jim wished with all his heart that he could just disappear. Apparently word got around fast amongst the clans and his embarrassing failure in the market was already juicy gossip. "We all know about it, my good fell-ow," Red continued mercilessly. "That was the worst nickin' I've ever heard of! I mean seriously, it was pathetic!"

"Yeah, pathetic!" his lunks chimed in, guffawing ridiculously. There was nothing Jim could do but hang there uselessly and grow madder and more humiliated with each barb.

"So what are you doing here, besides just … hanging around?" Red and his lunks burst out laughing at his cleverness.

"Hanging around, that's —"

"Spot on?" Jim interjected angrily. Somewhere inside Jim's eleven year-old mind, he knew he should stop talking and just take what Red was giving him with gritted teeth, but Jim had taken quite enough, and in spite of his precarious position his mouth just kept right on interjecting. "Are you serious? That's the stupidest joke I've ever heard! I'm hanging around because … I'm hanging? Oh, yeah, that's spot on Red. Really brilliant! You're a genius. No really, I mean it. A regular court jester!"

As soon as Jim's mouth shut, he wished it had never opened. Red's face glowed bright as his hair. The lunks just stood there, wide-eyed, mouths hanging open like big dumb cows. Nobody spoke to Red like that. Nobody.

"Well, that's some real cheek comin' from the lil' cryin' boy."
Red's face trembled. "I saw you there, you wanker! Cryin' there on the
ground blubberin' like some loon! I bet — I bet your parents abandoned you 'cause you're so loony and you cry all the time!"

Red was shouting now, tears threatening in his eyes. It must have
been a long time indeed since anyone had made fun of him, and Jim
could tell he wasn't going to let that go easily. "I bet they were never
happier in their lives than the day you disappeared."

The knot swelled back into Jim's throat with a sudden ache and
his face grew hot and eyes got stingy. "You shut up about my parents!
You don't know anything about them!" Jim tried to keep his voice from
shaking and his chin from quivering, but it was no use. Red knew he had
the upper hand then and he was going to do anything but make this easy.

"I know that any dad or mum in England would want to get rid of
such a useless, cryin' mistake like you."

The lunks didn't laugh this time. Red didn't snap or smile. He was
serious and his pals knew it. Jim knew it, too, and as he hung there
his little heart broke all over again. The tears ran upside-down and
dripped right from his eyes to the ground.

Even the lunks looked away and started to back down the alley.
This was no fun anymore, they'd had had their fill. Red lingered for
one more satisfying smirk. "See ya' around, you monkey," he said, and
then just left Jim there to hang upside-down in misery.

After a few more moments of sniffling to himself, Jim heard Paul
and Peter scamper around the corner. "Wow, that was a close one!"
Paul exclaimed.

"We thought you were a goner for sure," Peter added. "Some
angels or something must love you, Jim! That's how lucky you were,
that's how lucky!"

Paul jumped on top of Peter's shoulders so they could reach up and
undo the tangled knot of vine around Jim's ankle, dropping him down
to the ground with an unpleasant bump.

"Sorry it took so long for us to get back," Peter said. "But we
had to go three more roofs over before we could climb down. But

wow! Somebody definitely loves … you …" The two brothers noticed Jim's face. It was certainly red from being hung upside-down, but tears drenched Jim's eyes and he must have looked as though he would never smile again.

"No," Jim said. "Nobody loves me." Then he got up and started walking down the street to the old shoe factory. Peter and Paul walked beside him, but Jim never looked their way or opened his mouth to speak. He stared at the tops of his shoes in silence as they scuffed along the dreary, cobblestone walk.

SIXTEEN

THE SHADOW PIRATE

When Jim reached the crumbly little hole to the cellar beneath the shoe factory he never even broke his stride. He walked right past it, eyes still glued to the ground. Better to leave on his own, Jim thought, than to be kicked out by the Ratts.

"Hey, Jim!" Paul called after him. "Where are you going?"

"Come back, Jim!" Peter also called from the hole, but Jim refused to listen. He knew the truth. When Lacey and George got back they would throw him out on his ear for all the trouble he'd caused them.

Jim had no clue where he was going, but he kept right on walking anyway, staring straight at the tops of his shoes and constantly wiping away his tears. Soon his nose began to run (as noses often do after a good cry) and he had to use his sleeve to wipe it since he had no handkerchief. Then his head began to throb (as heads often do after one's nose has run and eyes have cried for a long time) and Jim wondered if it were possible for a person to feel more loathsome than he did at that very moment. He had lost his box and the King of Thieves would pillage his father's treasure. Maybe Phineus had been right, Jim thought. Maybe Jim had never even deserved the noble name of Morgan.

Eventually, the crying eyes, running nose, throbbing head, and aching heart became too much and Jim could walk not another step. He stopped right in the middle of the street, looking around for the first time in some hours to see where he was.

Whether by luck or fate, somehow Jim had ended up by the bridge leading back toward his family's city home. Maybe his feet just remembered the way, or perhaps some cruel spirits somewhere thought it would be good for a laugh to rub the one place Jim desperately wanted to go, but had no hope of reaching, into his face. Either way, the mere thought of his home and his father felt like a punch in Jim's stomach and he could now add an aching midsection to his list of emotionally induced maladies.

Without a clue of what to do or where to go next, Jim stepped onto the bridge. It was quiet save for the soft sound of the flowing water beneath the walk - until a sharp caw broke the silence, the caw of a raven.

Jim saw him at the other end of the bridge, and in that moment all of Jim's worries and pains, from his aching heart to his running nose, froze solid with fear. As before, when James had first gone to his London home, here now on the bridge stood the dark pirate, the raven still perched upon his black-cloaked shoulder. He stood like a shadow that had decided to step off a wall to haunt the streets. His black hat was still pulled down low over his face and his sword hilt still protruded from beneath the edges of his greatcoat.

Jim stood petrified. This form of a pirate, this shadow pirate, terrified him as much—no, more—than even the memories of Bartholomew Cromier. But this time, unlike at his home, there were no bushes or corners behind which to hide. The pirate stepped across the other end of the bridge. Jim held his breath. Perhaps the shadow would miss him and keep walking. But the shadow stopped and turned his head toward the far end of the bridge – to look right at Jim.

Jim trembled from head to foot. The icy fear began to crack and split from the heat of a deeper surge of terror. He and the shadow pirate stood still at each side of the bridge, staring at each other for a long moment.

The pirate started across the bridge, walking straight for Jim.

There was no mistaking it, Jim knew. The shadow had been seeking him at his house, and now it had found him on the bridge. The freeze of fear that imprisoned Jim to his spot finally shattered and from somewhere inside himself Jim found the strength to run.

He had no idea where he was going, but he whipped around corners, dashed through alleys, and tore down streets that had no names. Jim looked over his shoulder, sure he would find the shadow just behind him, but when he turned a corner he ran right into a set of open arms.

"Get off, get off, let me go!" Jim cried, twisting and turning. But much to Jim's surprise, the arms never fought back. Instead, they let him go. Jim fell rather unceremoniously into a pile on the sidewalk.

"Jim!" a familiar and sweet voice said. "Whatever are you doing?"

Jim looked up. Lacey stared down at him with a look not too unlike the one she wore the first time they had met.

"I ... I was just ..." Jim looked around. There was no trace of the dark pirate anywhere. The fear trickled out of Jim, slowly replaced with the miserable pride he had been feeling before his incident on the bridge.

"I was just leaving," Jim finally managed, getting to his feet and starting to walk off again.

"Leaving?" Lacey asked with a snort. "It'll be night soon and being out here like this will only get you sick."

Jim, having been crying for some time, then terrified out of wits, and now just miserable again, was in no mood for any kindness or

sweetness to spoil his ugly misery. He walked over to a large rain barrel that had leaked into the street and stared down into the puddle,
refusing to look up at Lacey.

"Good," he said and folded his arms. "I hope I do get sick. So sick
that I —"

"Don't you even say that, Jim Morgan!" Lacey scolded sharply. Jim
could picture her eyes changing the way they had before, and, for some
reason, that made him almost want to smile. "You should be ashamed
of yourself, just running out on us like this!"

"Running out on you?" Jim nearly shouted. He finally looked up
at Lacey, who, as he had guessed, was now sporting a very cross look
indeed. "You and George were just going to kick me out of the clan
anyway after today. Admit it!"

"Kick you out?" George said over Jim's other shoulder, his smiling face suddenly appearing as well in the reflection on the puddle of
water. "Why in blazes would we kick you out? You just started!"

"Why? Why!?" Jim shook his head, throwing his hands up in the
air. "Isn't it obvious? I'm useless, absolutely useless. I couldn't get my
own breakfast. I couldn't even take one lousy apple without spilling a
hundred others. I almost got us caught by Butterstreet. I couldn't run
two blocks without nearly passing out. And then I almost got myself
killed trying to jump across the rooftops. Red was right, I'm just a big
mistake ... and it's no wonder ..." Jim felt his throat and eyes burn
again as the last words made their way out. "It's no wonder I was the
biggest disappointment my father ever had!" he blurted, and more
tears erupted as he did.

"Oh, Jim." Lacey put her hand on Jim's back, and any crossness
fled her eyes, which filled up with kindness again. "I'm sure that's not
true."

"It is," Jim said, sniffling and trying to stop crying. "I heard people say so with my own two ears."

"But did you hear your father say so?" George asked.

"Well, no ..." Jim admitted.

"Well, then, how do you know for a fact that it's true?"

"Well," Jim said. He had never thought of that before. "I guess they could be wrong ..."

"And besides," said Peter, who sidled up to Lacey. "It's not exactly like Big Red speaks the gospel truth, if you know what I mean."

"He's a dunderhead, Jim!" Paul chipped in as he too, appeared as a reflection in the puddle beside his brother George. "He's the one pick-pocket on the street I'd hand over to Butterstreet meself!"

"Now that's something we can all agree on," Lacey said. "Big Red is a brute!"

"He used to wet the bed at St. Anne's orphanage, that's what I heard," Peter said.

"Probably still does," George added, and for the first time that day, Jim smiled and laughed a slobbery laugh beneath his running nose and tear-stained cheeks.

"You probably still do too, George," Paul said with a laugh.

"I never wet the bed, Paul, that was Peter!"

"IT WAS NOT!"

Lacey and Jim laughed again, and when Jim looked down he saw five faces staring back up at him from the puddle instead of just his one, and for a reason other than fear, the aches and pains inside him drifted away.

Together the children walked back to the hole, laughing and jok-ing the entire way, though Jim kept one ear out for the sharp call of a raven. Jim knew his situation was still dire. The box that held his father's secret was in the clutches of the King of Thieves (who some-how knew something about the treasure no less,) a shadowy pirate was apparently chasing him around London, and he was sleeping in a cellar beneath an old shoe factory with a gang of thieves. But even the cellar, Jim surmised, was a safer place than any other from the dangers that surrounded him of late.

SEVENTEEN

THIEVIN' 101

ll right, Jim," George said as he stretched and loosened up his arms and hands. He cracked his knuckles and twisted and turned his back and shoulders and even did a couple of jumping jacks to get his blood moving. "I think we started all wrong last time."

"You know," Paul added. "With the apples and all."

"Yes, he knows we mean the apples Paul!" Peter chided his brother when he saw Jim's cheeks flush with leftover embarrassment. "No need to bring that up."

"It's okay," Jim said and took a deep breath. The four boys stood around the corner of an alleyway in downtown London as hundreds of pedestrians walked to and fro on the streets before them. Jim's stomach tightened up a little with nervousness as he thought about his incident at breakfast a few days before, and he was less than eager to experience that kind of trouble again. But he had to get his box back and it seemed that this was the only way.

"It is okay!" George said encouragingly. "Because my brothers and I put our heads together over the last couple of nights and have come with ..."

Peter drummed his hands rapidly on his legs until the three of them leapt together with their arms outspread and smiles glowing.

"... the Official Ratt Brothers Course to Thieving and Pickpocketing!" they cried together.

"By George!"

"Peter!"

"And Paul Ratt!" After each said his name they bowed simultaneously with a flourish, their hats in their hands.

Jim couldn't help but laugh, clapping politely for their showmanship. "I'm proud to be your first student," he said.

"I still don't know why I have to go last," Paul grumbled, slapping his hat on his head.

"Because you're the youngest!" the other two said together. "And besides," George said. "You get to say: 'Ratt' at the end of your name, which is more than Peter gets to say."

"Yeah," Peter said, as if that fact had just dawned upon him. "That IS more than I get to say. This is bollucks!" And he threw his hands up in outrage.

Jim thought he was about to witness yet another Ratt brother brawl and swore to himself that the three brothers would end up being more famous for their scuffling than for their thieving, but George spotted what he wanted to see in the streets and called Jim over, effectively forestalling the inevitable fisticuffs.

"Looky there, Jim," George said, pointing at a rather tall lady, who was either noble herself or married to a noble family, Jim noted. She wore a huge, pink dress that absolutely billowed out from her waist and ruffled down to the ground. And in spite of the fact that she wore a gigantic brimmed pink hat, a servant scuttled along beside her with the sole purpose of holding an umbrella over her head to protect her delicate skin from the harsh sun.

"It's a good thing that umbrella's there," Paul said with a smirk.

"Why?" Jim asked.

"Because with her nose held up that high she'd go blind staring right into the sun." The boys laughed and Jim had to admit it was true. For the first time he wondered if that is what he and his aunt had looked like from the outside not so long ago. If it was, Jim thought to himself, it suddenly looked far sillier than it did noble.

"Okay, Jim," George said with unmistakable confidence. "You are about to witness the perfected Welshman's Waltz!" He slid out onto the street and blended with the crowd as Jim and the other Brothers Ratt watched intently from the safety of the alley. Like a hunting hawk George glided through the crowds, weaving in and out of the bustling rows of people until he was headed straight for the woman in pink.

"George really is the best pickpocket in all of London," Peter said, and Jim heard true admiration in his voice. "He knows all the moves!"

"Yeah," Paul chimed in. "The Dragons only steal more 'cause there's more of them. But they're jealous of the skill set, have no doubt. Look, here he goes!"

Jim leaned in over the Ratts shoulders to see the action. George walked with his hands in his pockets as though he had not a care in the world.

"He's not even looking at her," Jim said. "He's headed right for her! They're going to crash!"

"That's the point," Peter said, a wicked smile spreading across his face. George did indeed run right into the woman in pink, but instead of knocking her over or being knocked over himself, he deftly wrapped his arms around her and spun them both around as gracefully as a ballroom dancer before twirling off behind her.

"Watch where you're going you filthy little boy!" the woman shrieked, trying to wipe some imaginary dirt from the front of her dress.

"Well!" George mustered up the most indignant look on his face and turned his nose up as high in the air as the woman's. "Excuuuuse ME!" Then he wiped his rags of their own imaginary dirt, stomped his foot, and strutted off down the street. In a moment's time he crept back in the alley, flipping a fresh and shiny silver coin back and forth over the back of his knuckles.

"That was brilliant!" Jim exclaimed.

"It definitely was one of your better performances, George," Peter said with a nod.

"The main thing is, Jim," George said, looking Jim right in the eye. "You've got to put their mind on somethin' else. Distraction is a thief's best friend."

"That's good n' all George," said Paul. "But I think style may be just as important. For instance, I prefer the Welshman's Waltz with the English Finish, myself."

"What's that?" Jim asked, but George was already out on the street and headed in a beeline for a stuffy merchant's wife dressed all in satin. He crashed into her, spun her, and twirled away - except this time when the lady cried out about a filthy little boy, George took off his hat and bowed low to the ground.

"My lady," he exclaimed. "The pleasure was all mine!"

Jim laughed so loud from the alley that their hiding space was compromised and they had to flee a constable's deputy for three blocks. But, they all agreed later, the laughs had been worth it, and in the back of Jim's mind a small glimmer of hope suggested he may get his box back after all ... just maybe, if nothing else went wrong, that was.

EIGHTEEN

BARTHOLOMEW CROMIER

Many, many miles from London, where Jim Morgan was taking the first steps toward becoming a master thief under the tutelage of the Brothers Ratt and living with them in their cellar beneath the old shoe factory, Bartholomew Cromier stood alone atop the gray tower overlooking his family estate on the hard coast of the sea where the waves crashed against the rocks from morning until night – Shade Manor.

The bricks in Shade Manor's walls and the tiles on her many roofs were so dark they leeched the very light from the air, and the billowing sea mist, like a never-ending fog, turned the stones blacker still. Brown ivy, more dead than alive, crawled up the walls facing away from the ocean and all the trees in the orchards grew fruitless and crooked. Even the fountain water, cascading over the stone saint in the courtyard, trickled down the carved face like forlorn tears.

Travelling folk would walk for miles just to skirt around Shade Manor, and nobles and merchants alike, living in the nearby towns, whispered among themselves that the dark manor was not only one of the dreariest and coldest places in all of England – but that it was also cursed, and perhaps even haunted.

Bartholomew Cromier, however, cared nothing for rumors or for travellers, nor for ghosts or for curses. His cold heart and steely mind were too far bent toward he and his father's dark purposes to bother with such trivialities. Even at that very moment, his raven-black hair dampened from the sea mist and his coat whipping in the icy wind, Bartholomew silently brooded over he and his father's incomplete vengeance against their old enemy, Lord Lindsay Morgan. The fact that Lord Morgan's mysterious treasure had somehow slipped through their fingers drove Bartholomew nearly mad. It had been one week to the day since Count Cromier had told his son that the treasure was not at Morgan Manor, and by that seventh day Bartholomew had brooded himself into a whirlwind of silent fury.

"What do you mean it's not there?" Bartholowew had shouted as loud as he dared at his father.

"Just that," his red-wigged father had replied, stomping his foot. "The treasure isn't there. Not that I expected it to be hidden beneath the parlor, mind you. But some clue or map to the treasure's location should most definitely have been on or near Lindsay Morgan's person."

"What do we do now?"

"We wait!" his father had shouted back.

"WAIT FOR WHAT?" Bartholomew had screamed as his father stomped away. But since then there had been no more shouting – only silent plotting, stewing, and slow-boiling frustration at the top of his tower, glaring out over the colorless, angry sea and the black rocks drowning in the tide. Not only had Bartholomew refused to speak during that entire time, he had refused to eat as well, and he had grown more pale and gaunt than ever before. Beneath his raven-black hair and his piercing blue eyes, the young captain looked more ghoul than man.

"All of our carefully laid plans," he muttered to himself occasionally, often followed by either "ruined!" or "all for nothing!" Then he would shake his head and furrow his brow and go back to brooding and glaring.

However, on the seventh day, it finally seemed as though whatever Count Cromier had been waiting for had finally happened. Up the narrow steps that circled the inside of the gray tower, one of the servants came, stepping out into the mist, a candle rack in hand, to tell Bartholomew his father requested his presence – urgently.

"All for nothing," Bartholomew muttered to himself, shoving past the servant with a grunt and skulking down the stairs, through the mirthless halls of Shade Manor to his father's study.

Yet, as daring and dangerous as Bartholomew Cromier was, and however dark his mood, he forced a calm veneer over his face. For the only person more devious than Bartholomew, was his father, Count Cromier – the Red Count. Batholomew paused at the study door and took a steadying breath to cool his temper. Unfortunately for Bartholomew, a shrill, yet mannish voice shattered his delicate calm the moment he opened the door.

"Oh, hullo Barty!" Margarita Morgan shrieked as Bartholomew stepped into the study. Bartholomew only hoped that the slamming door behind him and the roaring fire in the hearth drowned out the sound of his teeth – which were grinding. "So good to see you again, Barty!" Margarita bellowed, hoisting up a nearly empty bottle of wine. "Let's toast the young man's health!"

Even more infuriating to Bartholomew than he and his father's failure to find the great treasure was the knowledge that ever since Lindsay Morgan's demise, Dame Margarita had been living like a queen in Morgan Manor, ceaselessly throwing opulent parties and gossiping all days of the week with her ridiculous friends from London. And when she wasn't doing so at Morgan Manor, which was bad enough for Bartholomew, she was doing it here at Shade Manor, which was worse.

She was dressed in a finely made gown from Austria, a silver tiara atop her blonde wig, and jangling jewels garishly draped about her plump neck and wrists. Bartholomew was about to spew some nastiness in retort to Margarita's toast when a graveled voice rumbled from the study's desk.

"I have good news, my son."

Bartholomew's father sat at his dusty old blackwood desk, a mess of ancient books and tattered scrolls strewn before him. The drawn curtains blackened the room's shadows into pitch and the sharp firelight deepened the color of the Count's red curls into a dark, blood red.

"Sit down."

Bartholomew skulked over to his father's desk and slumped into a leather chair, trying his best to hide the murderous fury in his eyes.

"What I'm about to tell you is secret information from the King's own network of spies," the Count said, tracing the purple scar on his face with his finger.

"O-o-oh," cried Margarita from divan upon which she sat. "How I love secrets! Do go on, Cromie, go on then!"

Bartholomew rolled his eyes. He hated when Margarita called his father 'Cromie' almost as much as he hated when she called him 'Barty." "Perhaps we should wait, father," Bartholomew said with a sigh, flicking his eyes to the side of his head twice in Margarita's direction.

"Oh," the count replied, smiling crookedly. "I wouldn't worry about that." And then, right on cue, a loud thunk echoed from the divan. Bartholomew looked over just in time to see Dame Margarita slump back against the wall and fall directly to sleep, snoring loudly. "She's been enjoying herself all afternoon," said the Count, sneering. "I think we have our privacy now."

The Red Count, named so as much for his murderous reputation as his distinctive wig, leaned across his desk, locking eyes with his pale, dark-haired son. "Robert S. North has been spotted in England. Headed for London."

Bartholomew stared back at his father. "Really? That's nice ..." Bartholomew could contain his rage no longer and finally exploded.

"Who the devil is Robert S. North and how does it affect our current predicament one whit?"

Instead of yelling back, the Count smiled his crooked smile once again and leaned back in his chair, stroking his jagged scar. "Robert S. North is the given name of Dread Steele, Lord of the Pirates."

"Dread Steele?" Bartholomew's yell faded into a startled whisper. "Dread Steele ... in England?"

A cold wind swept through an open window somewhere deep inside Shade Manor, blowing into the study, shivering the fire, and crawling a chill up Bartholomew's back. Dread Steele was a name that all those who lived on the coasts of England knew and associated with fear.

"The most terrible pirate to ever sail the seas," Cromier said quietly, staring off into the whipping flames. "A master of disguise, and a brilliant swordsman and shot. It is said he holds influence over the winds on the seas, that he knows more than a man should about black magic, and even that he has allied himself with a talking Raven he uses as his spy. I have seen enough not to doubt these tales."

"Father, please!" Bartholomew snorted. "That's all bog water ... isn't it?"

"As brave as you may be my son," Count Cromier said softly. "You have not seen some of the things I have seen in this world ... powerful forces at work."

"Well, as fascinating as this all is, father, what does it have to do with us?"

"Isn't it obvious, Bartholomew?" Count Cromier leaned across the desk once more, the firelight wreathing his hideous scar in red. "Dread Steele has come for the treasure!"

"Dread Steele knows of Lindsay Morgan's treasure?" Bartholomew wondered aloud.

"Yes, he does," the Count confirmed, sinking back into his chair, into the shadows. "What you must remember my son, is that Lindsay Morgan and Dread Steele were the fiercest of foes. Their hate was borne many years ago, when they were still young men. But you see they know each other - better than even friends might know each other. Add to that the fact that Dread Steele is notorious for his ability to find treasure so carefully hidden that no man alive should be able, and one arrives at one inescapable conclusion -"

"Dread Steele knows where the treasure is hidden," Bartholomew finished the thought, his icy blue eyes flashing.

"Possibly," Cromier confirmed. "Or he is searching as we are – but either way, he may have a clue or piece of information that we lack … that we need."

"What do you want me to do, father?" Bartholomew asked, deathly solemn, his hand gripping his sword handle tightly.

"Go to London. Do what no man, not even Lindsay Morgan could do in all his life – capture Dread Steele. We will make him talk."

"He would not join us?" Bartholomew asked. "If we offered to split the treasure?"

"No!" Count Cromier half laughed and half shouted. "Trust me, my son, there is no sharing this treasure. It is too great to be possessed by more than one."

"What will you do in the meantime?"

"I will go back to Morgan Manor and dredge the forest and the river. I have been thinking of late - only one person escaped our clutches that night, dead as he may have ended upon his flight."

"The boy - James Morgan?"

"Yes, doubtful as it may be, it is possible the boy has escaped with the secret to a treasure more vast than he could ever realize. And if I find young James Morgan alive, he will tell us what he knows or he will wish that he had died that night. I care not for the cost to my soul, one way or another that treasure will be ours!"

NINETEEN

A NEW PLAN

P icking a lock is an art, Jim," Peter said matter-of-factly as he and as his two brothers, Lacey, and Jim stood outside a locked, warehouse door in an empty alley. After a few weeks of picking pockets and increasing his skills on the streets, Jim, according to the Ratts, was ready to start on breaking and entering. It was now November and quite cold outside, and a few flurries fluttered through the gray air and down to the street. "It's like … painting a picture," Peter continued.

"You've never painted a picture, Peter," George said, crossing his arms in front of him, the look on his face letting his brother know how much better he thought his class on pickpocketing had been.

"I KNOW that, George!" Peter stamped one foot and growled. "I'm just saying it's *like* that. It was an example. Now I'm teaching this class, so piss off!"

"Well it was a poor example, that's all I'm saying."

"If you can give a better one then you pick this lock and teach Jim how to do it!"

At this George just sighed and rolled his eyes, but he never moved for the lock and shut his mouth. Jim imagined this was because it was George himself that had said there may not be a better lock pick in all of Europe, much less England, than Peter Ratt. Peter had a particular sort of mechanically inclined mind that loved nothing more than to take everything in the world apart, put it all back together, and know their workings from the inside out.

"Anyway, Jim," Peter said – nearly shouting Jim's name to make sure that Paul and George would know he wasn't talking to them. "Picking a lock is like painting a picture because you've got your ... er ... paper thing that you paint on," he pointed to the locked door.

"Canvas," Jim corrected, but not in the snide way he would have a couple of months ago.

"Right, canvas! And then you've got your brushes." Peter pulled out a small fold of leather from his back pocket and flipped it open. Inside were several thin strips of shiny metal. Some were short and straight like a pin; others crooked or twisted or even curled around in little twirls. All the little tools gleamed in the gray light of the winter day and even Jim's eyes widened when he saw them. They were the nicest things the Ratts owned.

"Those are brilliant!" Jim said. "Where did you nick those beauties?"

"Actually didn't nick them at all," Peter said proudly.

"He won them," Paul added.

"Some bloke on Windsor Avenue once said that he was greatest lock pick in all of England and had developed a tool for every type of lock ever made," George explained. "People challenged him left and right for years, but with no success. Then Peter came along."

"Boys," Lacey sighed as the Ratts and Jim stood there regarding one another with a certain pride. "Can we just get on with it already? I, for one, am freezing!"

"Right then," Peter agreed, turning to the locked door. "The *key* to opening any lock, Jim," - Peter turned back and winked to his brothers, who laughed ridiculously at his clever pun as Lacey groaned and hopped up and down to stay warm - "is knowing how it works inside. That lets you know how to trick the lock into opening without the key. When you know where to place the pins and apply the proper leverage ..." He stuck the pins into the lock hole and gave a neat little twist, smiling at the sound of a loud click. "And in we go!" He turned the knob and threw open the door with a wide grin.

"That was excellent!" Jim clapped with enthusiasm but was nearly bowled over by Lacey, who was tired of all of the boys' self-congratulations and, like any sensible person, just wanted to get warm. "But what is this place anyway?" Jim asked as they all stepped inside.

His question was answered as his eyes adjusted to the dim light. It was a warehouse: a warehouse for locked chests, locked cabinets, and locked drawers all stacked in rows and piled high in columns lit by dust-dancing streams of gray, winter light. Jim looked at Peter and saw a greedy little smile splayed over his cheeks. It was a lock pick's heaven.

The little Ratt clan practiced all morning and into the afternoon. Jim and Lacey had finally (and after several stuck and pinched fingers) gotten their first locks open and that so pleased everybody that they decided to call it a day. They snuck out the rear of the warehouse and as usual left all the unlocked chests and drawers wide open. The poor owner of the place often came into work to inspect his wares after these little sessions and swore to his wife that it was the ghost of his old business partner come back to torment him for removing his name from the sign outside after he died.

Not to be outdone by the particularly well-taught class on lock picking by his brother, George, on the way home, demonstrated the rather tricky Russian Nose Pick n' Flick technique for distracting an unsuspecting mark. It was a somewhat sticky method that Lacey called entirely disgusting, but George effectively employed it to relieve a rather grumpy and ill-tempered merchant of a gold chain from around his neck.

When the children arrived home and started a fire with a couple of pieces of coal in their makeshift little stove, George took his newly acquired necklace, a distinguished cross dangling at the end, and tossed it into the drawer with the various other coins and knickknacks they had thieved throughout the month – and all awaiting "sharing" with the King of Thieves at the upcoming court.

"One more for the chief," George said with satisfaction.

"And one more day closer to finally getting out of this dreadful place," Lacey said, inching closer to the stove for warmth.

"You, know, I've often wondered why the king doesn't have us steal more regular money," Paul asked to no one in particular. "I would think we could save up faster that way, but all he really seems to care about are necklaces and pendants."

"I guess they fetch a higher price than coins," Peter mused.

Just then, a candle light went off in Jim's brain and he suddenly recalled what he saw while hanging upside-down by the ankle outside of the pawnshop window only a couple of days earlier.

"It's because he's looking for one necklace in particular," Jim said aloud.

The Ratt brothers stared at Jim, quite surprised, and Lacey said: "Now Jim Morgan, you've just gotten here. How you could possibly know what the King of Thieves is looking for? Nobody even knows where he goes in between sessions of court."

"I do," Jim said. "He goes to the little pawnshop on Barque Street with the little round man from the gypsy's country, and he doesn't care a fig about the coins. He tosses them aside and compares all the necklaces to a picture of one in a book because he's looking for that particular one. And he has my box there too! I must have forgotten all about it after Red and the Dragons roughed me up, but I saw it all while I was hanging from the ivy that day we ran from Butterstreet and his lot!"

132

Jim got very excited as he told the story. Hardly a month ago he would never have believed he stood even a chance of getting his box back from the King of Thieves. But his new friends' training had given him a taste of success and Jim was beginning to believe that all kinds of things were possible. Jim's energy immediately infected the Ratts, as it tends to infect all little boys who are in love with adventure and intrigue, and, with mischief gleaming in their eyes, they leapt over to where Jim sat.

"A pawnshop!" George said, smacking his own head with his hand. "That makes perfect sense. That's where he could trade the necklaces for money for our escape!"

"But if he's really planning nothing but our escape, why is he bent on finding that one particular necklace?" Lacey asked, a fair bit of grownup skepticism in her voice.

"It must be something he lost before," Peter said. "And he's trying to get it back."

"Or maybe it's an extra valuable necklace," Paul suggested. "One that'll fetch loads more than all of the others put together!"

"I don't think he wanted it for money, Paul," Jim said, though in truth he knew for a fact what the old king wanted with it: for his father's treasure. But for one reason or another Jim kept this to himself. "He seemed rather keen on finding it and keeping it for himself. And the little man with the gypsy accent seemed very upset that they hadn't found it yet. He had a book that seemed to tell all about it and had a picture of it. If we could see that book, we could know why he was looking for it."

"Fat lot of good that will do us," said George, who started laughing. His brothers joined in, slapping their knees. "A book, he says! Then we could know!"

"All I can think of to do with a book is toss it in our stove for a little extra heat," Peter said.

Jim felt a little stung by this sudden mockery, as excitement had been building up inside him. He crossed his arms over his chest, scowling. "What's so funny about that? And why in blazes would you want to toss a book into a stove?"

"Because, Jim," said Lacey, as tired of the Ratts' uproarious laughter as Jim was. "None of us can read. No one in the entire king's court can read except for a few of the Owls, so even if we got that stupid book the only place we could go to get someone to read it for us would be a church."

"And they'd toss us back into St. Anne's orphanage or school the moment we popped up on their doorstep," Paul added, shaking his head.

"What are you talking about?" Jim threw his hands up. "I can read!"

The Ratt brothers stopped laughing, their jaws hanging open like baby birds waiting to be fed, and Lacey arched her eyebrow high over her eye in disbelief.

"You can read?" she asked, then folded her own arms and scowled as darkly as Jim. "Prove it!"

Jim shrugged, hopped up, and walked over to the pile of potato sacks they used for a bed. He picked one up and analyzed the letters stitched into the burlap. "Dunning's Potatoes of London, in operation in England since 1652," he said and threw the bag down, smiling widely and ridiculously pleased with himself.

"Jim!" George and the Ratts leapt to their feet. "This is absolutely brilliant! How come you never told us you could bloody read?"

"I guess I never thought about it," Jim said, suddenly feeling very good about having such a rare talent (and once more wishing he would have paid attention to the myriad other things that he could have learned when he lived as a nobleman's son).

"Can you write, too?" Paul asked.

"Sure can," Jim said. "And if you want, I can teach you how to read and write while you teach me how to thieve."

"You would … teach me how to read?" Lacey asked. Her blue eyes went wide, and all of the skepticism seeped out of her face. In those days not many women learned such things as reading and writing, but

Jim wasn't quite old enough to have been poisoned by such discriminations and gladly agreed.

"Brilliant!" George cried. "Well, what are we waiting for? Let's go!"

"Go where?" Jim asked.

"Well, it's like our father always used to say -" George began.

"You didn't know our father, George," Paul and Peter said together.

George didn't seem to hear them. "No better place to practice the art of thieving than the real world! That's what he said, all right. Let's get to the pawnshop on Barque Street and see about this necklace for ourselves!"

"I'm not so sure this is such a good idea, George," Lacey said. "The King of Thieves seems very dangerous, even if he is going to help us escape. Besides, what good will it do for us to break into his pawnshop?"

"We've got Jim, Lacey," George said. "He can read the book for us and we can know what the old king is up to. Now quit fussin' and come on!"

Out the hole, they tumbled into the streets where the night grew steadily darker and colder, and where the first true snow of the year began to color the city a ghostly white.

TWENTY

THE AMULET OF PORTUNES

By the time Jim, the Ratts, and Lacey arrived at the pawnshop on Barque Street, the snow had deepened enough to bear their footprints. Night had fully darkened the world and only a few streetlamps cast flickering light and wavering shadows over the empty roads.

Jim shivered as he drew close to the building. The shingle that read "Pawnshop" creaked and swayed in the cold wind and the shutters clapped against the brick walls. Jim remembered the first time he descended into the shadowy streets of London and how the houses there had seemed to have faces. The snow, that had by then accumulated over the windows and door of the pawnshop, lent it the frightening eyes and cruel mouth of an old man with bright white eyebrows and a thick mustache who hated even the sight of little children.

"George," Lacey said with a shudder, "let's wait until tomorrow. It will be warmer in the sun ... and more cheerful." She looked at the old man's face on the building and shivered again. But the Ratts had lived nearly their whole lives on the streets of London and if they saw the cruel face of man on the building they simply imagined it was another snobby lord who required their special attention to be taught a lesson.

"Just think about what we could find in there," George said. "There's a reason the King's looking for that medallion and I want to find out what it is. And besides, Jim's box is in there. If nothing else, we could nick that and be on our merry way!"

That was all the convincing Jim needed. He took a deep, icy breath and tried to feel brave. His father had been brave, he reminded himself, and that deep-seated feeling of being a disappointment pushed Jim all the more to break into the pawnshop and take back what was his.

"Open the door, Peter," Jim said. "Besides, it'll be warmer inside, Lacey," he added with a smile.

Peter hopped in front of the door and peered into the keyhole. He cracked his knuckles, loosened his arms, pulled out his leather case of metal pins, and got to work. It was apparently a tougher lock to pick than the one on the warehouse door, but Peter was no amateur. In a few moments the latch popped and the door swung open with a long groan.

Warmth blew out from inside the store, inviting the children inside. The coals that still burned in the stove, however, splayed sinister, red light over the trinkets and odds and ends decorating the pawnshop shelves, and in the shadows the jewelry glimmered like glowing animal eyes in the forest. Jim gulped hard at that memory, but he reminded himself he was no longer going to be a coward and took the first step through the door. The others followed, and, almost by itself, the door creaked behind them, clicking shut with a loud pop.

The children jumped and huddled close together. "Sorry about that," Paul said, although a little unsurely. "I bumped it a bit, I think."

"You think?" Lacey asked with a scowl, but after few moments no further sounds belied the presence of anyone else in the shop but the children, and they proceeded to have a look around.

All manner of curious things that desperate Londoners had traded away for a few much-needed coins filled the shop from top to bottom. For those who have never been in a pawnshop, they really are very sad little stores. Every object on every shelf once belonged to someone with no choice but to trade those precious items for less than half their true worth, just to scrape by for another month.

There were smoking pipes and empty satchels for tobacco; pots and irons for cooking; fine sets of silverware; and rows of teapots and cups and saucers. Lacey found a wedding dress hanging in the corner. It looked nothing short of heartbreaking to see it there, knowing that the woman who had worn it had been forced to give it away for the sake of her family. Nevertheless, Lacey imagined taking it for herself and wearing it one day. Then she pushed those thoughts out of her mind with a fierce shake of her head. She couldn't steal that dress. For some reason it seemed wrong, even for a thief.

The boys, on the other hand, found some pistols, overcloaks, tricorn hats, and even a set of cruel-looking knives, all of which they had no problem trying on and making like a band of fearsome pirates.

"Arrgghh!" Paul growled as he spun around to reveal an eye patch he had found. He wore it over one of his eyes beneath a tricorn hat, brandishing a rusty pistol in each hand. The boys burst into laughter but Lacey immediately shushed them quiet.

"Shut up, you dingbats!" she whispered rather loudly. She seemed to want to stomp her foot again but resisted the temptation for fear of the noise it would cause. "Do you want to let the whole street know we're here? Let's find what we want and get out of here and back home. Put that stuff away! These are people's things that are as poor as we are and that's against the rules! Now come on!"

The boys begrudgingly put their new playthings back, George mumbling something akin to "yes, mother" under his breath, but the glow of the coals in Lacey's flashing eyes silenced his grumbling quickly.

"I think it's back in the rear office," Jim said. They crept behind the counter and through the door at the back of the shop. Another stove full of red-hot embers lit this smaller room and its walls practically shimmered like a cave of diamonds. Necklaces and medallions hung on every hook and in every corner of the room, gleaming silver and gold in the light of the stove. The Ratts' eyes went wide and they licked their lips.

"It's a treasure!" Peter said.

"Surely we almost have enough to get out of here," George said.

"More than enough," Jim said, furrowing up his brow. "If the King of Thieves traded all these in for money we'd have more than enough to sail all of us to the Far East and back again."

"Then why doesn't he do it?" Peter asked.

"I'm not sure he's ever going to, Peter," Lacey said, a sudden sadness sweeping over her face. "If Jim is right, then all he really cares about is this medallion, and he's using us to help him find it."

"And when he gets what he wants," Jim added gravely, "I think he'll leave the clans behind."

"Don't you say that, either of you," George barked. "We are leaving here and the King of Thieves is going to take us with him! We stole a lot of this rich stuff and it's ours as much as his! What could be so important about one medallion anyway that he would lie to us like that?" Jim could hear his friend's teeth grinding. George was so angry that in the dim glow Jim could see his hands balled up into fists at his sides.

"Maybe this could tell us," Paul said. He stood over by a desk beside a bookshelf. An empty inkwell, a dry old quill, a candlestick on a stand, and a thick book sat on the desktop. "Can you read it, Jim?"

"Not in this light," said Jim, shaking his head. Almost immediately a small yellow flame glowed in the room. George had found a slender lighting stick and used it to light the candle on the desk.

"George, no!" Lacey whispered harshly, but George was upset and little boys (and even grown men) tend not to listen to reason when angry.

"Just keep a good lookout, Lacey," George said without looking at her.

Lacey harrumphed a complaint but crept over to the window just the same to stare out of the office, straining her ears for the slightest sound of approaching trouble.

Jim stood beside the desk as the light from the candle brightened over the pages of the book. On the far page, the hand-drawn image of a peculiar medallion came into view. "This must be it," Jim said.

"What does it say?" George asked, all three Ratt brothers leaning in close over Jim's shoulders as he began to read the words.

"Of all the great treasures lost in the wreck of the mighty galleon, *Fortune*, off the coast of Spain, none was as grievous to me as the loss of the Amulet of Portunes," Jim read. "This charm came to me at a great cost and possesses a most unique power. The amulet holds the power to unlock anything that is locked and to unbind anything that is bound, whether it be chained, barred, locked by key, or even that which is bound by magic."

"That could come in handy," Peter whispered, his eyes gleaming. "Especially for a thief."

"But I have not lost all hope," Jim continued, "It is said that a commoner, an able seaman by trade, found the medallion, and having wasted its powers to unlock a cabinet of whiskey, drank himself silly and lost it in a game of cards in London, where it still passes from hand to hand in that town's many streets."

"That's what he's up to," Paul said. "He thinks eventually one of us will nick this amulet of whoever for him so he can unlock anything that his heart desires."

"But he already has all of this treasure," Peter said, looking around again at the wall full of gold and silver chains. "What could he possibly need to unlock?"

"What couldn't he unlock?" Jim said, secretly thinking about the fate of his father's treasure. If the King got his hands on the Amulet, he could open the box – and then open whatever security keeping his father's great treasure safe. "He could have any treasure he wanted."

Peter and Paul's eyes lit up with dreams of unlimited treasure, but Lacey, on the other hand, didn't believe a word of it. "Boys! I mean, seriously, have you ever heard of something so ridiculous? A magic necklace that can unlock anything? It's absurd!"

"Well I didn't think magic was real until that gypsy cursed my box!" Jim argued, snapping out of his reverie in a sore temper.

"It's not the same thing and you know it, Jim!" Lacey crossed her arms and the two of them were about to have a real corker of a fight when Peter noticed something through the window that the arguing Lacey had missed.

"Say," he said. "Were those footprints there just a second ago?" But the answer to his question was the loud clink of a key sliding into the keyhole of the pawnshop door.

"Hide!" George ordered as he snuffed the candle out.

"I haven't had a class on hiding!" Jim said, on the verge of panic. But George had already thought of that and as his brothers and Lacey disappeared behind shelves or cabinets or desks, George flung himself and Jim against the wall behind a curtain and told him to keep quiet.

The front door opened with a groan and shut with a clap as it had when the clan had snuck in themselves. Two sets of creaking footsteps made their way toward the back room. The door to the office opened and Jim couldn't help but shift ever so slightly behind the curtain to peek through a slit in the fabric and see what was going on.

The King of Thieves, wearing his tailored half-coat with the tails and his silk hat, walked in first. The red glow of the coals cast long shadows on his furrowed brow and his sharp jaw and his large, hooked nose. His dark eyes glimmered beneath the edge of his hat, peering around the room suspiciously.

"Are you absolutely sure you saw a light in here, Wyzcark?" the King asked, walking to the desk where the candle and the books sat.

"I know vat I saw," Wyzcark muttered, the squat man waddling into the room behind the King. "There vas a light ... and shadows. I swear it."

The king lit the candle and picked it up from the table with his long spindly fingers. He held it forth toward the shadows, but the children were hidden neatly enough to avoid his sight. The King arched one eyebrow over his large, dark eye and sighed. "Well, maybe it was ghosts," he said dismissively.

"Humph," Wyzcark said with a grunt. "Think what you like, but ve must be more careful than ever! Ve can't afford any lapses or mistakes now, not when ve're so close!"

"On the contrary, my little friend." The king smiled, setting the candle back down on the table. "Once we find the Amulet, we will be able afford as many lapses as we like."

"Don't be so cocky, oh King of Thieves," Wyzcark said with just enough mockery to prick the smile off of his tall friend's face. "Even though the amulet has supposedly been spotted, ve have yet to verify that fact. And even if ve do, ve have yet to steal it for ourselves."

"Oh, don't worry, Wyzcark, my skeptical friend." The smile returned in the form of a sneer on the King's face. "The little dogs I have running my errands may be dirty street urchins, but they have sharp eyes and sharp ears. They're eager to please me and afraid to make me angry. I showed Big Red and his Dragons the picture of the amulet and they verified what they saw, and that the old sea salt wintering at the Wet Rock was wearing it. It all makes perfect sense! The reason we didn't come across it by now was because the latest owner had been out to sea, and now that he's returned it won't be long before those grimy grubbers have my prize and the riches of the world will finally be open to me!" The king's eyes burned mad and hotter than the coals for a brief moment, until his fat comrade's suspicious voice broke his trance.

"Your prize?" Wyzcark asked, trying to draw himself up as tall as he could - which wasn't very tall, truth be told.

"Our prize, our prize, Wyzcark," the King said, soothing his friend with his best, honey-dripped tone.

"Just remember that," Wyzcark said, pointing a finger at the king's chest, which stood a full inch above his head.

"Oh, I'll remember." The king's tone grew so deep as to nearly become a growl. "Believe me, I'll remember."

The two men were about to leave when the king stopped suddenly and turned back to the table. He reached over his workbench and pulled away a false panel to the wall, withdrawing a single object from the hiding place there. Jim nearly leapt out from behind the curtain when he saw what it was – his box. The King also took the book from the desk and tucked it beneath his arm.

"Just in case the ghosts decide to come back, eh, Wyzcark?" The King said. The two men laughed to themselves and the king blew out the candle before leaving. The door shut behind them and the children were alone once more.

Cautiously, they emerged from hiding and gathered together in the center of the room. Lacey checked the window and watched as the treacherous King of Thieves and his fat business partner stalked off through the snow.

"They've got the box!" Jim lamented, punching his fist into his hand.

"But more," Peter said excitedly. "The Dragons have seen the necklace from the book. Some old guy is sporting it around the docks."

"One thing's for sure," Paul added. "We've got to make sure and get that amu-thingy before they do!"

"No problem for us," Peter said. "After all, we are the brothers ..."

He turned, expecting George to jump into the performance, hat in hand, ready to pick up their cheer, but instead, the leader of their little clan was standing by the wall. His slight shoulders were slumped and his thin face was hidden beneath his cap, which seemed to have grown in size to hang down low over his mousy face.

"George, you missed your cue," Paul said, but George said nothing in return.

"George, whatever is the matter?" Lacey asked, moving to stand by her friend's side. But George pulled away and nearly ran for the door.

"Nothing's the matter!" he snapped. "And if you sods want to keep wasting your time, be my guest, I'm going home."

Lacey and Jim looked at each other in bewilderment, but George's outburst seemed to come as a great blow to his brothers, and Peter and Paul's shoulders slumped nearly as low as George's had been and they trudged out of the store to follow him.

"Mates, where are you going?" Jim asked. "Mates?" But it was no use. Jim and Lacey walked back to the little home beneath the shoe factory in silence.

James had found out more than he'd imagined he would about his box – and the King of Thieves's interest in it. But, he thought miserably, as he followed the dragging footsteps of his disheartened friends in the snow, he may have lost his only means of stealing of it back.

TWENTY–ONE

CORNELIUS DARKFEATHER

When Jim and Lacey finally crawled through the hole and into the cellar, they found the forlorn Brothers Ratt huddled around the makeshift stove, faces buried in their hands. Jim and Lacey plopped down beside them in the fire's warmth, but for the longest time none of the children said anything at all, until George finally spoke, almost too quietly to hear.

"What did you say, George?" Lacey asked.

"He lied to us," George said. Even in the flickering light of the coal Jim saw his friend's chin quiver and heard the thickness in his voice. "He lied to us." After that, George would speak no more on the subject or about anything else for that matter. Of course Paul and Peter, being as loyal to George as best brothers always should be,

147

followed suit and the Brothers Ratt sat the whole night by the stove without saying three words to anyone at all.

When Jim awoke the next morning, he hoped that perhaps a good night's sleep had cured his friends of their disappointment and all would return to normal - but this was not to be. The night before had been one of the coldest in London in recent memory, the snow having fallen through the night into the morning. The burlap bags the Ratts used as bedding were about as soft as rocks when it was freezing outside, and being half-frozen to death in the morning is enough to put anyone in a horrible mood, which is exactly what it did to the Ratts.

Instead of quietly moping about they immediately set in on one another over the most trivial matters.

"That's my hat, Paul!"

"George, quit hogging all the space by the stove!"

"Peter, did you just blow your nose into this rag? Because that's my shirt, you cur!"

Jim mostly kept quiet during these arguments because they weren't the same lighthearted fare he had come to expect from the brothers. When they shouted at one another they meant it and when they fell to blows they hit hard as they could. Jim wasn't sure why, but it made his stomach churn and tighten up in little knots to watch them behave this way. Lacey, of course, tried to help, but Jim thought she only made things worse.

"Boys, boys, stop this nonsense this instant! What's come over you, really?" Lacey said late in the afternoon after the Ratts' latest row.

"Oh, yes mother, we'll just pretend that there's not a problem in the world," George said, a nasty pout on his face. "What would you have us do next? Bath time? That would be perfect because then I could freeze my ears shut so I could go five seconds without hearing your nagging voice!"

Lacey shut her mouth, only a slight whisper of a breath escaping her lips. Jim knew immediately from the surprised look in George's eyes that George wished he could take those cruel words back. But he was so inexplicably miserable that he refused to apologize. Then

Jim saw something he never expected to see in a hundred years. Lacey, the toughest girl he'd ever met, began to cry. Now, to her credit, she never blubbered or wailed. But her face twitched and quivered and she had to clench her jaw to keep from making a sound. Despite her best efforts, two tears, one from each eye, slowly fell down her cheeks and dripped onto the floor. Then, without a word, she turned on her heel and ran as fast as she could out the hole and into the snowy streets.

"Well, that was right nice of you, George!" Jim shouted.

"She had it coming, all bossing us around and all." George refused to look up at Jim, but just crossed his arms and plopped down in front of the stove. "She's been doing it since the first day she got here and we was tired of since then! Weren't we, boys?" George asked his brothers, but they only stared at the ground without saying much at all.

"Well, aren't you going to go after her?" Jim asked incredulously when the three brothers continued to sit there without moving. "I mean, not so long ago you came after me, and Lacey's been your friend longer than I have."

"Things are different now!" George barked, and once again Jim heard the huskiness in his friend's words.

"So?" Jim shouted back at him. "Why should you care if anything at all is different? You're the Brothers Ratt, the greatest thieves in London, remember?"

"Well, we quit!" George snapped with finality, staring straight ahead into the orange fires of the burning coals in the pitiful makeshift stove. Jim felt a pit form at the bottom of his chest, like a place that had been full just a moment before and was suddenly found empty, and his throat hurt and stung.

"Fine then," Jim said quietly, then slipped out of the little hole that was the door of the empty cellar beneath the old shoe factory.

Jim kicked through the snow on the streets of London until his shoes were thoroughly wet. He began to shiver, and soon his fingers and toes became sore from the cold. Thick ribbons of white draped all of the buildings along the streets, from the roofs to the doorframes. The city seemed nearly empty, as though all of the houses had bundled up tight and wrapped imaginary arms so close around themselves to keep warm that all of the people who lived inside were trapped until spring. A cold wind gusted down the streets, stirring up the snow into a chilling mist and blowing it into Jim's face. He shuddered deeply. Soon the cold took a cruel hold on him and Jim began to feel about as miserable on the outside again as he was within.

Only a day ago Jim had imagined breaking into the King's pawn-shop with the Ratts and Lacey, finding out what the wily thief was up to, and stealing back his box. After reading about the amulet, Jim had even thought about somehow stealing it for himself and using it to open the box – turning all his troubles into nothing but an unpleasant memory. But all of those dreams had fallen apart. The King of Thieves still had the box and Jim's new friends teetered on the verge of giving up everything they lived for.

Jim was turning these heavy thoughts over and over in his mind when he heard snuffling and halting gasps from around the corner of a building up ahead. He poked his head around the corner and, sure enough, found Lacey, bawling her eyes out, her poor little shoulders shaking up and down from her sobs. Jim coughed politely into his freezing hand to let her know that she was not alone.

The second Lacey heard the cough she straightened up and stopped crying, hurriedly slapping the tears from her cheeks. "Jim Morgan!" she snapped as she whirled around. "Don't you know how rude it is to sneak up on someone like that?"

"I was just seeing if you were all right," Jim said.

"All right? I'm fine!" She put her hands on her hips, trying to smile as if she hadn't a care in the world, but her eyes and cheeks were so puffy and red that she looked more miserable than ever. "Why would I even care what those stupid boys have to say about anything? And besides, how I'm feeling is none of your business, Jim Morgan."

"Fine then!" Jim threw his hands up in the air. "Just be by your-self! Everyone can just be by themselves!" Jim turned on his heel to storm off dramatically, but the minute he turned, a wet, sloppy snowball plastered itself all over Jim's unsuspecting face. "What the -?" Jim exclaimed, until he was cut off by the most awfully familiar laughter.

"Great shot, Red!"

"Yeah — right on ... the nose!"

"Right on the nose, brilliant! I can't believe it! Right on the nose!"

As the leftover remnants of the snowball dripped slowly away from Jim's eyes, down his nose, and off his chin, he saw the bright red flare of Big Red's tangled hair and his freckled face, laughing as hard as he could and surrounded, of course, by his faithful entourage of lunks.

Jim sighed and shook his head, trying to find a way to form the burning hatred in his heart for Red into some fierce words to hurl at the taunting Dragon and his cronies. But just when a zinger of a biting retort made its way from Jim's brain down to his lips, another volley of snowballs pelted his face and chest until he was covered in wettish white dust.

"Where are the rest of the rodents?" Red asked with a snort while his lunks cackled behind him. The four Dragons had all reloaded, Jim noticed, and stalked toward him and Lacey, packing the snowballs tighter and tighter in the palms of their hands. It only took a moment for Red to notice the puffy red eyes and flushed cheeks on Lacey's face. "Awww ... is de wittle baby cwyin?" he mocked, and Jim felt heat bloom in his chest and face.

"Leave her alone, Red," he said, clenching his fists at his sides.

"You know, that's the thing about you Ratt clanners," Red growled, tossing a hardened snowball up and down in his hand. "If you ain't blubberin' like some toothless infant, you're pickin' fights you can't win. And that's why I just can't stand any of you. But 'specially not you, Jim Morgan. Don't know what it is, exactly, but you don't belong here. Somethin' about you ... wouldn't surprise me a bit if I found out you was some son of some rich family who tossed you out 'cause they just couldn't stand the sight of you any longer."

"Don't talk to him like that!" Lacey snarled, stepping up right beside Jim and absolutely breathing fury toward Red and his goons.

"See what I mean?" Red said with laugh to his lunks. "She's finished cryin', now she's ready to fight us. I mean, seriously, a girl, fight us?" The four bullies laughed hysterically and shook their heads. "Gimme your snowballs and grab em!" Red ordered. In a blink the three goons grabbed Lacey and Jim - two had Jim's arms and the third squeezed Lacey tight in a bear hug. Jim and Lacey twisted and squirmed as best they could, but it was no use. Red laughed, setting two of the snowballs aside and gripping the others in his fists, one in each hand. "Now for some proper fun," he said. "Here, lemme offer you some refreshment."

With an enormous leer across his freckled face, Red smashed the snowballs into Jim and Lacey's faces at the same time, rubbing them in deep until the two were spitting and sputtering dirty snow out of their mouths.

"One of these days, Red!" Jim swore furiously. "One of these days I'm gonna ... I'm gonna ..."

"You're gonna what? Cry on me again?" Red taunted, then laughed again.

"Well I know what I'm gonna do!" said Lacey, staring right into Red's laughing face. "I'm gonna knock your block off!"

Red's hysterics only increased and he bent down for the other two snowballs. "Tha'll be the day!" Red said, lining up his last two snowballs with his victims' faces for a second smashing. "But in the meantimes, I think you'll just have s'more snow!"

"I think not!" a shrill voice suddenly announced from absolutely nowhere. It caught Red so by surprise that he gasped and dropped the two snowballs that were about to be lodged into Jim's and Lacey's faces. "Unhand them, you curs!" the voice cried again. Jim and Lacey, along with Red and his Dragons, peered about the snowy and empty streets for their would-be rescuer, but not a soul was in sight.

"I said let them go or you'll receive the walloping of a lifetime, you freckle-faced fop!" the voice challenged again, and while it sounded quite confident and fierce, Jim couldn't help but notice something not altogether right about it ... it was so high, so shrill and, Jim thought, not completely natural.

"Who are you?" Red shouted, a dose of fear in his once sneering face and laughing voice.

"Who am I?" the haughty voice retorted. "Why, I am a comrade of those who scale the white-capped peaks of the seas! I am a dealer in derring-do and dashing deeds, and a trader of terrible tumbles for tyrannical tosspots ... much like yourselves. I have traveled the lands of the world and have seen life through eyes on the ground and eyes in the sky. If you have a lick of sense under that red mop on top of your head you'll release these two or face my wrath!"

"Face your wrath?" squealed Red, he and the Dragons craning their necks and turning themselves dizzy looking all around for the owner of the mysterious voice. "Well, why don't you face us?" Red finally dared, and Jim thought he was trying to sound braver than he actually felt.

"So be it: Prepare to be undone!" the voice shouted, and suddenly ... suddenly ... well, Jim still didn't see anyone.

Red managed to crack a smile. "This is a trick, isn't it?" he said, regaining some of his swagger. "It's just one of you Ratts using a trick voice, aren't you?"

"Eh-hem!" the voice said with a cough. "First of all, I'm right here." The six children - Jim, Lacey, Red, and the three Dragons - followed the sound of the voice down to their feet, where sat a big black bird at the end of a trail of hopping bird prints in the snow. Jim saw the confused looks on the others' faces and imagined the same on his own. Was this some kind of joke? But then the black bird opened its beak and the voice came out.

"And secondly," said the bird. "I'm not a rat. I, you chattering churlish child, happen to be a raven!"

"Red?" the lunk holding Lacey said, his eyes as big as two moons on his face. "Is that bird talking to us?"

"Well to whom else would I be speaking, you half-wits?" asked the raven. "Now unhand these two or I shall be forced to give you the thrashing you deserve!"

"Thrashin'?" Red said with a snort, and it seemed to Jim that he was suddenly over the rather surprising fact that a bird was talking to him and more insulted by the notion that it thought it could take on Big Red and the Dragons and win. "You're just a stupid bird!" Red picked up one of the dropped snowballs and raised it high over his head. "Now you'll 'ave a taste of what they was gonna get!"

"So be it, boy," the bird said calmly as Red rocketed the snowball straight down at its head. The raven sidestepped the white projectile and - Jim could hardly believe it- actually managed to form a little smile at the edges of his beak. "Don't say I didn't warn you. Now have at you, poltroon!" The bird shrieked an epic, avian war cry and launched itself into the air, right at Red's face.

"Get away!" Red shouted, but it was too late for him. The raven beat its wings - flapped them right in Red's face - and perched itself in the nest of curly, red hair and repeatedly pecked the top of Red's head. "Get it off, get it off!"

"Sorry Red!"

"Can't do it, mate"

"Just following your original orders, which were brilliant by the way, and getting away!" Red's yes men scattered this way and that, disappearing into the alleyways and empty streets. Red himself was the last to escape the raven's fury, running all the way back to the Dragon hideout, crying at the top of his lungs and waving his hands frantically over his head.

Jim and Lacey stood breathlessly in the middle of the snowy street, still not quite sure they believed what they had just seen. But, with the flapping of wings, the talking raven indeed reappeared and fluttered down onto the snowy street beside them.

"Mister raven, thank you!" said Lacey, clapping her hands and seeming not the least bit unnerved by what had just transpired before her. "Someone finally gave that Red a piece of what he deserved!"

"Lacey!" Jim shouted with incredulity. "You're talking to a bird!"

"Well, of course I am silly," she said without even a bat of her eyes. "He spoke to us first if you don't recall, and, if you missed it, he also just saved our necks. And you should always say thank you when someone helps you," Lacey insisted. "So thank you, mister raven, thank you so much."

"You're most welcome, my lady," said the raven with a neat little bow. "Your manners are impeccable. And please, call me Cornelius, Cornelius Darkfeather."

"But birds don't have names," Jim muttered, remembering snippets of biology lessons that some poor professor had tried to teach him in his old life.

"Oh, and I suppose gypsies don't have real magic either, do they?" the raven retorted.

"How did you know about that?" Jim demanded, hands on his hips.

"A little bird told me," said Cornelius with a raven sneer on his beak that made Lacey laugh out loud. "And as it happens, not all animals have names, just the ones that talk, and there are several of those about in the world - I can assure of that, young sir."

"But ..." Jim was about to argue matters further with the raven, but realized that he had been exposed to real magic himself. If there could be spell-casting gypsies and enchanted amulets, then why not an animal or two that knew how to talk? "Sorry about that," Jim finally said with a sigh. "But the last couple of months have been more than a bit odd for me, you know."

"I'm sure they have, my boy, I'm sure they have," Cornelius said, hopping a bit closer to Jim, staring at him with his black-within-black eyes. "You know, we weren't sure at first," the raven continued, as much to himself as the children. "But, now that I've got a better look at you, we're a tad bit surer you're him, aren't we?"

"Sure he's who?" Lacey said, looking back and forth between the bird and Jim.

"Why, his father's son, young miss," the raven said and Jim saw a knowing look pass over its beaked face.

"You know about my father?" Jim knelt down into the snow to better look the raven in the eye. "Wait a minute!" Jim snapped his fingers. "I've seen you before! Twice actually - on the shoulder of the man in the captain's coat! Who is he and who are you?" But instead of

155

answering Jim's sudden onslaught of questions, the raven turned his back and hopped away.

"Well, time to go," the raven announced, crouching down to spring into the air.

"Oh, don't leave, mister raven!" said Lacey.

"Hey, I asked you a question!" Jim shouted, but the raven just looked back for a moment, smiled, and sprung up into flight above their heads.

"Actually you asked me several questions. But fear not!" Cornelius the raven cawed from the sky, circled once before flying away. "We shall meet again!" Then, with much flapping and cawing, the big bird soared off into the mackerel sky.

"What a nice bird," Lacey said happily as the two of them watched the raven fly away over the rooftops of London.

"Oh, yeah, compared to all of the nasty ones you've met," Jim threw in, still quite miffed that he had no idea how the raven knew so many details about his dire situation.

"Now don't you start too, Jim," Lacey said. "We have enough grumpiness waiting for us at home if you don't remember."

"I remember." Jim kicked some snow at his feet and finally tore his eyes away from the place in the cloudy sky where the bird had flown away.

"And what are we going to do about that, anyway?" Lacey asked.

"I don't know, Lacey," Jim said, starting for home with Lacey beside him. Jim stuck his hands in his pockets and his mind slowly returned to the unhappy thoughts that had occupied him when he first started this oddly eventful walk. "Do you think maybe they'll just get over it and get back to normal?"

"Peter and Paul, maybe," Lacey said. "But without George, they won't ever really be the same. They do what he does if you know what I mean. And all George ever talked about was the day we would leave here. He talks about liking life on the streets and being happy with stealing coins and apples, but when you get to know him a bit more you realize he's just trying to act tough for his brothers. All he really wants is for them and us to find something better, you know?"

"Yeah, I do," Jim said, suddenly feeling a little guilty for only thinking about how his dreams were falling apart and not giving a thought for what George must be feeling. George had been betrayed by someone he trusted, just as Jim had been tricked by Aunt Margarita. So before he and Lacey reached the hole in the cellar beneath the shoe factory, the two of them decided to be patient with the Ratts and see if their funk would wear off before long. But Jim's mind also lingered on the appearance of the talking raven – and on the frightening memory of its owner, the Shadow Pirate. Whatever they were up too, Jim imagined, he was sure it was hardly good news for he and his friends.

TWENTY–TWO

CHRISTMAS IN LONDON

As it turned out, the raven's appearance had not accompanied immediate disaster for Jim, but riding out the Ratts' slump was a task easier said than done. George remained as intolerable as ever, although he had ceased saying mean things directly to Lacey. Jim imagined George still felt fairly bad about what he had said before, but nevertheless, his poor mood did nothing to improve the spirits of Peter and Paul, who mostly just sat around saying little and doing less. While all that might have made life in the little cellar nothing but misery for Jim and Lacey, the situation actually resulted in an unforeseen benefit. Since the Ratts were no longer in the business of thieving for the majority of the food and necessities, it fell to Jim and Lacey to improve their own skills and pick up the slack.

At first, the results were mixed (which might be more than fair to poor Jim), the rewards were meager, and many attempts ended with a mad dash from Butterstreet and the King's Men. But as the cold winter wore on, Jim noticed more and more that he had to flee less and less. His fingers became deft at thieving and his eyes grew sharp. But more than that, Jim became pluckier by the day and more daring and adventurous than he'd ever been. He tried new maneuvers and even invented a couple of his own to relieve some of London's wealthiest of a bit of their treasure. There was one in particular he liked called the Kaiser's Underpants, which would have made even George proud.

As for Lacey, she began to leave kernels of corn and seed outside the little hole in the cellar every day, and sure enough, every once in a while Cornelius the raven would drop in for a bite and some friendly words with the young girl. Yet Jim was nothing but suspicious.

"How do you know where our hole is, bird?" Jim demanded one day.

"His name is Cornelius, *boy*," Lacey said, petting the raven on the head. "He really is rude, isn't he, Mister Cornelius?"

"An absolute tragedy of manners," the bird harrumphed. "A metaphorical shipwreck of chivalry!"

But Jim hardly cared. He didn't entirely trust the bird – and still feared his shadowy master. Those two knew something … something the bird wasn't telling Jim. Whenever Cornelius would ask Jim questions about his latest misadventures or about his life before, Jim purposely ignored the raven and insisted that he had to go out and lift some more coal for the stove.

But on days when Jim and Lacey weren't out thieving or making small talk with their new friend, Jim also made good on his promise to teach Lacey to read - but only Lacey, for George and his brothers refused to participate in such rubbish (even though when George stepped out or went to sleep, Peter and Paul would lean in extra close and pay more than a little attention). It was slow going at first for certain, and both Jim and Lacey got frustrated enough with each other to stomp to opposite sides of the cellar and sulk for a bit, and this

- coupled with the Ratt's already sour disposition - made the cellar at those times a most inhospitable place to be indeed.

On one such inhospitable day, after Jim and Lacey (with Peter and Paul, who told George that they were tired of doing nothing all day and broke out in spite of his grumblings to help) had lifted enough coal, a couple of loaves of bread, and a strip or two of jerky to last them for a few days, the two of them left the Ratts to their arguing and wrestling and stepped out into the early evening for some air.

Snow drifted down ever so lightly, the winds were calm, and the cold felt somewhat less than deathly. The streets of London were strangely crowded for this time of evening and all of the windows of the shops and inns were alive and blinking with freshly lit candles. Jim and Lacey breathed deeply as they came to a market square. The smells of fresh baked breads, cinnamon on roasted apples, and crackling meat on spits drenched the air. Lacey looked about curiously as Jim stuck his tongue out to catch a snowflake on the tip.

"It's awfully busy tonight, isn't it, Jim?"

"Yep," Jim agreed keeping his eyes fixed on his next snowflake.

"Oooh!" Lacey suddenly stopped, jerking Jim back by his coat sleeve and causing him to miss his snowflake. "Here's another one I want to try!"

"Again?" Jim said with a groan, but Lacey ignored him.

"T-t-t-imothy of Dunkrick - no, I mean, Dunkirk ..."

Jim tapped his foot on the ground as Lacey kept on spelling out the words to Timothy of Dunkirk's Barber Service shingle. She must have read almost twenty five signs in the last two days and Jim wondered if it were possible to unteach her how to read so that they could get to where they were going in less than three hours.

"Jim, isn't reading wonderful?"

"Oh, yes, extraordinary," Jim said wryly, watching as crowds of people streamed into a cathedral not too far away. "Is it Sunday already, Lacey?"

"I don't think so, Jim — oooh, another one, look at this one, look at this one!" Lacey dashed over to a nearby shop where the owner had cleverly twisted some branches into the shapes of letters in the window. "That's so beautiful, Jim! Let me read it!"

"If you must," Jim grumbled. He didn't even bother to read the sign himself, but instead tried to catch another snowflake on the tip of his outstretched tongue.

"Happy Christmas," Lacey slowly made out.

"I'm sorry?" Jim said, having not quite heard her in his snow-catching efforts.

"Happy Christmas!" Lacey cried and clapped her hands together. "Jim, that's why everybody's about tonight, it's Christmas Eve! Happy Christmas!"

"Oh, I suppose it is," Jim said and started walking on down the street.

"Now Jim Morgan," Lacey suddenly put on her motherly tone and rushed up beside Jim as he walked. "I said Happy Christmas to you and you didn't say it back! Don't you like Christmas?"

"Well," Jim replied with a casual shrug, not really thinking about what he was saying, "I used to, but you know, there aren't really presents or parties or things like that out here. So I guess I wasn't really looking forward to it. Especially not this year."

"Out here? What do you mean by, *out here?*" Lacey crossed her arms, her blue eyes flashed like lightning.

"Er … nothing, I just meant …" Jim tried to backpedal as fast as he could and make up something to smooth things over, but he knew that once Lacey's eyes blazed bright and bold there was little chance of getting any words in edgewise.

"My family never had any of those things: gifts, or parties, or a big cooked goose, or anything, but we still had Christmas! We sang songs and we told stories, and it was the most wonderful thing in the world!" Lacey's eyes started to get wet and her chin quivered a bit. Jim increasingly felt a sore feeling in the pit of his stomach.

"Lacey, that's not what I meant -"

"Oh, you shut up Jim Morgan! Now you know good and well that we haven't pestered you at all about where you came from or what was in your stupid box, but just because you had certain things *back there*, doesn't mean that we weren't also enjoying ourselves *out here*."

"Oh, now come off it, Lacey!" Jim barked back. "You know that's not what I meant. In fact, why don't we go get some things and have a little celebration of our own? It will be fun! I'll get some muffins and buns and a bit of roasted bird and you could get some roasted apples and a bit of green stuff. Who knows, maybe it will cheer up the stinkers back at the cellar." Jim tried to smile but Lacey's tearful eyes suddenly erupted into all-out crying and she stomped her foot in rage.

"Jim Morgan!" she screamed. "We can't steal on Christmas! Oh, you just don't get it at all, do you? Oh, I'm so angry I could scream!"

"You already are, if you can imagine," Jim said timidly, and then Lacey really did scream and turned on her heel toward home.

"I'm going home, Jim Morgan, and you can just stay out here and freeze for all I care!" Then she stopped and turned around to glare at him one last time. "And Happy Christmas!"

Jim let out a long sigh and just scuffed his feet on the snowy cobblestone as he shook his head.

"Tricky creatures to understand, aren't they?" an unnaturally squawky voice said from somewhere above Jim's head. He looked up to find Cornelius the raven perched atop a nearby shingle, leaning against the wall on one wing like a street urchin on a corner. "I once composed a poem of the beauty and incomprehensibility of women after I had met the most perplexing mermaid. Would you like to hear it?"

"There's no such thing as mermaids," Jim said sulkily, kicking at some snow at his feet.

"This coming from the boy with the magically locked box conversing with the talking raven," the bird replied.

"Fine then," Jim said. "Even if there are mermaids I still don't want to hear about it." He turned on his heel and started down the street, but Cornelius fluttered over his head and landed on the corner of the next building's roof.

"Feeling a bit rotten, are we? A pity considering the holiday."

"Oh, not you too," Jim said with a sigh.

"Oh, my dear boy, but I have had such Christmases! I could regale you with the tales of the feasts and the joys … ahhh." The bird sighed with the memories. "It really is a magical time of year."

"Oh posh!" Jim shouted up at the bird, now feeling especially grumpy. "There's no such thing as … as …"

"Magic?" The raven smiled and shook its head. "Now Jim Morgan, we both know better than that don't we?"

"Well I don't see what's so wonderful about it. It's just another day as far as I'm concerned."

"Is it now?" Cornelius said, fluttering down to the windowsill of the next shop. Jim walked up beside him and looked in through the frosty glass. It was a toyshop. Wooden tops and rocking horses and straw and cloth dolls lined the shelves inside. A couple stood by the wrapping counter and put a few coins into the shopkeeper's hands. From the look of their clothes, which were about as tattered as the Jim's, Jim imagined those coppers may have been the last coins those people had. But smiles decorated their faces as the shopkeeper carefully wrapped the wooden soldier in cloth and handed it across the counter to them.

"Those in there certainly believe in the magic, don't they?" Cornelius offered, looking away from the window and into Jim's face. He opened his beak to say more, when the door to the shop opened and a man in a fine winter coat with a fur-lined hat atop of his gray head came out of the store with several packages beneath his arms. His plump old face was flushed with the cold, but he smiled in the mist of his breath. He looked over at Jim, who was now staring into the shop window all by himself, for Cornelius had fluttered up to the roof when the man had looked their way.

"Happy Christmas, young man," the old gentleman said to Jim.

"Happy Christmas, sir."

"Shouldn't we be running along home, now? It's awfully cold tonight."

Normally Jim and the Ratts told such marvelous lies when people asked them about home and parents, to keep off the suspicion, but for some reason those lies failed Jim completely. "I … I don't …" was all Jim could say before the huskiness in his voice stopped him from talking.

The man looked at Jim from underneath his thick hat and bushy white eyebrows for a long moment, and Jim wondered if he was thinking of a way to trick Jim into following him to St. Anne's or to Butterstreet's. But then the gentleman smiled and reached deep into his pocket with his free hand. He pulled out an entire crown and held it out toward Jim. Jim Morgan knew already that he was a proud fellow, but that night, in the falling snow, he reached out and took the large coin in his cold little hand.

"Peace on earth, good will toward men," the old man said rather quietly. "Happy Christmas, son."

"Happy Christmas, sir," Jim said again, and the old man smiled and walked away into the night. The huskiness in Jim's throat did not go away. It thickened ever so slightly and it suddenly felt like an invisible hand pinched his nose and made his eyes water.

Jim looked into the store window again and then back down into his palm. For the first time in many months, Jim had money that was his own. It was not stolen, but it was given. It was all his. For a quick second he wondered what fantastic things he could buy with an entire crown all to himself. There were the tops, and the wooden soldiers, and oh, look, sweets ... but then, just as he was about to rush into the store, another thought stole into Jim's mind. He dwelt on that thought for a time, and then a smile spread across his face and some warmth came from inside his very self, and the cold of the night suddenly felt not so oppressive and deep.

Jim burst into the hole of the cellar with snow falling off his shoulders and hat. "Hello, George, Peter and Paul!" he cried. "Happy Christmas!" Now, ever since the death of his father, Jim had been a rather serious boy, but just then he could not keep the smile from his face. The way the three Ratt brothers stared at him as he leapt into the light of the stove, Jim for a moment, thought that they didn't even recognize him.

"Happy what?" George said rather sulkily, but Peter and Paul smiled back as though they'd been waiting to smile for weeks and only now just found the joy to do so.

"Happy Christmas, I said!" Jim repeated. "Didn't you know? It's Christmas Eve!"

"Who bloody well cares?" George seemed intent on staying as cranky as possible, but Jim remembered that he felt that same way staring into that barrel of rainwater until the reflection's of his friends' faces appeared beside his.

"Well, I do." Jim kept the smile on his face. "And now you have to as well."

From behind his back, Jim pulled out four packages wrapped in brown paper and tied up with string.

"What are those?" Paul asked eagerly, but Jim could tell he already knew and just couldn't believe it.

"They're presents, Paul," Jim said, handing both Peter and Paul one of the gift-wrapped presents each. The two boys stared at Jim, then at each other, then they tore the brown paper to bits.

"Toy soldiers!" they cried together and immediately engaged their wooden troopers in battle with each other before laughing out loud and seizing Jim in a giant bear hug.

"Thanks, Jim!" Peter said.

"Happy Christmas, Jim!" Paul's smile covered the entire bottom half of his face.

With all the shouting and joyous ruckus, George wandered over to where his brothers and Jim stood on a carpet of shredded paper. He looked at Paul and Peter, playing happily with their toys, then he looked at Jim, and then he looked down at the other brown paper-wrapped gift in Jim's hand.

"Jim ... I ..." Jim heard the thickness in George's voice.

"George, you silly goose," Jim said, pushing the package into George's hands. "This is a small thing, really. Without you, I don't know where I'd be right now."

George took the package and opened it up. It was a tricorn hat, maroon with gold threads along the edges. George stared at it for a few moments and then threw his cap off and set the hat on his head. With a sprinkling of awe in their eyes, Jim, Paul, and Peter gazed at George in his new hat.

"George, you're -" Peter began.

"- just like a gentleman of London." Paul said, finishing the thought. George blushed a bit, and for the first time in weeks, like his brothers, he smiled, and some of the old Ratt mischief seeped back into his eyes.

Then Jim looked past the Ratts to a pile of potato sacks in the corner, where Lacey sat with her arms folded and a rather sour countenance on her face. Jim walked slowly over to her, the last package in his hands.

"I told you earlier, Jim Morgan," Lacey said without looking at him. "I don't steal on Christmas and I don't want anything that was stolen on Christmas."

"So do you think I lifted the wrapping paper and string as well and tied them up in the middle of the street with no one noticing?" Jim said and Lacey looked up at him. "I didn't steal them, Lacey. And I didn't get them with money that I stole. It's a real present. A real one. Happy Christmas, Lacey."

Jim watched as Lacey's angry face slowly melted into a believing smile, and she took the package into her hands and slowly unwrapped it. She undid the little string and peeled back the paper with such care so that not one corner or edge was ripped or tattered. When she found a little cloth doll, with blonde yarn hair, resting in the crinkled folds of the paper, she looked up at Jim with wonder in her eyes.

"But Jim, how ... ?"

"It's Christmas, Lacey. It was magic." Then Lacey leapt up and squeezed Jim around the neck. In a moment, the three Ratts were squeezing as well, until the five of them were one big twisty pile of arms and tattered coats spinning around in a circle in the light of the orange coals.

"I'm sorry, Lacey," George said. "I'm sorry I've been such a brat."

"Oh, Happy Christmas, George!" Lacey said, and the hugging went on for quite some time. And in the midst of it all, a thought lit upon Jim's mind as soft as a snowflake on his tongue. Even if he failed to gain back his box, and even if he failed to find his father's treasure and pay back those fiends the Cromiers and his treacherous aunt, something in the back of Jim's mind told him his life could still turn out somehow for the better. As long as he kept these new friends – his best friends – close, anything was possible.

TWENTY-THREE

THE CAPTAIN AND THE CONSTABLE

The sun rose and glared brightly off the thick blanket of freshly fallen snow that covered the roofs and streets of London. It was now January and Constable Edmund Butterstreet stepped up to the office in his freshly cleaned and ironed uniform, rapping the shingle above his head that read "King's Men." The snow on the shingle cascaded down over him like his own personal snow shower and he smiled and whistled the tune to his favorite Christmas carol.

Despite the cold, winter was one of Butterstreet's favorite times of year, mostly because of Christmas and New Year. He was one of those types that somehow managed to keep his holiday spirit deep into February, when most had long since abandoned it and hoped only for the warmth of spring. But Butterstreet so loved the Christmas services

169

and the choirs, the foods and the gifts, that he remembered them most of the year until the next Christmas, and often tried to spread a bit of holiday cheer to all he knew, even the criminals.

"Good morning, Thomas," Butterstreet said to the deputy at the desk as he walked into the office.

"Morning, constable!" Thomas replied as he warmed his hands by the coal stove. "Hope you're ready to start early today, you have a visitor waiting for you in your office."

"A visitor? This early and in this kind of weather? Now what could this be about?" The big constable stepped back into his office and, as Thomas said, found his visitor waiting for him. He was a pale man, tall, with raven-black hair tied back into a tail. He wore the uniform of a captain of his majesty's navy with a sword by his side and stood at the window, staring out into the snow with his cold blue eyes. After a moment, Butterstreet recognized him from some rather unpleasant business some months ago.

"Ah, Captain Cromier, is it?" Butterstreet said merrily, holding out his hand to shake Cromier's. Bartholomew turned and, ignoring the offered hand, instead went and sat down behind Butterstreet's own desk. Now, this might have infuriated many men and led to some sort of argument, but Butterstreet was a man of common birth himself who was used to the way of things. Besides, it was still the Christmas season as far as Butterstreet was concerned and there was no use in letting an arrogant nobleman ruin his spirits. "Well, good morning, sir and welcome to our little office."

"Good? Hardly," Cromier sneered, quickly assessing the quaint office with its unvarnished wooden furniture and plain walls. "I'm going to get straight to the point Betterstraight."

"Butterstreet, sire," Butterstreet said politely, but as with his handshake, this was ignored.

"I have a serious problem that requires your full attention."

"It is my duty to mind this city from this office to the docks on the Thames, captain," Butterstreet replied. "How may I be of service to his majesty's navy?"

"There is a dangerous pirate of the seas in our fair city, Bitterstraught," Bartholomew said, standing and strutting about the office. "He is a scourge of the Channel and the Atlantic, but he has made the mistake of wintering in London for a time and was spotted heading this way some weeks ago. In fact he may already be here now."

"And which pirate may this be, that I'm looking for, captain?"

Bartholomew set his jaw and said the name with a dramatic turn: "Captain Dread Steele." Unfortunately, he finished said flourish only to find Butterstreet erupting in a roar of laughter.

"Captain Steele? *The* Dread Steele?" Butterstreet held his big sides as his rumbling laughter filled the entire office. Even Thomas in the front office smiled when he heard the thunderous sound. "Oh, forgive me sir, but I think you'd have better luck catching old Father Noel handing out sticks and coal to the gangs of thieving children I chase than catching that one!"

Bartholomew's alabaster cheeks pinked fiercely, and he tapped his index finger on the pommel of his sword. But then he pulled his jacket straight, swallowed some of his enormous pride, and spoke through gritted teeth. "And why is that ... do you say?"

"Captain Steele comes in and out of London as he pleases, sir." Butterstreet ceased his laughing, a serious look blooming in his merry eyes. His voice lowered as though what he was about to say should not be said too loudly. "Oh, he's a crook all right, and a buccaneer, but he's a charmer, that one is, and a master of disguise to boot. I've heard he can appear as nearly the likeness of any person he desires and sound like them too. Some even say he does this through the powers of the black arts and that he has wizards, witches, and talking animals for allies. Even the great Captain Lindsay Morgan, God rest him, couldn't catch Dread Steele noways. Gawd, I may have arrested the man once before, thinking him a regular thief and then let him go the next week."

"Nevertheless," Bartholomew said, the lines around his lips tightening. "There will be rumors of his comings and goings, whispers floating about the criminal underworld of this city. I suppose you can pick up pieces of that, at least, can't you?" Bartholomew's tone was as demeaning as possible, and he made his way toward the door, angry as he could be with the inefficiency of this particular constable. But Butterstreet simply smiled again.

"Oh now that I can do, sir," Butterstreet said with a nod. "I'm sure all the gangs from the Clawed Rabbits - a real nasty crew of Irish toughs - all the way down to the litt'luns like the Brothers Ratt and their new friend Jim Morgan will hear something about the arrival of the great Captain Steele to our shores."

Bartholomew froze at the door to the office, standing as still as a horrible, ghoulish statue for a long moment before slowly turning his head back to the constable. "What did you just say?"

"Oh, I was just commenting on how all the criminals will have heard something about the arrival of Captain Steele. Just won't be all trustworthy that's all ..."

"No, no, no!" Bartholomew stepped slowly back into the office, sticking his hook-nosed face and piercing blue eyes right up under Butterstreet's droopy mustache. "*Who* did you just say?"

"Why the Brothers Ratt, sir, and their new member, a lad by the name of Jim Morgan. Newcomer to the game, really. A fair-looking boy to be honest. I would say at first blush that he bears the appearance of a nobleman's son, by the cut of his hair and the look in his eyes, but he can't be, not running about with the like of the Ratts - they're as common as I am, sir."

Bartholomew stared into Butterstreet's face for a long moment, his blue eyes wide and watery from a sudden lack of blinking. He finally turned away from Butterstreet and walked back toward the window. "It's unlikely - a long shot," Bartholomew mumbled to himself, and Butterstreet furrowed his brow and strained for a better listen to the captain's soft words. "... one in a thousand, a prayer really, and how I abhor praying — but could it be?"

"Do you know this boy?" Butterstreet asked, no longer smiling and staring intently at the dark-haired captain's reflection in the window. The constable knew the looks in men's eyes, and what they meant. And he didn't like the hungry glare in Bartholomew Cromier's unnerving blue eyes, no, not one bit.

"This boy, this ... Jim," Bartholomew said slowly. "He stole something from a good friend of mine. Something important."

"Well, they are rather good picks of the old pocket if you know what I mean, captain."

"I need you to find this boy, Butterstreet," said Cromier, and the constable did not miss the fact that Bartholomew had finally gotten his name right. "And when you arrest him, I want him held here until I am notified. I will deal with the boy personally. Do you understand?"

"Yes, sir," said Butterstreet, nodding slowly. "And as for the pirate?"

"I will remain in London until we find both of these criminals, and I will see to their fates in person." With that, Captain Bartholomew Cromier marched out of the office with his head held high and his shoulders back, as though he had just been promoted captain all over again.

Butterstreet watched him go and shook his head just a little. He would do what the young captain asked (he would lose his job or worse if he didn't), but Butterstreet was more than a little disinclined to enjoy following these particular orders, much more than a little. Something told him that if the young captain got a hold of Jim Morgan, the unfortunate lad would end up far worse off than reading schoolbooks or singing in the church choir.

TWENTY–FOUR

THE INN OF THE WET ROCK

The very same day that the pallid Captain Cromier visited Constable Butterstreet's small office, Jim, Lacey, and the Ratts made their way to the docks on the Isle of Dogs. It was still as cold as a winter day could be in London, but the sun was shining and that gave the small clan at least a little warmth in their threadbare coats.

After Christmas, the Ratts had decided to come out of early retirement and return to thieving full time. This was good news for Jim and his hopes of finding the Amulet before King of Thieves could get his conniving hands on it. From what Jim and the Ratts had heard at the King's court, and much to their delight, the Dragons had still failed to swipe the amulet from the old man who supposedly possessed it, and even better yet — it was rumored that very same old man still lurked about London's streets.

"I really don't like the idea of going down here, even in the daytime," Lacey worried as she crunched through the snow beside Jim.

"And I still for the life of me can't figure out why," George said, making sure to add a extra H sound to all of his vowels so he could see his breath steam in the cold air.

"Well, first of all, the docks are very dangerous," Lacey said in her best mother voice. "My mum used to tell me it was full of all sorts of slimy characters. Pirates, killers, thieves, and even kidnappers."

"Hold on a sec," Jim interrupted. "Aren't we thieves?"

"Not thieves like us, Jim!" Lacey started to get that spark in her blue eyes again and Jim focused a little more on walking than on her face to diffuse the bomb before it exploded. "You know what I mean! And the second thing is that this is the area of town that the Dragons usually work, and we don't want another run-in with them."

"Dragons? Heh!" Paul said confidently. "I'm not worried about them."

Jim laughed along with George and Peter at Paul's bravado, but he shivered just a little bit harder all the same at the thought of Big Red unloading another fist into his face.

"Besides that," Lacey continued with rolled eyes that simply proclaimed: boys are so stupid. "How are we even going to find one supposed old sea salt in an entire town's worth of old sea salts?"

"Well, the king did say he would be at the Wet Rock," Jim said hopefully. "And for some time too, by the sound of it."

"Exactly!" said George. "We'll just post up at the Inn of the Wet Rock and the other spots all around there, and when we spot the old coot with the amu-what's-it about his flabby old neck we'll give him the old Punch and Judy, nick the necklace, and be on our merry way!"

George made it all sound so easy that Jim actually smiled and picked up the pace with a little added confidence, but, of course, Lacey immediately spoiled that happy-go-lucky moment with a dose of reality.

"If it were so easy, then don't you think the Dragons would have stolen the medallion by now, hmmm?" She made her "hmmm" extra long to let Jim and George actually sense how much longer she had thought about the situation than them. "Obviously not!"

"Oh, obviously, professor," George sneered, and jumped up to slap a snow-laden shingle so that it showered Lacey with snow. She stuck out her tongue (and not in the way to catch snow flakes.)

"Well, whatever the case," Jim said, now balancing the encouraging thought of having the amulet stolen in a blink of an eye with dealing with a possible no-win scenario, "that amulet may be the only chance. At the best, if we get the amulet and I win the box back, I can open it myself with the amulet's magic."

"And at the worst?" Paul asked.

"If we get the amulet, maybe I can trade it for my box."

"Even if that means that that old slimer, the King of Thieves, gets the key to untold treasures?" Lacey asked incredulously. Jim looked at his friend and for a brief moment, thought about telling them all he knew of the treasure – but once again, something inside Jim prevented him from divulging what little he knew of his father's secret yet.

"Believe me Lacy," Jim said. "I'll be more than happy to throw a wrench in that fiend's plans. But I have to get my box back first. And if going to these docks and snatching this amulet from the old salt is the only way, then that's the way I'm going."

The Ratts cheered Jim on, but Lacey gave the back of Jim's head a long and disapproving glare all the way down the next block and a half. Soon, however, they reached the docks, and it became immediately apparent that Lacey's mother knew what she was talking about after all. The docks were packed end to end with the dirtiest scoundrels and cheatingest scum to ever carry swords and spyglasses on the decks of ships both pirate or worse. It was by far one of the least appropriate places for children of the clan's age to be wandering about by themselves. So, naturally, the Ratts loved every minute of it.

"Whoa! Look at that!" Paul exclaimed as a crusty old sailor hobbled past. Jim had no idea what was so spectacular about the man until

177

he heard a peculiar click in place of the snowy crunch with the man's steps. And there it was, an actual peg leg.

"Wicked!" Peter and George said, grinning ear to ear with delight.

"How dreadful!" Lacey shook her head with pity, but the Ratts and Jim were already absorbed in the other strange sights and sounds of the docks. They saw buccaneers with real eye patches, parrots and monkeys atop their shoulders. They stopped and listened to stories told in circles of sailors gathered about fires over cups of warm ale. The boys sucked in every last detail of the adventures, full of magically induced storms, ghost ships that haunted the seas, mermaids, sirens, islands of native and wild warriors, treasure in unbelievable quantities, and dozens of other spectacles of the unnatural sort.

At one point, George even risked a hearty "Arrgghh!" in greeting to a passing pirate.

"Arrgghh!" the scruffy sailor growled in return, and the boys nearly fell over themselves in giggling glee. Lacey wasn't enjoying herself nearly as much as the others and walked sulkily behind them with her arms folded, scowling crossly. The Ratts loved the pirates themselves, but it wasn't until they walked through a break in the crowd that Jim saw something that took his breath away.

It came gliding toward the dock from out on the water, perhaps half mile away, fresh on the river from the sea and visible only as a ghostly silhouette in the mist. Its sails were out and grabbing at the wind, billowing proudly over the deck. The bow pointed like an arrow toward the shore and sliced through the water like a happy fish swimming home. It was a great vessel of the ocean, a mighty ship of the sea.

Jim suddenly remembered the shore by his family's home. He remembered running through the sand, a little wooden replica of the real-life ship before him in his hands. That memory skipped like a rock on a pond through Jim's mind and landed on another remembrance: standing on that same beach with his father for the last time. Jim remembered being so sulky then and a lump formed in his throat. For now, having been thrown out into the wild world with no home and no family, something in his heart yearned to be on the deck of that ship with the waves beneath his feet, as though that would some how bring him closer to the father he would never see again.

"Hey, Jim!" George called. "We've found the Wet Rock! Let's go!"

The Wet Rock was just a warmer and smaller version of the docks outside. Fires burned in the stone hearths and packs of weary seamen gathered around their warmth to eat and share wild tales of adventures both true and invented from long journeys on the vast ocean. The children stood by the entrance and scanned the wide room. Lacey sighed and shook her head.

"Exactly what does this man look like again?" she asked with more than a hint of irritation.

"Well, he's old," George said.

"And crusty, most likely," Peter added.

"Probably a bit shaggy and worn out, I'd guess," Paul nodded.

"And I would think he would be wearing the amulet," Jim said finally.

"Ah, yes," Lacey said, nodding with a huge sarcastic grin on her face. "That definitely narrows the search down a bit. It should be only seconds before we find him in here. No one else fitting that description for miles!" She stomped her foot emphatically. "We're never going to find him - this is ridiculous!"

"There he is," Paul said just as Lacey was about to launch into a tirade of I-told-you-sos. Lacey followed Paul's pointing finger, as did the others, and sure enough, sitting on a bench by a table full of the roughest and swarthiest pirates they had yet to see was an old man with a white beard and shaggy white hair. He wore a faded blue and red greatcoat and a cracked and worn bandolier over his shoulder that carried a rusty, dented cutlass. And sure enough, around his neck, hung the Amulet of Portunes, glimmering in the firelight.

"I don't believe it!" Lacey screamed, seemingly as much from fury that the Ratts had found the old man so quickly as from disbelief.

"You see, Jim," George said, polishing his dirty nails on his dirty shirt. "Leave it to us, and you'll have your box back by the end of the week. There was never really cause for concern. This is going to be like taking candy from a baby."

George had the others idle beside one of the nearby fireplaces as he flexed his fingers and rolled his shoulders to loosen up. "I figure the old Gregorian Gooseneck should do the trick for the old bag," he said confidently.

"He's going to get a drink from the barkeep now," Jim pointed out, and off George went. As he had seen his friend do so many times before, Jim watched George dodge and weave through the crowd, past pointed crooks of elbows and beneath outstretched arms the master thief glided like a falcon descending upon its prey. As for the prey, Jim watched the old man lean up against the bar while the barkeep gathered up two arm's-full of ales.

"Poor old blighter," Jim said to Peter and Paul.

"Doesn't even know what's coming," the two agreed in unison, nodding their heads in near pity.

Then the moment was upon them. George came in from behind the old salt as silent as a ghost, and as he walked by he craned his arm over his head to pluck the amulet neatly by its chain from its owner's neck. Jim, Paul, and Peter could hardly contain their excitement and anticipation as they expected the powerful talisman to soon be in their possession. But, at the last possible moment, just when George's fingertips brushed the clasp of the chain, the old man snatched up his ales, turned on his heel, and spun back to his table.

The sudden turning motion threw George completely for a loop and, trying to adjust his footing so he wasn't caught behind the old man red-handed, he ended up stumbling face-first into a stubble-chinned pirate with two pistols in his bandolier, spilling the rough-hewn sailor's ale all over the both of them.

"Oy!" the pirate erupted from his stool. "Watch where your goin' you scurvy runt or you might jus' find yourself tanglin' it up with the squids and fishes o' the deep!"

"Sorry, sir, sorry!" George babbled, then quickly ducked back through the crowded room to stand beside his friends.

"Like taking candy from a baby, eh, George?" Lacey said smugly, and it looked like George wanted to slug her. But he was a professional and quickly composed himself.

"Just a spot of bad luck, that's all," George said, smiling at his comrades and shaking his shoulders loose again.

"Of course it was," Paul said as he cheered his brother on and slapped him on the back. "Won't happen twice, that's for sure!"

"No way!" George agreed. "Time for the Prince Charles!" he proclaimed, and once more made a swerving path toward his target.

The pirates gathered about the old man were laughing and carousing with tall tales and crude jokes all around as George approached. As sneaky as a snake he sidled up beside the old man, laughing along with the distracted men. When the old man took his turn to tell a limerick (something about a one-toothed mermaid and a blind swabbie with an old barrel of rum) George burst out laughing in hysterics and slapped the old man heartily on the back. On the fourth slap, just the beat he timed to snatch up the amulet, the old-timer must have suddenly spied a coin on the floor because he reached down and George's swipe sailed clean over his head and instead smacked right in the face a black bearded fellow with a fierce-looking bandana cinched about his forehead.

Jim gasped and thought for sure his friend was done for, but George quickly ducked, and the bearded pirate blamed one of his fellows - which resulted in a brief but rather brutal scrum and the loss of a couple of teeth and a bloodied nose. George scrambled back to the fireplace lookout as confounded as Jim had ever seen him.

"Bad stroke of luck again?" Lacey said rather nastily and arched her eyebrows as high as they could reach.

"Oh, step off!" George thundered, and his brothers slapped him on the back to encourage him into battle once more.

"Of course it was rotten luck," Peter said. "Lightning never strikes three times though, so our father said! You've got him on the ropes!" He encouraged George with a smile but then flashed Jim a wide-eyed look of puzzlement behind his brother's back. This was not going according to plan.

All afternoon George threw everything he could at the wily old pirate: the French Telescope, the New World Noose, the Kaiser's Underpants, an Arab Cherub Surprise, even the faithful Russian Nose Pick 'n'Flick (which sent an unfortunately deflected bogey into the one remaining good eye of a one-eyed pirate, which again resulted in a quick spat of flying fists and chairs).

Finally, George staggered back to the fireplace on wobbly legs, breathing hard like a boxer who's seen the close-up of his opponent's fist one too many times. "Tricky old bushy beard," said George with his hands on his hips as Paul wrapped an arm around his brother's waist to support him and Peter fanned him with a bar towel. "I just need a breather ... I've got him right where I want him!"

But Jim saw George's dazed expression and knew there was no use in going back at it the same way. "Look, George," he said, putting one hand on his friend's shoulder. "You've given it a great go, but obviously the salt's got the beat on the pickpocket angle. Maybe we should try a new angle? Paul?" He gave the smallest Ratt brother a nod. "What do you think?"

"I think this is the perfect place for a Carnival Gag, now that you mention it, Jim," Paul said, and George nodded in resigned agreement.

"Let's give it a try."

"Ladies and gentlemen, if I could have your attention!" Paul's voice cried to the bustling crowds of the inn only a few moments later. He stood on a bench not far from where the old pirate and his friends sat and held his arms out wide like a mousy circus ringmaster.

"None of those in 'ere lad," a sour voice jabbed from beside a far fireplace to the rough laughter of Paul's audience.

"Right you are!" Paul said without missing a beat. "Let's try this then: roughnecks and scalawags! Listen up!"

"Arrgghh!" The audience raised their tins of ale and laughed at the plucky young Ratt.

"Well," Lacey whispered to Jim, who stood with George and Paul behind the table that Paul had claimed for his efforts. "That got their attention anyway."

"Call a spade a spade and all that," Jim agreed, though he wasn't sure he enjoyed having all the eyes (and some not in pairs) in the room upon them.

"It seems to me that there are some of you lucky salts in here with a bit too much gold for your own good and other foul-fortuned blokes about with not quite enough!" Paul bellowed.

"You're right there, lad!" a particularly scruffy pirate cried, and the room again erupted in laughs, jeers, insults, and brags.

"Well, seeing as how it's a bit cold to settle your differences outside ..."

"I've set'led more than my fair share inside, young'n," an aged pirate with more scars than hairs left on his head said in a deadly tone as he picked his teeth with the biggest knife Jim had ever seen.

"Yes ... I can see that ..." Paul gulped, staring for a long moment at the old fighter with wide eyes before remembering his audience and flashing a forced smile. "Well, for the rest of us then ... I suggest a game. It's very simple. Here in my hand, I have a marble." He held the shiny little ball in the air for all to see. "I will hide said marble under one of three bowls. Guess the wrong bowl, and you lose a piece of your treasure ... guess the right one ... and leave with your pockets a little heavier than when you landed in London town ... and I'll even throw in the marble! What d'ya say?"

"ARRGGHH!" the crowd cried, and before Paul had time to say dead-men-tell-no-tales, the longest line of unshaven, thieving scoundrels any of the children could have ever imagined formed up in front of the table.

"Born showman, that Paul is," Peter said with an appreciative nod. "Trust me Jim, what me and George do for locks and pockets, Paul does for the old con game! Watch and learn."

Paul leapt down from the bench and pushed the sleeves of his coat and shirt up past his elbows. He flashed a smile and rolled the shiny marble across the back of his knuckles before the first eager sailor in line, a squat man with pocked cheeks, a thin beard, and a huge bald spot surrounded by lengths of his mangy hair. The round pirate plucked a fat gold earring off his left ear and slammed it down on the table.

Paul tossed the marble beneath one of the bowls with a neat flick of his wrist and like a master musician on some sort of strange instrument whirled the bowls around on the table, crisscrossing and looping them in figure eights. The poor sailor tried to follow the dancing bowls so closely that his eyes began to dance in their sockets.

"Which bowl then, friend?" Paul said when he finally stopped, but the sailor was so dizzy that he just groaned slightly and keeled over on the spot.

"Next," Paul said curtly, and the line erupted in howls of laughter and approval. The pirates and seamen liked this game, that was for certain, but they apparently had no idea who they were playing against. Jim watched closely as Paul used all manner of distracting tricks and methods to keep the pirates guessing. He dizzied some, pestered others with inane conversation about albatross droppings, or just outsped their eyes with the amazing dexterity of his hands. Jim had to admit, he was deeply impressed by the display. Even he failed to follow the hidden marble and had guessed wrong in his mind every time he thought he knew which bowl it lay hidden beneath.

After about an hour or so of Paul's game, a nice pile of treasure accumulated on the table beside the tricky bowls. Rings and charms, bejeweled knives and chains, earrings and silver belt buckles all glistened in the firelight of the inn. Peter and George already figured that spending the loot on pocketfulls of candy would be a fine consolation even if they failed to nab the amulet. But, just as Lacey was about to chastise the greedy boys for how pointless that would have made this entire trip, two gnarled hands slapped down before Paul at the table and the old man in the blue and red greatcoat leaned in close. The amulet dangled temptingly from around his neck right before Paul's eyes.

"Pre'ty good game ye' got goin' 'ere, laddie," the old man said in a crackly voice. His crafty smile revealed a rough set of crooked, yellow teeth, and his breath was tinged with more than a hint of dank seaweed.

"Right we do, sir," Paul said, gulping nervously, for the old man's eyes were still sharp as daggers and stared over the faces of the five children, studying them intently. Jim thought the old salt paused for just a second longer when he reached Jim's face, but then the pirate turned his attention back to Paul, who said: "Care to play?"

"Aye, I do, but what do ye' think I should be wagerin'?" The old man smiled with half his mouth and his scruffy chin, covered in scraggly white beard, quivered as though he were about to laugh.

"How 'bout that necklace?" Paul asked, some of his charm failing a bit under the old-timer's intense scrutiny.

"Oh, this little trinket?" The old man played with it in his fingers for a bit before turning his half-smile into a whole one. "Why not? T'isn't worth much to me anymore," he said as he unclasped it and laid it on the table. "Not like something I'd need to keep under lock nor key, if ye catch my meaning," he chuckled slowly, and Jim and Lacey caught their startled gasps in their throats.

Could the old man know what they were up to, Jim wondered. But he was hardly sure whether the old man could even know what a powerful talisman he had, as he was betting it so casually in what was obviously a rigged game.

Paul wiped his sweaty hands on his pants and once more danced the marble over the back of his knuckles before flicking it beneath one of the bowls. "So, from London originally, sir?" Paul asked, trying to distract the unnervingly sharp salt as he whipped the bowls around as fast he could.

"Truth be told, Laddie," The old man said as casually as if he were catching up with an old friend, his eyes never once leaving the bowls, "I've made port 'n so many bays 'cross the map o' de earth that me old mind can't even remember de place I first left from. The sea is my wife, my family, my home ... all in one, and she's taught me everything an old man could hope to learn." At the last word he slammed one hand down on the table with one hand and snatched Paul by the wrist with the other.

"Hey! Get off!" Paul cried.

"I'm just playin' the game, young sir." The pirate stared right into Paul's startled eyes, grinning smugly. His gold tooth, the third from the middle, gleamed brightly. "And I choose ..." He waved his free hand playfully over the bowls. "This one." But instead of pointing to one of the bowls he seized Paul's hand and forced it open to reveal the shiny marble resting in its palm.

The line of yet-to-play sailors - and especially the crowd of losers - roared in protest at the realization that they had been duped by children. They pressed in around the table with rage in their eyes.

"Looks like I'll be keepin' this." The salt smiled, dropping the amulet back around his neck before leaving with a wink and a wave to the young thieves. Fortunately, the pirates and sailors took their treasure back instead of exacting painful revenge on the tricksters, but the innkeeper tossed Jim, Lacey, and the Ratts out into the cold evening and refused to let them back in after all the trouble they'd caused.

"Well that went well, didn't it?" Jim kicked a pile of snow in aggravation toward the shut door of the inn.

"Boys." Lacey tried to turn Jim and the Ratts in her direction but they were too caught up in their own self-pity to hear her.

"Yeah," George said glumly. "Not only did we not get the amulet, we didn't get any other loot either, and of course we almost got relieved of our lives by that mob in there."

"Boys!"

"No one's ever guessed before!" said Paul, shaking his head. "I can't believe it! No old man's got eyes that sharp. I swear he was like a falcon or something with those eyes!"

"Booooys!"

"Yeah, there's definitely something funny about that salt, that's for sure," Peter agreed, still ignoring Lacey. "Did you see the way he was looking at us? Something queer about him for certain. Like he knew what we were after or something."

"BOYS!" Lacey finally screamed and Jim and the Ratts at last turned to her, throwing their hands up with a chorus of "What!" on their lips. But that question was answered immediately – by the gold-toothed smile of the crafty old pirate, the Amulet of Portunes still dangling on the chain his neck.

"Greetins' my little friends," he growled, and from the shadows of the alley beside the inn, a troupe of the pirate's friends appeared in the fading light of the winter evening. At that moment the Ratts and Jim did what any brave young men would have done in their position - they unleashed the most girlish screams of panic ever heard in London before or since.

"Run Lacey! Run!" Jim cried as they tried to make a break for it. But it was no use. Jim's heart sank into his stomach. The old salt's friends were too fast for even the fleet-footed Ratt Clan, and in a moment they had the children wrapped up in their sinewy arms, calloused hands clapped over their mouths.

"Hello, boys and girl," one with a black beard said, leering at them. "What do you think we should do with 'em, MacGuffy? Boil em? Skin em? Or just plain, old run 'em through?"

Jim's mind raced though the unpleasant pictures of each of those morbid suggestions. But even more awful than the wild fear coursing through his body, was the ache in Jim's heart, knowing that once more he had missed the mark and ended up yet again in another hopeless situation.

"Well," MacGuffy mused, another toothy smile spreading over his face. "It's the captain's treasure they be seekin', so I think it's the captain they should be meetin!' Take them to the ship."

The pirates cackled and growled with mad glee at this suggestion and with hard shoves toward the docks, bustled Jim, the Ratts, and Lacey off into the cold darkness of the night.

TWENTY–FIVE

CAPTAIN DREAD STEELE

Beneath the massive winter moon, the burly pirates marched the Ratts, Lacey, and Jim, who did his best to stick his chin out and give the scalawags as little as possible to laugh about, through the snow. The small procession, led by MacGuffy, made its way through the alleyways of the docks down to the water, where a creaky sloop bobbed up and down on the black, lapping water.

"Not much of a pirate ship, really," Jim said as snobbily as ever. "In some countries they call those fishing boats."

George and Peter laughed; but Paul and Lacey cringed. Jim hardly cared if he was earning himself some rather brutal treatment. He was sick and tired of all his bad luck and was about ready to let someone else have a rotten time for a change. But the pirates, especially old MacGuffy, laughed right along with George and Peter.

"That's a clever little monkey isn't he?" MacGuffy said. "Maybe the Cap'n'll keep you as a pet. But whether alive or stuffed and mounted we've yet to see." He added the last part with such a wicked grin that Jim, no matter his wretched outlook at the moment, decided it prudent to keep his mouth shut for the next little while.

As they walked up a rather creaky gangplank, Jim heard the squeaky chimes of an organ grinder whistle and hoot in the night air. The pirates and their prisoners stepped aboard and the source of the music suddenly appeared. He was a huge lump of a pirate with a faded bandana cinched about his big head. Dirty hair not much rustier than Big Red's fell out from beneath the bandana in greasy dreadlocks and his filthy beard hung in braids from his chin as well. The somewhat musically inclined pirate sat on a barrel of grog and happily spun the grinder's handle, cranking out a tune and cracking a nearly toothless smile all the while.

An entire crew of pirates - who took little notice of the cold air - littered the sloop's deck in waistcoat jackets with threadbare scarves wrapped loosely about their necks. Some of them rested their hands on the pommels of cutlasses or on the grips of pistols at their sides. Others twirled and balanced knives on the tips of their deft fingers. The lot of them gathered mostly around a couple of small stoves that glowed with orange and white coals. They joked and laughed, or sang old pirate songs to the organ grinder's tune. Despite his situation, Jim couldn't help but feel that they were a happier bunch than most of the people he'd seen in the darker streets of London these last months.

On their way to the main cabin, MacGuffy found a particularly old pirate who was thicker around the middle than anywhere else on his whole body. The plump buccaneer was slumped up against an empty beer barrel with an even emptier cup loose in his fingers, snoring loudly. A black raven sat on the beer barrel eating what seemed to be corn from the top of the old pirate's top hat.

"Not even a proper parrot," George whispered to Jim, but the raven looked right at the two boys and winked.

"Cornelius?" Jim whispered, he and Lacey exchanging startled looks. But the clever raven flew off to the topmast without saying a word.

"What did you say?" George asked, but Jim just kept his mouth shut, wondering what the blasted, talking bird was doing hanging about here.

MacGuffy, meanwhile, kicked the old pirate's thigh with the toe of his boot and shouted, "Avast Mister Gilly!"

Gilly snorted and flew suddenly awake. "FIRE THE CANNONS AND HOIST THE JOLLY ROGER!" he roared with a slurred voice, and all of the pirates had a good laugh at the old man's expense.

"Caught you nappin' again, did I, Mister Gilly?"

"I'm no' on watch, Mister MacGuffy," Gilly said slowly and through his nose, as though inflicted with the worst of all colds. "I was jus' havin' a nap 'ere and dreamin' about somefin … somefin a long time ago …" He furrowed his brow and clenched his teeth trying to remember, and Jim thought his head might pop off if he kept it up. But, he eventually released all his pent-up efforts with a deep sigh that flapped his old lips. "But it seems to 'ave escaped me, naturally, sir."

"Well if you ain't on the watch, then who it be?"

"I," announced a voice as deep and rumbling as thunder. The boys and Lacey craned their necks to look up at the huge man who stepped before them. The ship's deck groaned beneath his weight, for he was as tall as a doorway and at least as broad. His head was shaved bald and his skin was as a black as midnight. Strange scars swirled beneath his dark eyes, the like of which Jim had never seen before. The huge man crossed his arms over his broad chest and smiled down at old MacGuffy.

"Ah, Mufalme." If old MacGuffy was at all intimidated by the big man he showed no sign and slapped the watchman on his huge bicep. "Excellent choice to have you on guard while nothing valuable is on board, excellent choice indeed."

Mufalme eyed the children suspiciously, and Jim was certain his eyes, which were a fantastic white against the man's black skin, lingered on his face for an even longer moment. He growled at old MacGuffy and put his huge hands on his hips. "I grow tired of your jokes old man. If this were my country -"

"But it ain't your country, now is it?" MacGuffy said with a smile, his gold tooth gleaming in the moonlight. "Which be a cryin' shame if ye ask me, for it would be a mite bit warmer if it were!"

"What do you want, old man?"

"Prisoners to see the captain."

"Prisoners?" Mufalme raised an eyebrow and sneered. "They look highly dangerous, MacGuffy. Perhaps you should have called for my help to round them up."

"Don't let the looks deceive ya, lad." MacGuffy smiled lazily and nearly laughed. "These be highly resourceful thieves yer beholdin' and they'll be meetin' the captain if ye don't mind."

"So be it," Mufalme finally agreed, stepping his giant frame aside to reveal a small set of steps leading down to the sloop's main cabin door.

MacGuffy and his mates rudely corralled Jim, the Ratts, and Lacey down the steps and into the captain's cabin. It was a small room, lit by a hanging lamp in the corner and furnished with only a table and an old leather chair. The single decoration on the walls was a large map that seemed to cover the entire known world. It was a rather fanciful map, Jim imagined, for it was populated with all manner of animated sea creatures and mer-people and odd monuments in places Jim had never heard of nor seen before.

"Wait here, darlin's," MacGuffy said with a leer. "The captain'll be with ye shortly." With that, MacGuffy and all of the crew but the black-bearded pirate and another - who must have been Chinese, Jim guessed, with a mustache that sprouted from each side of his upper lip like long vines of black hair - left the cabin.

It was awfully quiet in the cabin and the only sounds Jim heard were the faint hissing of the lamp and the soft lapping of water against the creaking ship.

"What do you think the captain'll look like?" Paul asked.

"Probably huge with a beard as long as I am tall and a necklace made out of human skulls!" Peter quailed.

"I saw a picture of a pirate captain once," George said, his face as pale as the man on the moon's. "He had a sword the size of a windmill blade and one of his hands must have been chopped off because he had a hook in place of it ... a hook!"

"Maybe the pirate captain is a she!" Lacey stomped her foot defiantly, but the fear in her eyes plainly told Jim she was wishing she had listened to herself instead of these stupid boys ... again. Of course the boys just stared at her incredulously, and Peter and Paul said something about that being the most ridiculous thing they had ever heard.

"This is serious!" Jim cried. "Besides, there are no such things as woman pirates!"

"On that point, young sir, you are mistaken," a low voice said behind them and the children nearly jumped out of their jackets in surprise. Jim whirled around to find the speaker and icy tendrils of fear crawled over his entire body. The pirate standing before them wore no eye patch, had no hook hand, nor a peg leg, and no parrot rested upon his shoulder. Instead, he wore only a charcoal great cloak, pulled up close to his chin and a black tricorn hat pulled low over his brow to mask his face in shadow. He was the one Jim had seen twice before. He was the shadow pirate.

"Welcome aboard my ship," the pirate said, and with that removed his hat.

His skin was permanently darkened by the kiss of the sun and both his hair and his eyes were as black as coal and streaked with lines of silvery gray. He was neither greatly tall nor overly short, and neither was he extremely large nor dreadfully thin. He was a man one could pass in the street and not remember after one block, but, Jim realized as he studied the pirate intently, if you took a good long look at him, his was a face you could never entirely forget: it was both calm as a breeze and violent as a hurricane in the same glance. Jim knew he wouldn't forget that face, for, with an even deeper chill, he realized he had seen it before, along with his father's and two others, hanging in a picture frame in his father's study!

"You ... you're the one I saw," Jim said. "On the streets ... but you were in the picture, the one in my father's study!"

"So, that's where that old painting went to," the pirate said more to himself than to anyone else. "I thought he would have gotten rid of that long ago." Then, just at the corner of his mouth, the pirate twitched a small breath of a smile. "Then again, he always held out hope, didn't he?"

"You knew him?" Jim now felt a rising heat in his chest burning the cold vines of fear away. "You knew my father?"

"Yes." The pirate nodded grimly. "I suppose he never mentioned me, though, did he? Never mentioned the name of Dread Steele?"

"Dread Steele?" the three Ratts exclaimed together, their eyes growing wide with wonder as Jim stood there like a statue trying to grasp the meaning of this sudden revelation. His father's greatest enemy, Dread Steele, had once been his friend, just like Count Cromier.

"The Lord of the Pirates!" George cried, and all of the fear from not a moment ago vanished from his face. "I've heard all about you. You're a legend!"

"Well, it seems you all have heard of me, but who are you?" Steele scanned the children's faces one by one, starting with Lacey. "A young lady." He leaned down and searched deep into Lacey's blue eyes with his own ink blacks. "You know, there truly are women pirates that sail the seven seas, my dear. But don't let that make you think that they're sweet or lovely like you. They're meaner than lightning and as rough as bark on a tree. Now, what's your name?"

"Lacey," Lacey said without even batting at eye. She set her little jaw and stared right back into Steele's face without a blink. "And don't think that just because I'm a girl that I'm sweet or lovely either. I'll knock the block off of any stupid boy that crosses me!"

"Trust us," the Ratts chimed in. "She will."

"I believe you," the captain said with a smile, then laughed, but it wasn't cruel or sarcastic laugh. In fact, it was one of the jolliest laughs

194

Jim had heard in a long time, like the way his father had laughed with Hudson that day on the hill that felt like so long ago.

"And you three gentlemen." The pirate captain stood tall again and crossed his arms, observing the three Ratt brothers like a dark-eyed sergeant at a military review. The Ratts immediately straightened up and snapped their shoulders back, their faces dripping with shameless idol worship. "Nearly three of a kind, I'd say. What are your names?"

The opportunity was too good to pass up. The Ratts took one look at one another and nodded. The time had finally come.

"WE ARE ... GEORGE ..."

"PETER ..."

"PAUL ..."

"THE BROTHERS RATT!"

"Thieves extraordinaire!" George threw in as they all stood together, arms outstretched with hats in hand and leaning over in a deep bow.

"Good improvisation George!" Peter exclaimed.

"We *are* thieves extraordinaire," Paul agreed happily, as though realizing how good that sounded for the first time. Lacey just shook her head in red-faced mortification.

"Yes," Captain Steele smiled and seemed to have a hard time controlling a sudden cough, covering his mouth with his hand. "Well, I am honored to be in the presence of such notoriety, for we pirates always honor those that live by the skill of their own two hands. Although it seems that you, along with some other local gangs, have been attempting to thieve from me."

"Not from you, sir," George said, and his brothers fell back into attention.

"From that old man."

"That old man is a member of my crew." The captain's face grew stern and nearly terrible for a moment. "And I consider an affront to any member of my crew, no matter how big or small, important or not, an affront to my own person and character." Fear began to creep back into the boys' faces, but no sooner had the brief storm boiled up in the captain's eyes than it blew away again and his formal politeness returned. "And what was so valuable on old MacGuffy that you thought worthy enough to scheme an entire inn full of bloodthirsty scalawags?"

"Well, sir," Paul began. "You see, he has this —"

"Don't tell him anything!" Jim interrupted. "Just keep your traps shut!" Now, all this time, while Lacey had been defiantly charming and the Ratts had practically fallen in love with the living legend before them, Jim's jaw had been tightening and his blood pumping angry red into his face. He'd been trying to put it all together, trying to fit the jagged edges of this mystery in place. But the only thought driving through his mind was that both Count Cromier and Dread Steele had been in that picture with his father, and that both of them somehow knew about his father's treasure, and so in some way, both of them had brought about his father's death.

"Ah," the captain said, turning his dark eyes on young Jim Morgan and studying him fiercely. "Taking the lead on things now are we?"

"I'm not the leader of anything," Jim snapped and glared right back, summoning up the nastiest stare he could muster.

"Those eyes," the pirate captain said quietly to Jim. "Now that I see them up close, I would know them anywhere. For they are the mirror image of your father's, James Morgan."

"Jim, he knows your name," George said. "How does he know your name?" The slightest hint of jealousy flushed the eldest Ratt's cheeks.

"Shut up!" Jim growled, failing to hold onto his rage any longer. "He knows my name because he knew my father. They were enemies a long time ago, but before that they must have been friends! And I'll bet you anything he's here because he had something to do with killing him!"

"Oh, Jim!" Lacey cried, covering her mouth with her hands.

Fast as a cobra, the captain's hand lashed out and snatched Jim up off the floor by the front of his shirt. "Never accuse me of that! NEVER!" the captain roared, his face was afire as though a match had been struck to a hidden oil well beneath his rough skin. Jim's defiant flash of anger melted into shivering fear and the other children shrunk back from the suddenly terrifying shadow pirate.

But after holding Jim under the fire of his gaze for a long moment the captain took a deep breath and set him back on the floor with a small shove. He stood up and turned his back to them all, straightened his coat, and ran a hand through his hair. When he turned to face them again, an icy calm once more covered his face.

"Never accuse a man of crime for which you have no proof, young Morgan," Steele said matter-of-factly. Jim just hung his head and refused to look up at the captain, wetness glazing over his eyes. "Even amongst Pirates it's unforgivable form. Now I on the other hand have several eye witnesses that can attest to the fact that all of you tried to steal this from my man MacGuffy." Steele pulled the amulet from inside his coat pocket, holding it up for the children to see. The round, jeweled medallion spun around on its chain, glimmering brightly in the lamplight. "The Amulet of Portunes, able to unlock any treasure a man's heart might desire." The captain stared at the medallion as though its gleam might hypnotize him. "Now what could five young children such as yourselves possibly want to unlock with this? Or need I ask, Jim Morgan?"

"I just want my box back," Jim spouted. "I just want back what's mine."

"I see," said Dread Steele, his eyes narrowing on Jim. "And I don't suppose this box would happen to have the symbol of a great pirate treasure engraved upon its lid, would it? And I also don't suppose that you count that very treasure in the lists of what is yours to be had!"

"What's he talking about, Jim?" George asked, looking back and forth between the Pirate and Jim.

"Ah, so you haven't told your friends, have you?" The Pirate smiled grimly. "That comes as little surprise to me, young Morgan."

"Haven't told us what, Jim?" Lacey looked at Jim, her bright blue eyes quivering.

Jim's mouth suddenly refused to work. He stared dumbly at his friends, his cheeks growing hot and red. Finally, he mustered a few shaky words. "I was going to tell you, honestly! I just —"

"Just chose not to?" Dread Steele interrupted. When Jim looked at the man's face, he found not the haughty, accusing smile he expected, but instead downcast eyes of the utmost disappointment – disappointment much like what had been in Jim's father's eyes on that beach not so long ago.

"Just chose not to tell them how your father knew the secret to a vast treasure?" Dread Steele continued mercilessly. "Just chose not to tell them how he had passed that secret on to you, and like the irresponsible whelp you are, lost it, and how you were using them to get it back ... all for yourself?"

"That's not true!" Jim tried to defend himself, but it was too late. He saw the blank, devastated looks in his friends' eyes.

"You lied to us?" George said, tears brimming. His brothers Peter and Paul seemed to be waiting for Jim to say something to convince them that he had planned on sharing his great treasure with them all along, but Jim had nothing to offer but regret.

"George, I'm sorry," Jim said, his own eyes stinging.

"It seems to me," Dread Steele announced, stepping between Jim and the Ratts. "That it is time for this evening end. "Murdoch," the pirate captain called for the rough-hewn sailor with the black beard. "Take the Amulet to where it will be safest. Put it in the Pirate Vault of Treasures."

Murdoch's eyes went wide with what Jim could only imagine was fear or surprise ... or both. "Yes, sir," the pirate finally stammered, taking the Amulet and immediately leaving to fulfill his duty.

"As for you." Dread Steele turned his attention back on the children. "It's obvious that your present ties are nigh already severed. Which is always the best time to make new ones. I think you three would make ideal pirates." He nodded at the Ratts, a hard smile in his eyes. But when he turned to Jim, the smile left and only the hardness remained. "You, on the other hand, have some obvious issues to work through." Then his eyes fell on Lacey. "And you my dear, really are sweeter than you'd like to admit, too sweet for pirating I'm afraid. Wang-chi, if you please, show our guests out."

The Chinese pirate snatched Jim and Lacey up by the backs of the neck and dragged them out of the cabin as the Ratts watched helplessly, George's eyes still filled with tears.

"No!" Lacey cried, tears instantly falling down her cheeks. "We have to stay together, please don't pull us apart!"

The captain grinned for a moment and Jim thought just for a second than he was going to let them go, but the grin slowly widened into a toothy, pirate smile. "Sorry friends, but this is called press ganging, not volunteering. Life is like a tide, young ones – it sweeps close to home and then far out into the great unknown again with little care for that which is caught in its pull. Time to say goodbye!" With a sweep of his arm, the captain shoved the Ratts back into the cabin and slammed the door behind him, locking it with a key as he followed Wang-chi out of the cabin.

"Please! Please don't do this!" Lacey pleaded, sobbing, but Jim had ceased his tears, summoning up all of his newly learned courage in fierce defiance.

"You pirate scum! I'll get you for this, just you wait and see!"

"I don't think so, young Morgan," the pirate king said almost sadly as Wang-Chi deposited the kicking and struggling children on the gangplank and pushed them down toward the dock. "Not only did I know your father, but I have also had the displeasure of meeting your aunt, though I doubt she knew it was me. If you're anything like her, which I believe you are, you'll have forgotten all about your supposed friends by tomorrow, and be back to worrying about the only person you truly care about - which is you. Goodbye, Jim Morgan."

As soon as Jim and Lacey's feet had touched dry ground, the pirates hoisted up the gangplank, trapping the Ratts on board and Jim and Lacey on the docks.

Lacey put her hands over her face, crying miserably. When Jim tried to put a comforting hand upon her shoulder she jerked away, refusing even to look at him. Jim felt cold despair wrap its fingers around his heart and just for a moment, thought of surrendering to it and giving up while he at least still possessed his life.

But as Jim stared into the dark, where Dread Steele stood on his deck, a salty wind blew in from the ocean, tugging at Jim's curly hair and kindling the embers of a long cold fire within his chest.

"This isn't over yet," Jim cried, balling up his hands into fists. "If you knew my father then you should know this is not over by a long shot!" With that, he pulled Lacey by the arm and stormed over the snow-covered cobblestones back into the heart of London.

"Where are we going?" Lacey finally asked.

"The last place I ever thought I'd willingly go," Jim replied, eyes straight ahead. "We're going to see the King of Thieves."

From the deck of the sloop, Captain Steele watched as the little boy and girl made their way in the cold. Around Steele gathered his crew: Mufalme, Wang-chi, Mister Gilly, and all the rest of the rugged men save for Murdoch, who had left on his errand to the Vault of Treasures. Even Cornelius Darkfeather sailed down on his black wings from the topmast, landing neatly upon the captain's shoulder.

"So," Wang-chi said, "that's Lindsay Morgan's son?"

"Yes," the captain said, and a disquieted murmur rose up among the tough sailors.

"Then why have we let him go?" Mulfalme rumbled. "Is he not the one you seek? Does he not hold the secret to that which Lindsay Morgan took?"

"Perhaps he is and perhaps he does. But first I must see whether he truly is his father's son ... or if he is too far gone. Cornelius!" the captain said, and the raven perked his up his head and hopped down onto the railing of the sloop's deck, looking up at the captain.

"Follow them," he ordered. "Report back to me all you see and hear."

"Sir," Cornelius coughed politely, "wouldn't it be best if we just told the boy -"

"Do as I say, bird," the captain growled, and with a shrill caw the raven took off into the air, following the small pair of footprints in the snow.

TWENTY–SIX

THE CONSTABLE'S PLAN

Right about the same time that Jim and Lacey were making their way toward the raucous court of the King of Thieves, Constable Butterstreet sat at the desk in his office, kept warm by the stove and wondering what his life might have been like had he'd become a gardener instead of a King's Man. But just as he pondered turning in his badge for a spade, Deputy Thomas barreled into the office, shivering cold with what looked like an icicle dangling from the tip of his nose.

"S-s-sir!" Thomas reported, then tried to click his heels together sharply. But the poor man shivered so badly that his heels just kept right on clicking like something akin to a jig.

"Thomas!" Butterstreet said, trying not to laugh at his deputy's ridiculous state. "What have you done with yourself, man?"

"W-w-well," Thomas stammered. "I-I was going back and forth betwixt watchin' the docks and watchin' for the children, then, whilst I was at the docks, the children showed up. Specifically, it was the Ratts and their pal, Jim Morgan, sir."

"The Ratts and Jim Morgan? At the docks?"

"Y-y-yes, sir! Hung about all day lookin' like they was runnin' a scam on some pirates!"

"Pirates?" Butterstreet stood. "What in blazes are they thinking running about with that sort? They could be in for more trouble than they realize!" Now, Butterstreet would never have admitted this to anyone, but the truth was he was actually somewhat fond of the pick-pockets he chased day in and day out, especially the Ratts. It wasn't that he approved of what they did (he still wanted to see them in school robes and singing in the church choir) but he had developed a rather soft spot for them, oftentimes remembering his own rascally deeds as a boy growing up in London.

"T-t-they may already be, sir!"

"What's happened, man? Spit it out!"

"S-s-o they was goin' after this particular pirate's medallion, and even though he out-tricked them more than once, they kept after it like it was the most important necklace in the kingdom. But that's when they got caught, s-s-sir."

"They were caught by the pirates?" Butterstreet rumbled. "Were they hurt?"

"N-n-not so much, sir. But the pirates marched 'em down to a sloop that they must be using as a base, and that's when he turned up, sir."

"He who, Thomas? Give me the details, man!"

"W-w-why, Dread Steele, sir."

"DREAD STEELE?" Butterstreet paced back and forth behind his desk now, the details of the deputy's story winding him up like a toy soldier.

"Y-y-yes, sir. I barely saw him on the deck ... a shadow of man, sir, like death himself! So, he lets Jim and the girl go, but seems he kept the Ratts aboard. But he also sent one of his men to take the medallion to this odd place not far from the docks on Farthing Street." Then the color in Deputy Thomas's cheeks paled away and his gaze grew far away. "Strangest building I ever seen, sir. That's to say sir, it seemed to me you'd never know the door to the place was even there if someone didn't show it to you. Somethin' not quite right about it ... like the city ended at the buildin's edges and a new place began, all just in its own four walls. Well, in went the man into this queer house, and then out in just a moment's time, but I assume he left the medallion there."

By then, Butterstreet was breathing like a bull ready to charge, his droopy mustache flailing in blasts from his flaring nostrils. "The pirates, the Ratts, Jim Morgan, a mystery medallion, and a haunted house? It sounds like a conspiracy as none other! Almost too much to believe, Thomas - but if what you say is even half true, this is the sort of case a man can retire on, it is!"

"W-w-what do we do sir?"

"We have to move quickly and take them all together! Now it seems to me that this medallion is at the center of it all, and if my instincts are correct, and they usually are ..."

"T-t-that they are, sir," Thomas agreed hastily, not wanting to be left behind in a case that was busy granting early retirements and all.

"Then I suppose that odd house on Farthing'll be the spot where we can pick back up on all of them again. Call out the men, Thomas! There'll be some arrests tonight!"

"W-w-well, sir, beggin' your pardon, but we are the men, sir, after Bob quit and all," Thomas said sheepishly.

"Quite right, Thomas, quite right. Then it comes to you and me."

"A-a-and what about the Captain Cromier, sir?" Thomas asked.

Butterstreet grunted distastefully. He had almost forgotten that it was the black-haired, pale-skinned captain who had assigned him these chores in the first place. "Well, I suppose we shall have to bring him, too, as he said he wanted to deal with Steele and Morgan personally."

"Not sure I care too much for the captain, sir."

"Me neither, Thomas, but you have your orders like I have mine and tonight we'll catch Jim Morgan, the thieving Ratts, Dread Steele, and his entire crew all in one swoop. It'll be a night the city of London will never forget!"

TWENTY–SEVEN

JIM MORGAN AND THE KING OF THIEVES

Jim led Lacey by the arm through the cold, empty streets of London in silence. Every once in a while he heard Lacey sniffle or choke back a sob, but other than that she said nothing. Jim shed no tears himself, but that familiar knot in his throat that plagued him whenever he thought of his father had returned.

Only a few hours ago, he had been so close to possessing the amulet, and with that, a step nearer to retrieving his box. But instead of gaining any ground whatsoever, Jim had lost everything he'd gained thus far. He was sure Dread Steele had played a part in his father's death, no matter what the pirate pretended to feel at the accusation. George, Peter, and Paul were now prisoners on that filthy sloop, and worse still, Jim thought, it was he, not Dread Steel who had most hurt his friends. Why hadn't he just told them his secret? Did so much of his old self still remain that he would fear to share this one secret from those who cared most for him? No matter how Jim tried to focus on what must be done to right all those wrongs, he could not forget the pained look on George's face.

Well, Jim thought, his free hand still bunched into a mean fist. This just couldn't stand. Jim had one card to play, and he was going to play it to win. But as he and Lacey neared the dark hole of the drain that led to King of Thieves' hidden court, Jim found the first dangerous hurdle he would have to clear. This particular hurdle had a bright red hair and a crew of tough lunks at his command.

The Dragons guarded the drain as though they'd been expecting trouble, and when Big Red saw Jim and Lacey approach, an ugly leer spread across his freckled face. "Well, well, if it ain't his lordship, Jimmy Morgan. Been havin' a late night cup o' tea with the King of England?" Big Red's face twisted up with so much wicked glee one would have thought that Christmas had come twice that year.

"Tea with the king! Great one Red!"

"Spot o' tea! Spot on is what that is, spot on!"

"His lordship, Jimmy Morgan? Brilliant, Red, brilliant!" Red's yes men laughed a little too hard at what Red hadn't exactly meant as a one-liner until he snapped his fingers and they immediately shut up.

"So," Red said, puffing out his chest and stepping up to Jim with that nasty smile still on his face - a smile that Jim knew meant nothing but trouble for him and Lacey. "Where's the rest of your lot? Did the mouse brothers get caught 'n a trap?"

"Just let us pass, Red," Jim said, but Lacey stifled another sob.

"They did get caught!" Red nearly whooped, and if it were possible his horrible smile grew even wider and his lunks laughed aloud, joining in the ridicule.

"Shut up, Red!" Jim spouted. "You're a right poltroon, you know that? But even worse, you don't have a clue what's going on, do you?

The King of Thieves is lying to you. He doesn't care about you, he's just trying to get this special amulet all for himself!"

The other Dragons kept right on laughing in Jim's face, except for Red. His cheeks grew crimson with fury and the smile burned right off his face. "You're the liar! The Dragons are the king's favorites and of all the Dragons he likes me best! I'm his right-hand man, he told me so hisself!"

"You're wrong, Red." Jim held his ground, trying his best to keep his hands from shaking. One way or the other, he had to get into the King's court, whether by Red – or through him. "He doesn't give two bits about you."

Well, that was it for Big Red. His ears lit up bright pink, and with a howl he drew back his big fist. Jim clenched his teeth, throwing his chest out and his shoulders back. It's a strange thing about boys: Sometimes they don't think about ducking or moving or even punching back. The manliest thing to do in Jim's mind at that moment was to take that punch right on the jaw and show Red that it didn't hurt one bit. Fortunately for Jim, Lacey had no such issues with pride.

Just as Red stepped in to launch his strike a small fist sped past Jim's shoulder and planted itself square on Red's nose. Much to Jim's surprise, instead of finding himself on the snowy seat of his pants, he found Big Red in a heap on his rump in the midst of his gang, holding his nose, tears starting, and eyes wide in shocked surprise.

"Really, Jim," Lacey said, wiping the tears from her cheeks with one hand and holding up a defensive fist with the other. "Sometimes you just have to do something, you know? I'll never understand boys, really! Now, who else wants some?" she challenged.

The other Dragons looked at Red, nose dripping blood, and then up to Lacey, blue eyes flashing behind her fists.

"After you," the first lunk said, stepping aside and motioned toward the hole with outstretched hands.

"Thank you," replied Lacey, and with that she ducked down and crawled into the drain. Jim looked up at Red's lunks, who were staring at him with completely confused expressions, and shrugged. "Girls, right?" he said with a smile, then followed Lacey down the drain.

"She, she hit me!" said Red nasally, holding his face.

"She sure did, Red!"

"Right on the nose!"

"You took that one like a champ, you did! Right in the face! Bravo, Bravo -"

"Shut up!" Red raged at the Dragons and clambered to his feet. With no other idea what to do, he followed Jim and Lacey through the drain himself, into the court of the King of Thieves.

The clans packed the court from wall to wall, just as they had the first time Jim had come. Once again the packs of wild children hung from the abandoned church's gargoyles and sat dangle-legged in the old warehouse's broken-out windows. The clothes on their dirty bodies were as mismatched and threadbare as before, and their faces and hands as sooty and filthy as Jim and Lacey's, kept warm by stolen scarves and mittens.

The King of Thieves, on the other hand, was dressed as sharp as a tack in his fitted jacket and his satin hat. A greasy smile stretched across his pale white face and his spindly fingers tapped together delightedly as the court echoed with the sound of shuffling feet and clinking gold of another session of share and share alike. Wyzcark sulked unhappily in the shadows, his patience for the long-awaited delivery of the Amulet of Portunes lost.

"Excellent! Excellent, my friends!" the king called out over the cacophony. "Rarely have I seen such a marvelous collection of charms, trinkets, coins, and jewels. Well done, well done, indeed." He patted the heads and shoulders of the last few thieves as they dropped off their contributions. "Soon, oh so soon, we will have enough. Enough to make our dreams come true. We won't be cold. We won't go hungry. We won't be chased and harangued and bothered and bustled. We'll find a place that's summer all year long and filled with fields of trees from which we'll pick our food and beneath which we'll sleep our days away!"

The children unleashed a mighty hurrah, clapping and cheering with all their might. Jim clenched his teeth and balled his hands into fists as he watched the smiling liar soak up the clans' adoration.

Jim remembered the first time he came to the King's court, how afraid he'd been. The King of Thieves had challenged Jim for the ownership of the box, and at that time, Jim had wanted no part in any of it. But just then, a bit of that wild boy that had waged imaginary wars on the beach outside the Manor by the sea came back to life inside Jim Morgan. One corner of his mouth curved into a rogue's grin and Jim readied himself to finally answer the King of Thieves with a challenge of his own.

"Now, if there is no other business for the evening," the king said as always. But this time, it was Jim Morgan's voice that interrupted.

"Actually, I think you and I still have some business, King!" Jim shouted, with Lacey, the Dragons, and Red (still holding his nose) standing behind him. The court of the King of Thieves grew quiet as a church and the fake smile on the king's face twisted into a real one, but not one that was very nice at all.

"Well, well, well," the king said, his tapping, spidery fingers coming to rest against each other and crossing like clenched teeth in a crocodile's mouth. "If it isn't my good friend Jim Morgan. Where are the Ratts, I wonder?" he said with a sneer.

"They're currently indisposed," Jim said quickly. "Down by the docks ... they're guests of some pirates from the Inn of the Wet Rock. Heard of it?"

The king's sneer twitched just a little. One half of his mouth fell into a frown while his eyebrow arched into a sharp point.

The king stepped slowly toward Jim and Lacey. "I see your time with us has done little to temper your haughty spirit, Jim Morgan," he said, his silky smooth voice growing rough and cruel. The king's black eyes twinkled unkindly in the moonlight. "What were you doing down by the docks?"

"Well, we weren't wasting our time looking for treasure you're just going to toss aside, we're we?" Jim stared right back into the king's face. "We were looking for the Amulet of Portunes!"

The king's mouth dropped wide open and Jim saw his squat little friend, Wyzcark, start in surprise from his shadowy hiding place beside the wall. "How do you know about that?' the king demanded, his calm control shattered with a sudden snarl. "How do you know?" he growled again, yanking Jim up close by his coat until they were face to face.

"We broke into his office!" Lacey shouted to the clans of thieves, now leaning in with piqued interest over this little spat. "He has this book; Jim read it. It talks about a magical amulet that can unlock anything! That's what the king uses us for. He wants us to find this amulet so he can steal huge treasures for just himself and his friend!" Lacey pointed accusingly into the shadow and Wyzcark tried to lean back even farther against the wall as the children's eyes found his usual hiding spot. "He doesn't even care about us. He's not going to help you. He's not going to leave us with one cent once he has the amulet!"

The clans murmured amongst themselves, looking back and forth between the king and his defiant challengers. Some of them, especially most of the Dragons, laughed Jim and Lacey off, but more than a few of the other began eyeing the King suspiciously.

"Silence!" the king roared, and with a flick of his eyes Red's Dragons rushed out and grabbed Lacey around the arms putting a hand over her mouth. "Lies! These are all vicious lies! Who is it that always keeps you out of school? Out of the orphanages? Out of Butterstreet's claws? Don't I always leave you with your own share of what you take? Do I ever even ask what you do with it?"

"It's not a lie!" Jim shouted, turning his head to the court as best he could with a fistful of his coat in the king's grip. "I did see the book. Just like Lacey said. The amulet is real! The pirates have it, and as soon as the king gets his filthy hands on it he's going to take all the gold and ditch us like an old hat!"

The restless buzz rose in volume over the clans. Children are marvelously natural lie detectors, but the King of Thieves was such an adept liar, such an artful con, and had been doing it so well for so long, that his hold on the clans was strong. However, Jim was the boy with the magically locked box, and never before had the King turned the Dragons on another clan member to quiet her before. Some of the suspicion in the children's eyes began to turn into outright mistrust.

Jim turned back to face the furious king, whispering fiercely to him. "I've seen it with my own two eyes, King. And if you ever want to see it with yours, you'd better be willing to make a deal."

The king took a good long look into Jim's eyes, and then a slow pan around the court. The clans were starting to grumble. They were beginning to see the holes in the King's lies and one by one their eyes brightened like clever little lamps as they got the picture. The circle of thieves around the King and Jim began to tighten as the clans pressed in angrily on every side. Even the Dragons held Lacey a little less firmly and searched the king's face for any evidence of trickery. Finally the King dropped his eyes back down toward Jim Morgan's defiant face and could do nothing to stop a small grin from forming on his long face.

"This is both a surprise and not, Jim Morgan," he said quietly. "I wasn't sure when you first came to us, but now I have indeed seen that you're a born criminal. You were made for this. You really are one of us." The sticky smile spread all the way across the king's pale face. "Now what are your terms?" He added the last part darkly.

"The clans get the gold - what's here and what's at the pawnshop. All you keep is enough to bribe the pirates to let the Ratts go. Me and Lacey go free. And I get the box back."

"You ask a great deal, Jim Morgan," The King said through gritted teeth, the smile slipping off his face.

"The Amulet of Portunes is worth a great deal, isn't it?" Jim growled right back.

"So it is. So it is."

The King of Thieves stood still for a long time, and Jim watched the conniving wheels of his mind turn and turn behind his eyes. The clans had drawn even closer by then, some even shouting and pointing accusing fingers toward the King and his Dragons. But just before a riot could break out, that slippery smile stretched wide across the king's cheeks once again and he dropped Jim down, patting him on the head and standing straight and tall before the crowd of crooks.

"Boys and girls ... ladies and gentlemen," the king all but sang in his honey-dripped voice. "This is really all just a slight ... miscommunication between Jim and myself." He laughed a little, then rushed on quickly with a nervous gulp when the clans failed to laugh back. "To prove to you how much I care, and that I would never take what wasn't rightfully mine: I believe I will take a turn to share and share alike!"

The king scooped up a huge handful of gold from the pile and tossed it into the crowd of thieves, who erupted with whoops and screams, their anger overtaken by greed as they snatched the falling coins and jewelry out of the air and off the ground. "Take it all! Take everything!" The King announced, and the throng of street pickpockets poured forward to take back their shares of the treasure, laughing and cheering. Even the Dragons, save for Red and his lunks, abandoned the King then, shoving other, smaller children aside to grab fistfuls of gold and silver off the ground.

"Don't stop there!" the King encouraged them, as though they needed it. "Run as fast as you can to the pawnshop on Barque Street. Break down the door! Smash the windows! Take all you find, it's yours!"

The grubby children shrieked with delight, and in less than two minutes the shining pile of trinkets and coins was wiped clean and the courtyard stood empty of everyone save the king, Wyzcark, Red and his yes men, and, of course, Jim and Lacey.

Seeing no point to keeping her quiet any longer, Red's lunks released Lacey and she immediately stomped her feet and spouted her fury at the king. "You should be ashamed of yourself! You've lied to all of us all along. How cruel? To make a bunch of kids think you'll help them escape these crummy streets when all you really cared about was finding that stupid amulet!"

The king took the brunt of Lacey's fury with a shrug. "Well, I did give them a refund just now, didn't I?"

"I suppose so," said Jim. "But is it worth all that for one treasure?"

"For one treasure?" The king's slick smile twisted up and snapped into a snarl. "All treasure!" His eyes grew wide and his face taut as a stretched rope. "You may not believe this Jim Morgan, but I began this life much as you did. Oh yes, we are not so different you and I. I know you are a nobleman's son. It takes one to know one, as they say. And all of us born into such lives are born thieves – born believing we deserve all that we ever desire.

"But for all the wealth my family possessed, for all that was promised to me from my first breath - it would never be enough – not once I learned of the Amulet of Portunes. I discovered it in a book in my father's library when I was a boy not much older than you. It became my obsession ... once I learned what it was and what I could do with it I knew I would stop at nothing to make it mine. After my father died, I spent all his fortune unearthing clues – gathering the tools and allies I would need to take all that I deserved.

"When I have the amulet I'll be one step closer to having all that a man could ever desire. I quested for this prize my whole life and I would break a thousand more little children's hearts just like yours to have it!" By the end of his declaration the King of Thieves' face was as pale as the snow, his eyes bloodshot and red as fire. His hands were clenched so tight that Jim thought his bony knuckles might pop right through his skin.

Jim stared at the king, not quite sure whether or not the man was going to lose complete control and go mad. But, slowly, as though remembering himself and where he was, the king calmed himself, straightening his coat and hat. He took one last deep breath and fixed his slippery smile back in place. "So, Master Jim Morgan, if you please, where is the amulet?"

"Where it belongs, I guess," Jim said smartly, though not too much so, for he had just seen the monster that lurked beneath the king's smooth exterior. "The captain of the pirates told his man to put it in the Vault of Treasures."

Now it was Wyzcark's turn to pale, and suddenly he looked as if he was about to lose his dinner. "The Vault of Treasures!" he cried. "Ve're lost ... finished!" He threw up his hands and started pacing about in circles, shaking his head.

"So, it does exist," the king said, much more calm than his friend Wyzcark, the gleam in his eye returning. "How very interesting."

"Interesting?" Wyzcark was beside himself with hysteria. "Interesting, says he! It may as vell be at the bottom of the ocean. All this time, all this planning, all this investment, vasted! Oh, ve are finished, king, finished!"

"Oh, shut up!" the king snapped, fixing his gaze on Jim's defiant face. "We're not done yet."

"What's the Vault of Treasures?" Red piped up.

"The Vault of Treasures," said the king, matter-of-factly, "is a hiding place in London for pirate booty. Constructed by the first pirates to ever set foot on these lands, the Vikings, and they built into it traps and obstacles of the most lethal variety. Some say they even cursed it with pirate magic." The king smiled even as Wyzcark came close to tears. "And as time has passed, each generation of pirates has added their own twisted measures of security to its formidable stock."

"Doomed!" Wyzcark wailed.

"Well," Jim said with a shrug. "Good luck with that, and all."

"Good luck?" The king smiled even wider, that wicked gleam still lurking behind his dark eyes. "Oh yes, you'll need luck to break in and take the amulet for me."

"Me?" Jim cried. "No way! I just told you where it is, so if you'll please hand over my box and enough coin to spring my friends, I'll be out of your hair forever – as we agreed. Besides, I don't even know where in blazes this place is, I just know that's where they took the amulet!"

"Oh no, Jim." The king shook his head grimly. "We have a new deal. I will put your precious little locked box into your hand, along with a bag full of enough gold to bribe any band of scurvy-ridden pirates for ten prisoners." The King leaned in close, peering deep into Jim's face. "But only after you've put the amulet in mine."

"But you just said so yourself!" Lacey all but screamed. "It's nearly impossible ... and lethal! And Jim already told you, we don't even know how to get there!"

"Oh, don't worry, Lacey, my dear. Leave the details to me." The king stood back up and once more calmly tapped the tips of his long spider fingers together. "We're all going together, and even I will lend my own thieving expertise to ensure our mission's success."

"All of us?" Red asked timidly.

"All." The king folded his arms behind his back, and the suddenly much-relieved Wyzcark, seeing that there would be plenty of others to brave the traps of the vault before himself, swept around behind the children, cracking his own little grin.

"Come then, young ones," he snarled. "Vaste not the hours given us!"

Jim sighed and marched along as Wyzcark herded the children out of the courtyard. He had made a gamble coming here and getting the King involved. If he won, he could not only get back his box, but set his friends free as well. But if he lost ... Jim gulped hard. Well, he didn't even want to think about that.

TWENTY-EIGHT

THE SEEKER

The strange little party made up of the King of Thieves, his henchman, Jim, Lacey, and what was left of the Dragons walked out into the snowy streets.

"So what are we going to do?" Lacey pleaded with the King. "Walk around London until morning asking everyone we meet if they wouldn't mind pointing us to the Vault of Treasures? We'll freeze to death before we find it, won't we?"

"You really should quit nagging, young lady." The king stopped in the middle of an empty intersection, looking about nonchalantly. "It really is most unbecoming of a young woman."

"Oh, but if I were a boy it would be all right, wouldn't it?"

"Just be quiet please," the king said without looking at her. He was looking at Jim. "What did you think Jim? That I had been searching

217

fruitlessly for magical artifacts all this time without success? Well, that wouldn't have kept me going, now would it? My thieves have not always come back completely empty-handed."

From around his neck the King withdrew a silver chain with a silver object dangling from its links. He leaned down and showed Jim a small, forged replica of a dragonfly.

"What's that for?" Jim asked, staring at the metal bug. The detail was impossibly intricate, down to the little veins on the wings that, though silver, were translucent in the moon's light.

"This finds places we know to be there, but not the where of the there," the king whispered, staring at the dragonfly with glowing eyes. Jim watched those eyes, and came to the unmistakable conclusion that the King of Thieves was not exactly sane. "The only trick is, you must know for a fact, beyond the shadow of a doubt, that the place you seek awaits you. And since you heard the pirate speak of the Vault with your own two ears, I think it would be best if you told the seeker where to fly."

The king held out the small bug and Jim kept right on staring at it. Then he flicked his eyes to Lacey and the Dragons. Their eyes were also fixed on the magical item, but their mouths were open and their faces were white.

"Don't do it, Jim!" Lacey finally cried, but Jim knew he had no choice. He turned his eyes back to the silver seeker.

"Find the Vault of Treasures," he said, and no sooner than the breath from his lips touched the wings of the dragonfly than it burst to life with a crackle of blue light. It zipped up into the air, twittering to and fro just like a live dragonfly until it blazed off down a street to Jim's right, leaving a bright blue trail of light in its wake.

Lacey, Red, the Dragons, and even Wyzcark gasped in surprise, but the king, who was no stranger to magic and mystery, wasted no time. "Quickly!" the king commanded, pointing after the already dimming trail of blue fire floating in the air. "We must not lose the path!" With Wyzcark pushing them madly from behind, the small band of thieves rushed down the streets and alleys of London, chasing after a sparkling streak of blue lightning.

After much pattering and stomping of feet down the cobblestone streets, the small cavalcade skidded to a halt in front of perhaps the plainest, most nondescript building in the entire city. The silver dragonfly floated in a bubble of blue light before a gray brick building between a bank and tailor's. When the king approached the dragonfly its glow dimmed and it dropped neatly into his palm, only a piece of metal once more.

Jim caught his breath in the cold air and was, in spite of the grim situation, still proud to see that Red and his lunks, and the king and his tubby little friend Wyzcark, were far more out of breath than he.

"This?" Wyzcark raised his hand toward the building with a face half-perplexed and half-gasping for breath. "This is the Vault of Treasures? I vas expecting something a bit more ... piratey."

"Or maybe just a sign out front that says Pirate Treasure's Here?" the king snapped.

"Pirate treasure here! That was a good one, sir!"

"Spot on the mark if I ever heard anything spot on before."

"A sign out front! Pirate treasure hidden here? Hilarious!"

With a tired sigh, Red snapped his fingers to stop his yes men from over yessing the King. It apparently wasn't easy leading a gang of lunks, Jim imagined without the slightest bit of pity.

"So what now?" Jim asked, hands on his hips. "I suppose we could knock since we don't even have a bleeding key to this place."

"Tsk, tsk, Jim my boy," the king said, staring at the building with greedy eyes and once more tapping his long fingers together at the tips in excitement. "They don't call me the King of Thieves for nothing. As it so happens I am somewhat familiar with the legend of the Vault of Treasures. As with most pirate treasure, whether buried on a hidden island or tucked away in the dark places of the earth, the vault employs neither guards nor traditional locks to bar intruders."

"No guards or locks?" Red asked breathlessly. "Well, then what are we waiting for?"

"He said no *traditional* locks," said Lacey, rolling her eyes in exasperation.

"What kind o' locks then?" Red said, rubbing his knuckles in his palm and glaring at Lacey.

"The same kind of locks buccaneers the world over have used for centuries, Red," the King said. "Booby traps! Pirates are anything if not overly romantic, aren't they? They believe anyone with the skill to pass their barriers is worthy of the treasure they seek."

"Booby traps?" Jim suddenly got a sinking feeling of what was about to happen. "What kind of booby traps?"

"Oh, only the most deadly," the king said with a smile, as though he'd thought them up himself. "And according to the stories, there are three here, each one a unique challenge. As the ancient pirate poem that tells of this place sings:

To those children of the sea,
Who under the black flag sail,
In the Vault face trials three,
Of magic, mystery, and travail.

Ah, how I love pirate logic!" The king laughed gleefully, cruelly pointing his ever-so-dark eyes in Jim's direction. "So Jim," he said, unfurling one spidery hand in the direction of the plain building that was supposed to be the Vault of Treasures. "After you, if you please."

"This wasn't part of our deal!" Jim stomped his foot hard on the street, staring right into the black, greedy eyes of the King of Thieves.

"But it is now, Jim!" the king cried, nodding to Wyzcark. The King's squat partner in crime snatched Lacey up in one arm, unsheathing a crooked little dagger that seemed old and worn enough to have committed many a dirty deed with its sharp point.

"Just some incentive, to keep you honest and ... on point," Wyzcark said with a grin and the lunks laughed like hyenas at the pun.

"Well, Jim Morgan." The king folded his skinny arms across his chest and stalked over to Jim, speaking in nearly a whisper. "We've come a long way, haven't we? I thought you too soft when I first saw your fair face in my court. And from what I heard from the outset, I thought I was right. But now look where you are. The fate of all your friends lies in your hands. Little Lacey here, and on some pirate ship, so soon to leave the docks I'm sure, the Brothers Ratt, quailing under their new master's lashes. And let us not forget your precious box, cursed with gypsy magic, hiding the secrets you hold so dear. So much at stake, and all you have to do to fix it, is that which you've been doing for the past several months, my boy. Steal the amulet and share and share alike, and the King will make all things right for you!"

Jim looked at Lacey. He could tell she was trying to be brave, and he knew she was, but that prat, Wyzcark, held her tight and let his crooked little blade glimmer in the moonlight. Then Jim looked at Red and the Dragons. They smirked at him, beside themselves with joy at Jim's predicament. Then he looked at the king, smugly tapping his foot and waiting for Jim to do what the King knew he must.

"All right," Jim said, swallowing hard. "I'll get it for you. But you have to promise to do what you said."

"Oh, Jim." The king looked hurt. "I swear it on my honor." But Jim didn't miss that thief's twinkle in his eyes.

Jim turned toward the building, which had a very plain door right in the middle of its plain wall. He glanced back over his shoulder once more at Lacey, still struggling in Wyzcark's grasp. Then, as quickly as possible, before his courage abandoned him, Jim rushed toward the door, grabbed the handle, and stepped inside.

TWENTY–NINE

THE HALL OF KEYS

J im half-expected a booby trap just inside the door. He closed his eyes tight, bracing for spikes to shoot up from the ground or a cannon ball to drop on his head. But only silence and the cold night air greeted Jim on the other side of the door. As the door creaked shut behind him, Jim slowly opened his eyes and beheld the last thing he expected in a Pirate Vault of Treasures. A tree stood in the center of a large, open courtyard. It was no dried-up trunk with dead branches covered in icicles - as all of the other trees in the English countryside looked just now – rather, pink and white blossoms burst from every tip of every branch, as healthy and alive as if it were the middle of spring.

"That same look crossed my face when I saw this tree for the first time," a voice said, accompanied by the flapping of wings. Cornelius the raven landed in the courtyard not far from Jim, staring at the tree as well.

"You!" Jim put his hands on his hips. "I guess I should thank you for nothing so far! Fat lot of good you've done me and Lacey!"

"I told you, boy," the raven squawked defensively. "I've over-stepped my bounds once already! If you knew the story of my life you would understand why I hesitate to do so again, which is what I'm about to do."

"How?" Jim asked, skeptically folding his arms over his chest.

"By telling you what you're about to get into, and by bloody well going in myself!" The black bird fluttered up onto Jim's shoulder and pecked him once, solidly on the forehead.

"Ouch!" Jim cried. "What in blazes was that for?"

"For being a presumptuous brat when someone is trying to help you! Now, look at that tree. See anything funny about it?"

"Besides the fact that it's blooming in the middle of bloody winter?"

"This is a magic tree, Jim," Cornelius continued, ignoring Jim's sarcasm. "It blew here as a seed over the ocean from a distant shore over a thousand years ago. As the seed grew into a tree, it longed for the ocean shores that once were its home.

One day, a sailor, a true buccaneer who loved nothing more than the freedom of the ocean, was being chased across the land by a wicked king from whom he'd stolen a great treasure. When the pirate could run no more, he came to rest at the trunk of this tree and decided to simply wait for the king to catch him and seal his fate. But the tree smelled the salt on the man's skin and the ocean wind in his hair. The tree opened up the ground at the base of its roots and gave the pirate a place to hide. From that day forward all free men of the sea have used this place to hide their greatest treasures."

"That's a nice story, Cornelius, but what does that have to do with me staying alive long enough to get the Amulet?"

"Everything! You see this is a magical place, Jim – a living place; the tree's magic courses through every brick in this building. I heard the supposed King of Thieves' story, but he was only half right when he said that pirates would give their treasure to anyone with the skill. The skill is important, but this place is like any other living thing. It weighs the intentions of those who seek their way inside, and if the intentions are right, if the soul is sweet enough, it may even help you find your way."

"Help me?" Jim said. "So it will let me take the amulet?"

The bird pecked him on the forehead again.

"Ouch!"

"Are you dense?" the raven asked. "I said that was only half of it - the skill is still part of the game. The vault has many rooms that hold many treasures. But the tree will guide the hunter to the room he seeks and through obstacles that will test only that seeker. Understand?"

"I think so," Jim said, rubbing the sore spot on his head. "But will you help me, Cornelius?"

"To pass the first two, yes. As best I can," the bird nodded. "But past the third, you must go on alone, Jim Morgan. Now, are you ready?"

Jim's stomach somersaulted in his gut, but somehow he managed a nod. "Ready as I'll ever be."

"All right then, my boy." Cornelius pointed his beak toward a doorway beneath an arch at the far end of the courtyard. "There's only one way left to go, and that is onward." Jim nodded grimly and stepped forward. He passed beneath the unnatural tree, the snow of winter crunching beneath his feet and blossoms of spring dangling above his head, like some half-forgotten dream. As Jim neared the door an ancient inscription carved across the rugged green panels appeared in the soft moonlight.

Beware all ye who enter here, dangerous magic lies within.

Jim swallowed hard and drew in a slow breath of icy air, knowing in his heart that to save his friends there was no other way but forward.

"In we go," Cornelius said quietly. "And Godspeed to us both."

The green wooden door creaked open with Jim's lightest touch and he stepped through into the dark room beyond.

225

Moonbeams crisscrossed the large hall that stretched open before Jim and a rather foul smell of something old and rotten stung his nose.

"Ugh!" Jim pulled one end of his scarf over his nose. Unfortunately though, it was as threadbare as the rest of his outfit and the putrid stink burned right through. "What died in here?"

"I'd put an eight piece on it being those chaps up there," Cornelius said. Jim followed the raven's upward gaze. Whole skeletons of long-gone intruders hung like awful Halloween decorations from wicked, long spikes pointing down from the ceiling.

"Gads, Cornelius!" Jim cried. "How'd they get up there?"

"Let's hope we don't find out," Cornelius replied with a ruffle of his feathers that may have been a shiver of fear. "Look ahead and I think we'll get an idea of what we're up against, my boy."

Sure enough, at the end of the hall stood a long table, and keys of every shape and size filled it from end to end. Some were made of gold and silver, others of rock or wood, and even some - Jim gulped when he saw them, out of old, white bones. Beyond the table, a lone door carved of red-stained oak sat dully in the cobweb-draped brick wall. It had a large, bronze handle with a deep black keyhole leering out above it.

Jim stepped cautiously around the table and walked up to the door. In the blue light of the moon he made out ancient, carved letters in the face of the door. Jim swallowed hard and read the old words aloud.

Open the door, Use the key,
escape thy death with guesses three.

"Well, that's plain enough," Cornelius cawed.

"Very plain," Jim quailed. "Pick the right key in three guesses or end up a set of bones up on the ceiling there. And oh right, you only have to pick from about ten thousand keys! Very plain indeed ... plainly impossible!"

"Stop that immediately!" Cornelius snapped, pecking Jim fiercely on the side of the head. "Your father was one of the bravest men to ever sail the seas, and I doubt he'd look too kindly on his son knocking his knees together like this, even in the face of death!"

"I'm not my father!" Jim cried, his nose and throat suddenly stinging fiercely. "And I don't think he'd be surprised that I was afraid. He didn't think too much of me, you see."

"Jim," Cornelius said softly this time, and instead of pecking Jim again, patted him on the head with an outstretched wing. "I know that's not true, for reasons you may not realize, I know that's not true. And I also know that you're not your father. But you're his son, and you've come a long way all on your own. Look at everything you've managed thus far! Fear is dwelling upon all the misfortunes the world may happen upon you. Courage is knowing in your heart all the wonderful deeds you will happen upon the world!"

Jim took a deep breath, straightening his shoulders a bit. "All the deeds I will happen upon the world," he said to himself as much as to the raven.

"That's right, my boy. Your father happened quite a bit on this old earth, and something tells me you've got it in you to happen more than a little yourself. Now there must be some clue amongst the keys to tell us which one it is. So let's get to it!"

"All right then," Jim said. He shook his hands and arms loose of any clammy fear and scanned the table full of keys. "Well, we get three guesses, so I think we should try the most obvious first. This is the Vault of Treasures for pirates. Bones are a symbol of pirates. So let's try this one."

He reached out and grabbed the most frightening of all the keys on the table: the full skeletal remains of a hand, the pointer finger carved into a key. Jim almost laughed when he thought of the jokes Paul would make with this little beauty (most likely using it to pick Peter's nose, no doubt), but the thought of his friends in the hold of the pirate ship reminded Jim of why he was here and what he had to do.

"A good guess, I'd say," Cornelius nodded. "Give it a turn."

Jim moved to the door and inserted the skeleton hand key, twisting it hard to the right. A loud crack reverberated through the hall and with a wall-trembling rumble the ceiling above fell, the skeleton-littered spikes diving toward Jim and Cornelius, crunching to a halt only a few feet above their heads.

"No!" Jim cried out, covering his head, but the ceiling once more held in place - this time close enough for Jim to look into the empty eyes of the skulls that hung there. "Well, that wasn't such a good guess." He breathed hard and felt his heart slamming within his chest.

"Apparently not," Cornelius agreed. "And that answers the question of how those poor blokes wound up on the ceiling."

"Yeah, the ceiling came down to them. Let's try again," Jim said, tossing the skeleton-hand key aside with disgust. "What do you think we should try?"

"Well," Cornelius said, studying the table of keys. "While skull and cross bones are indeed the symbol of pirates, this particular place has another symbol."

"The tree! Of course, Cornelius!" Jim cried happily. "How could I be so stupid? I bet the key to this door was made from some of the tree's own wood. And look!" Jim pointed to an elegantly carved wooden key with a red and white blossom on the end.

"Yes!" Cornelius flapped his wings in excitement. "This must be it! Turn it, turn it, and let's move on!"

Jim rushed with the key and slammed it into the keyhole, jerking it hard over. Another booming crack split the silence of the hall of keys and the spiked ceiling careened toward the floor once again. Jim ducked, cowering low with his hands over his head and even Cornelius looked away in terror, but once more the ceiling came to a skidding stop just short of crushing them. When Jim stood back up, the sharp points of the spines were close enough for him to prick his finger upon them.

"Wrong again!" Jim threw the beautiful wooden key against the wall in anger. "Now we only have one guess left and I have no idea what to pick!"

"I'll tell you this, boy," Cornelius said darkly. "Some wicked pirate must have had a hand in dreaming up this trap. Two wicked hands actually, which cuts out quite a few candidates I had in mind if you ask me. Since we're about to die I might as well tell you the story of Two Hook Henry. Now there was an unfortunate chap if I ever met one."

Jim ignored the poor bird, who was doing his best to keep their spirits up on the verge of disaster, and instead, morosely traced the unhappy events that had led him to this tragic end. But when he returned to the memory of standing in his father's study while the dastardly Count Cromier gloated, he suddenly drew in a sharp breath. "Two hands," he said.

"Yes," Cornelius said drolly. "Both of them, within two seconds of each other - never seen anything like it, unless you count the time that Blind Jake lost both his eyes in a knife-throwing contest —"

"No Cornelius!" Jim shouted. "A man's heart and a man's mind and man's own *two hands* are the only keys he'll need to any door in any lands," Jim quoted the stanza that the count had read off his father's picture frame.

"What's that?" Cornelius said. "Quoting old pirate texts? I was trying to keep things light at a time like this, but if you insist on being religious about the whole thing I know some lovely psalms about dying -"

"No Cornelius, don't you get it?" Jim said. "That's the riddle! You said this place knows who you are and tests you. The count read that old pirate saying in my father's study, and then Dread Steele said almost the same thing to the Ratts. Pirates believe that they have the keys to anywhere in themselves, in their own minds and hands. I think the answer is no key at all - just opening the door with my own hand!"

Without waiting for Cornelius to respond, Jim dashed over to the door and grabbed the handle.

"Oh, dear!" Cornelius crowed. "Are you sure? I mean are you sure?"

"Know in my heart what I can happen upon the world, Cornelius," Jim said, and, closing his eyes tight and breathing one last breath, turned the handle of the door. Another loud crack snapped the silence and Cornelius squawked loudly. But this was the cracking of the old door, and it swung out before Jim with a tired creak.

"Aha!" Cornelius flapped his wings and crowed like a rooster. "Brilliant, my boy! I knew you had it in you!"

"Thank you, Cornelius," Jim said, blushing for a moment at the praise and deeply grateful to have a friend at his side (or on this case, upon his shoulder.) But there was little time for congratulations, the door was opened and the second room of the vault waited on the other side.

THIRTY

THE ORCHARD OF BRONZE

I f it were possible, the next room was drearier and darker than even the Hall of Keys. Gray, stone blocks and black mortar formed the ceilings and floor, and three rows of bronze pillars stood throughout the room like limbless trees in a metal forest. More skeletons, draped in shreds of ruined clothing clinging to the white bones, gathered in sad little clusters around the bases of each pillar like tired workers who sat down for naps and never got up again.

"Well," Jim gulped, staring at the morbid scene before him. "At least there aren't any spikes on the ceiling."

"I suppose that's a silver lining," Cornelius agreed as he flapped down beside one of the long-dead raiders of the vault. "So I wonder what got these poor fellows."

"It looks like they just sat down and died," Jim said, turning his attention to the tall, bronze spires that lined the room. "And what about these? Some are taller than others and thicker, but they're just stuck in the ground like flag poles or something."

"A clue, I'm sure there's a clue," the raven cawed, flying back up to perch on Jim's shoulder. "Let's find the door."

They wandered through the orchard of bronze poles for a few moments before finally reaching the red door on the other side. On both the right and the left of the door, immensely heavy anchors of bronze hung by rusty chains from holes in the ceiling, balanced on their points atop small, stone perches.

"Strange," Cornelius murmured in Jim's ear. "No apparent danger, large spires all over the place, a counterbalance by the door, a whole slew of dead men telling no tales … I don't like this room."

"I don't like any of this," Jim said, studying the door. As with the door in the Hall of Keys, this one, too, was marked with carved letters of a riddle.

Feet flat, eyes sharp,
No flags on the poles, no halves, only wholes,
Solve the clue in guesses two.

"What does it mean, Cornelius?" Jim asked, staring hard at the door.

"You're asking me?" the raven said, ruffling his feathers indignantly. "These are supposed to test *you!* What do *you* think it means?"

"Well," Jim said nervously. This riddle was far more difficult than the last one. "I mean, I guess there's a key for the door, and it has something to do with the poles with no flags."

Cornelius stared at Jim. Jim stared back at Cornelius. "Well, that's just brilliant," the raven said.

"All right then," Jim said, more than a little affronted. "Let's hear your idea, Mr. Genius!"

"Well, for starters, I don't think the key is a traditional one like the last time."

"What makes you say that?"

"Firstly," Cornelius folded up his wings as though he was putting hands on his hips. "We already had a clue with keys like that and I doubt the maze would repeat itself. And second ... this door doesn't have a keyhole."

Jim looked at the door handle and, sure enough, there was no slot for a key. "Oh, I see," was all he said, for he was truly stumped by this one and could tell that Cornelius was too - which made him extremely grumpy with the dark-feathered bird and his know-it-all voice. "Maybe it will open like the last one did, just by turning the handle."

"That's highly doubtful," Cornelius said. "I already said, the vault probably wouldn't repeat either a method or an answer."

"Well we should try it, just in case," Jim said crossly, reaching for the handle.

"No, Jim, wait!" Cornelius shrieked, but it was too late: Jim had already grabbed the handle and gave it a sharp turn.

The door didn't open and the room was quiet as a tomb. "See," Jim said, actually a little relieved that nothing bad happened when he turned the handle. "It was worth a try. Nothing happened."

"Ah, yes, fantastic," Cornelius sighed. "Maybe all these blokes just starved to death from nothing happening!"

"Cornelius, you're not being very -" Jim was about to scold the bird when a loud groan rumbled from behind the walls. The boy and the bird froze. Then the groaning stopped and hidden holes in the stone suddenly erupted with spouts of water.

"What manner of devilry is this?" Cornelius flapped his wings in panic. Jim looked down. The water was already frothing up to his ankles.

"Well," Jim said matter-of-factly, "I don't think they starved to death, anyway."

"Excellent observation!" the bird cried. "We need to get out of here, quickly. Think, boy, think!"

"I don't know, I don't know!" Jim cried, the panic rising in his voice. "Maybe we can use the poles to knock the weights off their perches!"

"Try it, try it!"

Jim splashed through the water that was already up to his knees and tugged at the closest pole. "It won't budge!" he said after yanking at it several times.

"Try another, another!" the raven cawed. "Clue said three, so maybe only three move!"

Jim threw himself at two more spires, but not only did they feel firmly planted in the ground, his hands quickly grew slippery in the water and slid uselessly along the metal poles.

"This isn't working!" Jim slapped the water, now bubbling up around his waist, with an angry fist.

"Well, we'd better find something that works," Cornelius fumed. "I don't know if you've noticed, but ravens aren't exactly built for swimming!"

"Well I don't know if you noticed, Cornelius, but swimming won't help either of us when the water's over our bloody heads!"

"Oh, hang it all, hang it all!" The raven flapped his wings as the water crested Jim's chest and a pile of bones floated by in the water. "In the clue, the clue! There must be something in the clue!"

Jim tried to concentrate, but the rushing roar of the water and its cold waves now tickling his neck were making things more than a little difficult. "Okay, okay! Keep my feet flat and my eyes sharp," he said aloud. "Our flags have no poles."

"A key, a key, and something to do with the poles!" Cornelius squawked and now hovered up above Jim's head.

"Yes, I know it's a key that has something to do with the poles, Cornelius!" Jim raged as the water touched his face for the first time, the terrifying thought of that water covering his mouth, his face, and his eyes suddenly becoming dreadfully real to poor Jim. Jim grabbed a thighbone of a prior victim of the flooding room floating by in the churning waters and waved it at Cornelius. "And if you interrupt my thought process again you stupid bird, I'm going to knock your head up against one of these stupid poles and put you out of my misery!" And with that Jim swung and struck the closest bronze spire with such furious force that it gonged like a crashing cymbal louder than Jim ever could have imagined.

Jim looked back at the anchors around the door. They shook from the vibration of the sound, but not enough to be unseated from their perches.

"Cornelius, that's it! How could I be so stupid?" Jim cursed himself, for, fortunately, one of the few things he'd ever paid attention to in his lessons was music. "It's all in the clue! No halves, only wholes, no flags on the poles, keep flat and sharp. These are notes, notes in the right key! The keys are musical sounds that will knock the weights down and open the door!"

"Brilliant boy! Brilliant!" Cornelius cried. "Get to it, get to it!"

Jim wasn't a very good swimmer, but he used the poles to help himself stay above the rising water. From pole to pole he splashed in the water and struck them with the bone. Finally, he struck one of the right poles and the reverberating note sent one of the weights crashing into the water.

"Yes!" Jim cried and moved on to the next pole. But the water was rising fast and there were still many poles to choose from. Jim coughed and spit as he tried a few more, but he was running out of time. Soon the water would cover all of the poles and he wouldn't be able to swing hard enough to ring the notes.

"Hurry, boy, hurry!" Cornelius said, perched atop one of the highest poles, the water moving up fast. Jim was close to the last of the poles: it was surely one of the last two in front of him. But as he reached back to strike it, the wet bone slipped from his soaked fingertips.

"No! Cornelius, the bone!" Jim splashed into the water after the bone, but the waves carried it out of his reach.

From his perch, Cornelius swooped down and seized the bone in his claws. The valiant bird flapped as hard as he could to carry the bone back to Jim. The water had almost covered the last of the two spires.

"Cornelius!" Jim gasped, choking on the water that splashed into his mouth. Cornelius tugged the big bone back to within Jim's reach, but when he set it in the water a wave from the churning tide surged up and caught the poor bird unawares, sinking him under the surface.

"Cornelius! No!" Jim howled, but he could see the bird no more under the white froth and bubbles. There was no time to search. Jim turned back to the poles. There was only time to strike one before the water covered them both. Jim closed his eyes and swung at the one on the right. The crashing tone shook through even the water and with just enough force, dislodged the final weight. The door opened.

Jim felt the pull of water like powerful hands around his waist, dragging him beneath the surface. He gasped for one last breath and down he went like a bug caught in a drain. The water flipped and turned him, dragged and spun him, knocking him about and finally spitting him out the door and tumbling him into another hallway.

Jim sat up, coughing and sputtering and spitting up the foul water. He wiped the dripping foam from his eyes and face the best he could and looked around. Bones and piles of old pirate clothes were everywhere. Then he saw him: a haggard pile of waterlogged feathers in an awful heap. Cornelius's poor legs stuck straight up in the air and his proud beak was open with his little red tongue hanging out the side.

"Cornelius!" Jim cried, hot tears mixing with the cold water already running down his cheeks. Jim crawled through the muck and the bones to the soaked bird's side and picked him up, cradling him. "Oh, Cornelius," Jim sobbed, pulling the bird's still body close to his chest.

"I'm so sorry I said you were stupid. You're not! You're brave and you're kind. I don't think I ever would have gone with someone into a place like this. Especially not if that person was me. I'm so sorry, Cornelius, I'm so sorry."

"Sorry?" a small voice croaked from Jim's chest. "Sorry for what? You saved our lives."

Jim's eyes opened wide, and when he looked down he found the bird looking back up at him with dazed eyes.

"Cornelius! You're alive!"

"Yes, yes," the raven replied, shaking the water from his feathers - and all over Jim's face. But Jim was thrilled only to know that his friend was not dead. "I suppose it will take more than a little wetness to finish off old Cornelius Darkfeather."

"Cornelius, if you hadn't gotten the bone -"

"And if you hadn't solved the puzzle!" Cornelius reminded Jim. Warmth flared up inside Jim's chest and the shivering cold from the water went away. "Well done, Jim Morgan, well done indeed."

"Only one more puzzle to go," Jim said, climbing to his feet. He picked up Cornelius and set him on his shoulder. The room in which they stood was only a hallway between two rooms, only a few meters long with drains on the floor to empty the water and small slits for windows at the tops of the walls to dry it out. At the far end was a blue door.

Jim took a deep breath and made his way up to the door. Slowly, a carved symbol grew visible in the soft moonlight – a three-tipped spear before a pearl on an open shell.

"Cornelius, look!" Jim exclaimed. "That's the symbol on my father's box. This room must have something to do with his treasure."

"And that's not all," Cornelius said grimly, pointing his beak toward two words engraved just beneath the symbol.

"*Only one.*" Jim read off the door, and he swallowed hard.

"I don't think it would know if you came in with me, would it?" Jim suggested hopefully. "I mean, you're so small and sitting on my shoulder and -"

"Remember this is a magic vault, Jim." Cornelius shook his head sadly. "Somehow the tree will know. This room is meant only for you, and you'll have to go in without me."

Jim nodded gravely. He marveled at the fact that he never really thought he would make it this far, but here he was and now he had to go on by himself. "I guess it will be all right, then," Jim said, trying to chase away the doubts and fears that suddenly clawing at his mind.

"Yes it will, my boy. You've done marvelously thus far. Just remember, it is what you will happen upon the world, not the other way around."

"Right then." Jim tried to smile, but he was sure it looked only as convincing as it felt, which was not very. Cornelius flapped up to one of the small venting windows at the top of the ceiling and perched at the edge.

"I'll check on everything outside and wait for you there, my boy," the raven said at least half-confidently. "I'm sure I won't have to wait long." He was about to fly out when Jim called to him again.

"Cornelius!" The bird turned back to listen. "At least you saw me. At least you saw me this one time." Jim tried not to let his voice tremble. "I figured things out on my own and I didn't run away. I wasn't a disappointment ... not this time, and you saw me, didn't you?"

"Yes I did, Jim Morgan," Cornelius said softly. "With my own two eyes I saw you, and were you ever a sight to see. And not for the last time, I'm sure." And with that the bird hopped out the window and soared off into the cold night air.

Jim turned back to face the door, and with a shivering, deep breath, straightened his shoulders the best he could, turned the handle, and stepped through to face the final challenge.

THIRTY–ONE

A Standoff in the Street

While Jim was barely escaping death amongst the traps and magic inside the Vault of Treasures, matters outside the little building on Farthing Street began to grow just as dangerous.

It all started with Butterstreet's faithful deputy, Thomas, who had, as his constable had ordered, stood diligent guard across the street from the suspected pirate building, his knees and teeth knocking against their opposing sets in freezing, syncopated rhythm and his poor nose running into an icky icicle that dangled off its tip. It was from there that Thomas saw a blue flash blaze down the street and come to a hovering rest in front of the building like a mad firefly – which made the poor deputy nearly swallow his half-frozen tongue.

Like some sort of broken mechanical man, Thomas ran on frozen joints and feet all the way back to the constable's office, where Butterstreet sat in his stove-heated room drifting off into warm dreams of gardening.

"S-s-ir!" Thomas cried, shivering like a reed in the wind. "I-i-i-t-t-s h-h-a-ppening!" Butterstreet nearly fell out of his chair and immediately sent word to Captain Cromier, who had stationed himself near the city garrison and who himself nearly fell out of his own chair when he got the word, and who then called up an entire platoon of marines. Together, the captain, the marines, the constable, and his deputy marched down the street to the Vault of Treasures.

This armed force, moving with great haste through the city, might have fallen on the small group of thieves waiting outside the Vault of Treasures completely unawares, but The King of Thieves, a practiced burglar nearly all his life, possessed a keen sense of danger. Whether it was a change in the cold wind, a scent on the icy air, or the slightest tremor of marching feet upon the cobblestone streets, the King recognized the threat before it ensnared him, and without so much as a word of warning to his faithful Red and his Dragons or to poor Lacey, he and Wyzcark slipped into a shadowy alley just as the marines rounded the corner. Red, the lunks, and Lacey might have been able to make a run for it, but Butterstreet and Thomas had slipped up behind them, and there was nowhere to go.

"Sorry, friends," Butterstreet said, his big beard drooping low around his face. "But it looks like it's St. Anne's for the lot of you." Butterstreet clamped manacles around the children's wrists, but he did it with such gentleness and sorrow on his voice, that Lacey felt almost compelled to tell him not to worry, that it would be all right. On the other hand, not a trace of pity, sympathy, or goodness even touched Captain Bartholomew Cromier's pale face. Instead his blue eyes flashed murderous lightning.

"Where is Jim Morgan?" he snarled at the children, his gloved hand squeezing his sword handle threateningly. Red, courageous lad that he was, gave Jim up immediately.

"He's in there!" Red jerked his head toward the vault, and his lunks jerked their heads right along with him.

"Red, you coward!" Lacey shrieked, but Red was far too terrified, wondering if there was any way that he could talk himself out of this situation - then sadly realizing he wasn't nearly smart enough for that.

"Men!" Bartholomew Cromier shouted to his marines. "Criminals against the crown lie just beyond that door. And I shall have them! Prepare to enter!" The marines lined up smartly at either side of the deathly pale captain; readying themselves to charge the little building. Bartholomew, his black ponytail flowing in the cold breeze, gritted his teeth and prepared to draw his sword and lead the attack.

But just as the young captain drew the breath order his men forward, a throaty, graveled voice called to him from down the darkened street.

"Oh ... I wouldn't do that if I were ye," the voice said. It chuckled happily as its owner stepped from the shadows and into flickering reach of the marines' torchlight. It was MacGuffy, hands behind his back, walking through the snow as though taking a stroll on a pleasant spring evening.

"This is no concern of yours, old man," Bartholomew said dangerously. "And mind your tone when you speak to a man who holds the king's commission, or you'll wish you'd never opened your ragged mouth!"

The insults only widened the toothy grin on MacGuffy's face. "Oh, well, you see this does concern me, laddie. You see, yonder building you and your pretty little boys are plannin' to raid is private property."

"This building is suspected to be the property of pirates and scum," Bartholomew said, sneering.

"That it is, son," MacGuffy agreed, his ruinous smile stretching wide and growing just as dangerous as Bartholomew's sneer.

"Perhaps you failed to notice, fool," Bartholomew finally turned to give the old man his full attention, strutting along his row of grim faced marines. "But this is an entire platoon of his majesty's marines at my back. And if you claim any ownership, love, or concern for this place," Bartholomew said, "then that would implicate you as a pirate. And it would be our duty to treat you to the justice you deserve."

"Aye ..." MacGuffy said, laughing again as though Bartholomew's threat was a joke. The torchlight glimmered in his crazed, old eyes and he held up his gnarled fingers, snapping twice. "That it would, lad. That it would." Into the light, one by one, summoned by MacGuffy's signal and smiling as madly as the old man, the sloop's pirate crew appeared, pistols and cutlasses at the ready, the Ratt brothers in tow. Cornelius Darkfeather, who had seen the marines coming down the street from the air and had warned the pirate crew, cawed in the night as black-bearded Murdoch, huge Mufalme, Wang-chi, sleepy Mister Gilly, the fat organ grinder, and all of the rest plodded up the street.

The Marines, caught quite off guard, immediately shifted their formation from the door to face the oncoming pirates. Bartholomew and MacGuffy stood all but nose-to-nose in the snowy street, each with their men at their backs. The Ratts saw Lacey and ran, unchecked by the pirates, who were now more ready for a row than anything else, over to her side. The three brothers were so worried about Lacey and Jim that they didn't even care when Butterstreet looped them into the chains that held their friend.

"Lacey!" Peter said. "We thought we'd never see you again."

"Peter, Paul, George!" Lacey cried and, if it weren't for the chains about her wrists, she would have pulled all three of them into a gigantic hug. "We thought we'd never see you again, either!"

"Where's Jim?" George asked.

"That awful King of Thieves sent him inside, even though he knew there were dangerous traps in there. That coward!" Lacey nearly burst into tears at the thought. "He's been in there for so long, I don't know what's happened to him. I don't know if he's ever coming out again."

THIRTY-TWO

THE VAULT OF TREASURES

At first, the third room was far too dark for Jim to make out anything at all. He stood still and listened for any sound of danger, but his nervous breathing and the steady drip of water from his clothes, fingers, and nose onto the cold stone beneath his feet were the only sounds. Then, without warning, torches on the walls flared to life all on their own. Jim gasped in surprise at the whooshing hiss and snapping pop that crackled with the lighting of each flame. An orange and gold glow flooded the room and Jim let out a low whistle.

The flickering firelight glimmered off shining edges and sparkling surfaces of mounds of treasure: silver vases and gold bowls packed old wooden shelves, bejeweled necklaces and suits of armor hung from great hooks, beautiful paintings leaned against piles of ancient manuscripts, and jewels the size of Jim's fist spilled from great chests and lay scattered about on the floor.

"I'm in the vault," Jim whispered aloud as though Cornelius was still perched upon his shoulders. "I'm in the vault!" He whooped loudly, his voice echoing off the walls. "This is my father's treasure," Jim said breathlessly to himself. This is what he left behind – and he was right – it is a vast treasure!" With a broad smile Jim dashed through the cavernous room, staring at the loads of rich stuff and frantically searching for the Amulet of Portunes.

There were treasure chests full of doubloons, mannequins adorned in the crowns of foreign royalty, and emblazoned shields and swords of gold and silver with bejeweled hilts lying beside reams and reams of the finest silks and cloth from the world over. Jim had been born into one of the wealthiest families in all of England and even he had never seen a horde as opulent and magnificent as this one. It truly was the greatest treasure in the world.

Jim wandered about the sparkling room for a few more moments when he finally saw it, hanging on a hook on the far wall, dangling over a table of dusty maps rolled into massive scrolls ... the Amulet of Portunes.

Jim dashed over to where the amulet hung. He'd almost been crushed and impaled and drowned for this little necklace and now it was within his grasp. Jim reached out for it, nearly touching it with his fingers, when a stab of fear ran through his mind.

"What's the third challenge?" Jim asked himself out loud. "There's supposed to be three." He looked around and as he feared, at the far side of the Vault of Treasures there was a white door with a silver handle, two torches on either side.

Jim left the amulet and made his way to the door. Like the others, a clue was chiseled into the wood, but this one was much shorter and carved more deeply and harshly than the ones before. It said: *Only that which you deserve.*

"Only that which I deserve," Jim whispered to himself. It didn't make any sense. What was the challenge? He walked back over to the amulet. He looked at the medallion for a long moment before reaching up for it as he had before. But when his fingers touched the warm metal, a buzzing whirred to life in Jim's mind. Invisible bonds seemed to hold him in place and he felt as though to touch the amulet could come at the cost of some great and terrible consequence.

"It's harder once you read the door, isn't it, James?" a voice echoed in the vault, and the surprise of it snatched the breath from Jim's lungs. With a start, he leapt from where he stood and hid behind a pile of treasure chests near the middle of the room.

"It makes you wonder, doesn't it? What do you really deserve to take from here?" the voice said again, but this time, Jim didn't miss it. There was something familiar about that voice ... more than familiar, in fact. He had known that voice from the time he was a small boy.

"Phineus?" Jim said, poking his head around the corner of the chests. He rubbed his eyes and shook his head just to be certain. But, sure as the nose on his face, standing there in the same familiar, out-of-date jacket and knickers, glasses perched on the tip of his nose beneath his enormously bushy gray brows, was Phineus, the Morgan family's old tutor. The old man stood there, slightly bent over, staring at Jim as though nothing had ever happened since the last time they were together.

"Phineus!" Jim cried, rushing from his hiding place and running toward the old tutor to throw his arms around him. Jim never thought he would actually be thrilled to see the crotchety old teacher, but his heart was doing backflips.

The moment Jim reached the place where Phineus stood, however, the old tutor was no longer there and Jim wrapped his arms around nothing and nearly plunged face first into a pile of emeralds and rubies.

Jim looked back - Phineus stood behind him now, on the other side of the room from whence Jim had just run. Jim paled and suddenly thought he understood the horrible truth. "Phineus, are you ... dead? Are you ... a ghost?" Jim asked with a trembling voice.

"Not exactly," Phineus said gruffly, adjusting his glasses as he walked over to stand beside the Amulet of Portunes. "I'm more of a memory. In your head. But here, in this place, I can move and walk and talk and think, all on my own. Had you paid attention to the basics, young master, eventually we would have gotten to magic in your studies."

"You knew about magic?" Jim asked.

"I knew a great many things, James." The Memory Phineus leaned over and stared intently at the medallion, scrutinizing it as though its worth was more than dubious. "A great deal of trouble over this little trinket, wouldn't you say?"

"More than you know," Jim said. He wanted to take a step toward Phineus, to reach out and try and touch him again, but Jim was more than a little hesitant to stand too close to the memory or ghost or whatever it was.

"Actually I do, know, James. Or should I say, Jim," Phineus replied, looking from the amulet to Jim's pale and wide-eyed face. "You see, I'm your memory, so I have access to all your other thoughts, so when I ask my question, I'll know if you tell me the truth."

"A question?" Jim asked.

"Yes, of course, the third challenge is a simple question," Phineus said. "Or perhaps not so simple. Why do you deserve this Amulet? Why do you deserve even one doubloon in this entire vault? The fruits of your father's labors."

"Why do I deserve to take it?" Jim was a slight bit confused. "Because I passed the challenges! I made it through the hall of keys and the water-filled room of bronze trees. I didn't get crushed and I didn't get drowned, and now I get to take the amulet. That's how it works, right?"

"Yes, that's *how* you would be able to come by it, Jim," Phineus said. "But you still haven't answered the question. *Why* do you deserve to have it?"

"I don't understand. I'm here. I made it past the challenges. Doesn't that mean I deserve the prize?"

"Many have stood where you now stand, I believe," Phineus said. "The treasures they sought were certainly different and varied, but their misguided hopes were all the same. So few have been able to leave with that which they sought." Phineus motioned over to the corners of the room. There, hidden from view by the piles of treasure, out of sight to anyone focused only on what gleamed in the torch-light, several more skeletons sat in motionless doom. Their white, cobweb-laced jaws hung open from their skulls in forever-frozen maws of agony.

Jim sucked in a startled gasp. "Phineus, who were they?"

"Those who did not deserve that which they tried to take," said Phineus grimly. "Now, why do you deserve this amulet, Jim? It is a talisman of vast power and opportunity. You who so many times before forsook opportunity for quick and wicked pleasures." Phineus's eyes were suddenly accusing, burning bright in the firelight and staring hard into Jim's face. "You, Jim Morgan, seek an amulet with the power to unlock deep secrets, but you have had the keys to great knowledge and privilege your whole life, and you have tossed them aside like rubbish!"

"Forsook opportunities?" Jim shook his head, but inside he knew the Memory Phineus was right. "I ... I just didn't see then. But I've learned so much now, I've changed!"

"After everything was already lost!" Phineus yelled angrily. "You never listened! You made my life a living nightmare and almost drove one of the greatest minds in England to insanity! And for what? A good laugh?"

"An' what about me?" the deep Highland voice of Hudson, Jim's father's faithful valet, boomed in the vault. Still holding the cane that was a sword in his hand, the one he had used to save Jim's life before he had died, Hudson stepped out from behind a mound of treasure. "For my whole life, I served an 'onarable man. Your father. I braved dangers you could no' even imagine. Only to die defendin' a spoilt brat who looked at me as nothin' more than a common man, meant to bend my knees 'fore any person born to a noble family. Oh, I heard those thoughts in your head, Jim Morgan." Hudson glared into Jim's face. "I heard 'em and I know what you thought of me, boy!"

"Hudson," Jim was nearly in tears now. "I'm … I'm a commoner now. I live with commoners! I don't think those things any more. You have to believe me, I'm sorry!"

"But sorries don't take back the things we've done, do they, Jim?" a final voice said, louder and more authoritative than all the rest.

Jim's heart sank into his stomach and all the feeling left his fingers and his toes as a chill ran up his spine. This was the voice he had longed to hear again since that terrible night so many months ago. But now that it was ringing in his ears, he wished he could block it out. It was the voice of his father.

"And what was that you said to me the last time you saw me?"

Jim looked up. His father wore the last set of clothes Jim ever saw him in. His head was bare and his hair was pulled back away from his face to reveal angry eyes. "What was it you said, Jim?" the memory of his father demanded, and Jim looked down at his feet.

"I said I wasn't sorry," Jim said, his throat tight and thick. Invisible smoke seemed to sting Jim's nose and eyes. "But I was … but I am," he stammered, yet he couldn't look his Memory Father in the eyes.

"Sorry doesn't change a thing, does it, Jim?" his father snarled.

"You don't deserve this treasure you seek!" Hudson growled.

"You don't deserve this treasure!" Phineus barked.

Jim risked a glance up at his Memory Father, and he could tell by the look on his father's face what his words would be.

"You don't deserve this treasure, Jim," his father said. "You don't even deserve even this one medallion. You have no idea the trials and adventures I undertook to uncover such a great treasure as the one I intended for you, Jim. Nor do you know the pains I went through to keep the secret hidden for so many years.

"For so long, you were my greatest hope. This treasure was to make it possible for you to do anything your heart desired. You have no idea what your potential was, what great deeds you were meant to accomplish. But you are not the boy I thought you would grow to be. You are my greatest disappointment, Jim." Jim almost fell over. Those words struck him like a blow to his very heart. "You don't deserve the treasure," his father said again. "You deserve to be punished."

"You deserve to waste away like my time!" Phineus railed.

"You deserve to be left behind!" Hudson shouted.

The memory people closed in around Jim, their eyes full of anger and their lips full of all of the horrible things that Jim deserved. Jim tried to close his eyes and cover his ears, but there was no escaping his memories and their accusations. Jim fell to his knees, tears streaming down his face. He tried to find an answer, but he knew it was too late for that. He would go mad like the other poor souls who tried to rob this place, and he would end up another skeleton in the corner.

Jim suddenly lamented the fact that he'd failed everyone. Cornelius would be waiting outside, but Jim would never arrive. Lacey would be hoping against hope that Jim would come with the amulet and trade it for her life, but her hopes would be dashed. And the Ratts, locked up on the pirate sloop, would be dreaming of reuniting with the rest of their clan, but they never would.

Then, almost lost amongst the cruel voices of the memory people berating Jim, a soft sound rustled in the back of Jim's mind. It was quiet at first, almost too quiet to understand. Though steadily it grew stronger until Jim knew what the sound was - a chorus of new voices, whispering over the accusing ones of his father and the rest. New memory faces suddenly appeared behind Jim's closed eyes. Cornelius was there, and Lacey and the Ratts, but unlike the memories that now surrounded Jim, these accused Jim of nothing. In fact, they were cheering him on.

"You can do it, mate," George's voice said. "You're part of our clan. You're our friend, forever."

"I saw you, Jim Morgan," Cornelius said. "I saw you be brave and tackle the terrors of the vault. I saw your courage, young man."

Then, Lacey's voice spoke to Jim. "You taught me to read, Jim Morgan. You bought me a present and you stood up for me in front the Dragons. You're my friend, Jim Morgan. And I am yours."

Then Jim remembered why he came here in the first place.

"Wait!" Jim cried, looking up at the memory people surrounding him. "You're right! I don't deserve the Amulet of Portunes. And I know for a fact I don't deserve my father's treasure. They're not mine and I don't deserve them one bit!" Jim said fiercely.

"Well then," Memory Phineus said with a haughty laugh. "You should be locked up for trying to take a treasure you don't deserve!"

"But that's where you're wrong!" Jim cried, standing defiantly. "Because that's not the treasure I came here for."

"If you didn't come for the gold or the amulet," Jim's Memory Father stared at him thoughtfully, "how do we know what treasure you really came for?"

"Because of what Phineus said," Jim replied, wiping the tears from his face. "Because of what you said. You're my memories, you know what's inside me ... in my heart. And where my heart is, there will my treasure be also. Father, your treasure was out there, on the ocean ... but mine is my friends. They're in trouble right now and they need my help. I didn't come here for the amulet, I came here for them."

The memory people stared at Jim in disbelief. From nowhere, for there were no windows in the vault room, a cold wind blew, nearly snuffing out the torches on the wall and whipping at Jim's coat and hair. The wind smelled like the salt of the ocean and a sound like the crashing of waves thundered just before the wind died. Then, one at a time, the memory people surrounding Jim vanished like smoke off a match. No sooner than they had disappeared then all the treasure in the room vanished like clouds on the back of a fast wind, the mounds of jewels, the armor, the chests of doubloons – all of it faded into nothing, leaving only the Amulet hanging on the wall.

Jim's Father was the last to go. He stood there, hands behind his back, much as he had on the beach outside Morgan Manor so long ago. But there was a new look on his face now. "Well done," Jim's father said. "Well done indeed, my son." And as the memory version of Jim's father evaporated before him, Jim thought he saw the faintest trace of a smile cross his lips.

"Wait! Father don't go!" Jim cried out. He tried to grasp the wispy remnants of the memory before they faded. But they were like the fog in his hands. "Don't leave me!" Jim shouted again, but this time only his echo replied.

THIRTY-THREE

THE BATTLE

ven as Jim took the amulet down from the hook on the wall in the now empty vault, the faint smile on his Memory Father's face remained etched in his mind. Had he even seen it at all? Had it truly been there, or did it even matter since it wasn't his real father anyway, but only a walking, talking memory used by the vault to test him? All of these questions whipped around in Jim's thoughts as he opened the white door at the end of the room and felt the cold night air bite the tip of his nose.

Snow crunched beneath the soles of Jim's shoes, and he looked up to find that he was right back in the courtyard of the tree again. The white door was now the green one through which he'd first come. Jim observed the tree, its blossoms now closed in the moonlight, and he wondered if it was possible that he'd dreamed the entire episode up. But the amulet's chain was cold in his hand, and the memory of his father still stung him real enough. He padded through the snow around the tree and noticed his own pair of old footprints moving around the other side, and he couldn't help but marvel at what a tremendous adventure he'd been having since he'd run from his house those many months ago.

Jim came to the door at the front of the courtyard and pushed it open, half-expecting the Red and the lunks to jump him as soon as he stepped into the street, take the amulet by force, and leave him and Lacey to find a way to free the Ratts on their own.

But much to Jim's surprise, when the door opened to reveal the street before him, he found the Dragons in chains, along with Lacey. In fact, so were the Ratts! Jim scrunched his eyebrows in surprise, taking in the entire scene before him.

All the thieves, including his lost friends the Ratts and Lacey, were indeed in chains with manacles about their wrists, Constable Butterstreet and his deputy standing watch over the unruly lot. But not one of them noticed Jim in the least. Their eyes were locked on the street, and only when Jim followed their gazes did understand just how sticky the entire situation had become.

Royal marines stood face to face against a slew of mangy pirates, swords and pistols and bayonets glimmering in the light of the torches. At the head of the pirates stood the gold-toothed salt, MacGuffy. The old buccaneer's toothy smile was enough to give Jim a start, but it was the sight of the marine commander that turned Jim's blood to ice and scattered even all the thoughts of his memory father and the magical amulet in his hand. In the light of the torches, his pale hand gripping his sword, stood the black-haired captain, Bartholomew Cromier, the man who had once tried to kill Jim in his father's study.

The pale captain and the old salt stood eyeing each other in the street, their armed men itching for battle at their backs. The marines firmly held their ground, but their fair faces hardly matched the cocked smiles and crazed eyes of the wild pirate bunch across from them, yearning for a fight.

Jim watched all of this like a spectator at a boxing match until a raspy voice called attention to his presence.

"Well, well, Jim Morgan," the King of Thieves muttered as he slunk out of a nearby shadow. "You had it in you after all ... well done, my boy, well done indeed. But it seems we find ourselves in a rather precarious predicament." No sooner than the King of Thieves said this than every party involved in the fierce standoff noticed Jim's arrival, and nearly a hundred heads turned at once to find him there, and nearly two hundred eyes lit up with the glow of recognition.

Jim swallowed hard and suddenly felt as hot as he had just felt cold. Little beads of sweat popped up along his forehead as he stared out at the hostile crowd now glaring at him and the shiny object in his hand.

"Jim Morgan!" Captain Bartholomew Cromier set his icy cold sights on the boy, a sort of madness glittering in his blue eyes and glinting off the teeth of his wolfish growl. "You've caused me quite a bit of trouble since the last time we met."

"Not nearly as much as you've caused me, you murderer!" Jim's fingers and toes crackled with electricity and an angry heat blazed up from his chest, flushing his face a fierce red.

The captain stared at Jim, his cheeks still as pale as the winter weather. Then he smiled and turned to MacGuffy. "I'll tell you what, sir." The captain put on the airs of a merciful noble. "I'll do you a favor in exchange for a small token. You let me take the boy, to punish him for crimes against the crown, and I'll leave your special little place alone for the time being, which I'm sure will be plenty enough for your quick hands and feet to empty of all its plunder."

MacGuffy chuckled and his men laughed and chortled right along with him. "Well, that's migh'y generous of ye, my liege." MacGuffy arched his eyebrow high, staring fearlessly into the young captain's eyes. "But as ye said earlier, we be pirates. And as a general rule, pirates don' care too much to see anyone punished for crimes against the crown ... sir. An' it seems to me that the boy here is accusin' ye of some crimes of your very own ... and I find that more than a teensy curious, eh?"

Bartholomew bristled and, for the first time - even from where Jim stood by the door of the vault - the slightest tint of color heated the young captain's white cheeks. "I'm giving you a chance to walk away with your life, old man. What do you care for the boy? He's a liar and a thief. Keep your treasure, keep your lives, keep your tongue in your mouth, and walk away."

"I'm no liar!" Jim raged from where he stood. He no longer cared that there was nowhere to run or nowhere to hide. All he felt was his anger, and all he could voice was his outrage. "I saw you with my own eyes! You killed Hudson and you helped kill my father!"

Now this got the pirate's attention, and MacGuffy's teasing smile twitched with a bit more madness than glee. "It may come as a surprise to ye, captain," MacGuffy said lowly, so low that Jim could barely hear. "But we are more than a bit familiar with the boy's father. Lindsay Morgan was his name."

Bartholomew Cromier smiled a cruelly and leaned in close to the pirate, speaking as low as MacGuffy. "Yes, Lindsay Morgan, scourge of the Pirate Seas. Yes, I killed him and his man ... and you can thank me later."

"ARRGGHH!" MacGuffy suddenly cried as he whipped his old cutlass from his bandolier with blinding speed. Bartholomew Cromier, who claimed to be the best swordsman in the king's navy, barely evaded the blow, quickly brandishing his own blade in defense. "Undeserving murderer!" MacGuffy snarled and then called back to his men. "He admits to it! He killed Morgan!"

"ARRGGHH!" the gang of pirates cried into the night, and both they and the marines across from them readied their weapons for battle.

"What will you do, old man?" Bartholomew challenged. "You're without your leader and only this handful of men at your back. This entire city is full of garrisons of the king's men, guards, and soldiers! They are at my command! If he has any sense, your own captain has undoubtedly unanchored whatever ship he's hiding on and fled out to sea! Dread Steele, indeed. If he were here, that coward would have at least had the good sense to take my deal and give me the boy!"

"Would he now?" MacGuffy smiled again. "Why don't we ask him?" With three quick tugs of his free hand, MacGuffy pulled away a wig, a false beard, and a fake nose from his face. He straightened his back and loosened his shoulders, spitting a set of false teeth from his mouth.

Jim, the Ratts, and Lacey dropped their jaws nearly to the snowy ground at their feet. "Dread Steele!" they cried together.

Bartholomew Cromier's prideful sneer fell, and he took two steps back from the now dark-haired pirate captain that stood confidently before him. "The boy will go free," Steele proclaimed. "And you will pay for your crime! Have at you!"

The battle commenced. The pirates charged the marines and Steele and Cromier clashed together as the street suddenly filled with the sounds of shouts and cries and clangs and cracks.

Jim backed up until he hit the wall of the Vault of Treasures behind him. He saw Butterstreet swoop the chained children up into his arms and throw them back against the building, keeping himself between them and the melee in the street. Jim couldn't believe his eyes. MacGuffy, the old pirate, now the famed marauder, Dread Steele, attacked Bartholomew Cromier with all of the rage that Jim himself wanted to throw at the Captain. Steele seemed as crazed for justice as Jim was, and Jim thought back with confusion on the fury that had gripped the pirate when Jim had accused him of having a hand in his father's death. Why would Lindsay Morgan's oldest adversary fight so hard to avenge him?

Jim had little time to ponder this mystery, however, for as swords and clubs and muskets and bayonets clashed before him, he felt the King of Thieves and Wyzcark creeping nearly on top of him from the shadows of the wall.

Jim leapt back away from the two master criminals, lifting the amulet high above his head by its chain. "Back off, or I'll smash it on the ground! I swear I will!"

The King of Thieves and Wyzcark stopped dead in their tracks, and the king put up his hands as though deeply offended. "Why Jim, I'm disappointed! I would never steal something that has already been agreed upon between two thieves."

"You're a liar!" Jim leveled his finger at the King, pulling the amulet back just a bit farther over his shoulder.

"A liar?" The King formed the most believable hurt look on his face. "On the contrary, Jim Morgan. I am a man of my word. I made a deal with you, and I always keep my promises." The King reached behind his back and, from seemingly nowhere, produced Jim's box, still locked tight by gypsy magic. He held it up on the tips of his long, spindly fingers like a gift presented to a lord.

Jim's eyes lit upon the box and, without thinking, the hand that held the amulet dropped just a little.

"You see, Jim," the King said, his eyes glittering in the moonlight as they coveted the amulet in Jim's hand. "This is business. You did something for me, now I'll do something for you. Don't think me a fool Jim, for I don't take you for one. This box is the key back to the life you were born to, isn't it? A key back to the life you deserve."

Jim stared at the box. He couldn't take his eyes off it. As much as he hated to admit it, the king was right. It was all right there, Hudson had said so, so many nights ago. Even though the treasure in the Vault was gone, the box was all that Jim had left and perhaps his only means back to his old world of ease and comfort, of servants and clothes and riding lessons and harpsichord playing, of anything his heart desired.

"And Jim, for all the danger that you've faced on my behalf, for all the hardships you've suffered these past few months, I'll make a new deal with you. Use the amulet, Jim. Unlock this box. Take back what rightfully is yours. Then we can find new treasures together – as many and as much as we could possibly imagine! Believe me boy, I have never offered to share such power so wholly and completely as I offer to share it with you."

"Don't listen to him, Jim!" Lacey cried out, but Jim was deaf and blind to all else but the King of Thieves and the cursed box. Jim lowered the amulet even farther, his shoulders slack and his eyes fixed on his box.

"We could be kings, Jim Morgan." The king drew closer and closer to Jim, his voice low and comforting but his gleaming eyes fixed steadily on the amulet in Jim's hand. "Not false kings of thieves and gangs. Not rulers of hungry, dirty streets. We could be true kings. Rulers of lands and men we have never even seen or known before. Join me and leave the others behind. The box is yours. Untold treasures can be ours! I'll be like a father to you ... and you can be like a son to me. Unlock the box and take the first steps back to where you truly belong."

Jim's hand raised again - this time not above him, but before him. He raised the amulet to his eye level, between him and the box. A faint glow emanated from the center of the amulet. The glow reflected in both Jim's eyes and the King of Thieves'.

"Jim!" George called, but Jim was deaf to their words.

"That's it, Jim," the king coaxed. "Time to live up to your potential. Just wish with your heart, speak the name of the amulet, and the life you deserve will be yours again."

The glow around the amulet became a bright flame of green light. It flashed in the dark shadow of the night and lit the white snow at their feet with glimmering sparkles. Jim knew what he wanted, most of all in the bottom of his heart. He envisioned his life, where he would be, and with whom. He pictured it, all the way to his dying day, and he knew what he had to do. The amulet's light was almost blinding now, and the king and Wyzcark had to squint against the green blaze.

Jim held the amulet high and his lips moved as though under another's control. "I wish to unlock that which is held fast. I wish to unlock the desire of my heart ... my treasure ..."

"Yes Jim!" the king cried. "Do it!"

Then something happened the king did not see coming. Jim whirled on his heel and thrust the amulet toward his chained friends. "PORTUNES!" Jim cried with all his might, and the chains about the wrists of the Ratts, Lacey, and even Red and the Dragons disappeared in a flare of green light.

"No!" the king cried, for Jim now hurled the amulet through the air to dash it against the cobblestone street. The King forgot all else and stretched out for the Amulet with his spidery fingers. But it was too late – the medallion crashed into the stony street and broke apart, shattering to pieces in a blazing, green explosion.

Down on his knees clutching at the broken shards of the amulet, the King raged and howled and cursed. Jim feared what the King would now do, as madness fully gripped him. But as the King breathed murder towards Jim, the escaped green fire that flowed from the ruined talisman climbed up the King's spidery fingers, snaking it's way up his long, skinny arms.

"Foolish boy!" the king rasped, his face shaking with fear as he tried to swipe away the green light that now so quickly enveloped him. "Look what you've done! It could have been so easy. The treasure was in our grasp – it could have been ours – it could have been ..." The King never finished those words. The green magic consumed his entire body and in a final brilliant flash and puff of green smoke, the King of Thieves disappeared into nothingness.

"Look at vat you've done!" Wyzcark leapt out from where he was hiding, his crooked little dagger glinting in his fat hand. "You've cost us everything, Jim Morgan!" Wyzcark pulled the blade back to strike, but just then, from nowhere, Constable Butterstreet and Thomas, his deputy, jumped in between the boy and his attacker.

"You'll not be hurtin' these children on my watch, jackanape!" Butterstreet rumbled. "They're-gonna-sing-in-my-church-choir!"

The two King's Men were about to seize the fat, little thief, but Wyzcark slashed out with his knife, backing Thomas and Butterstreet away for just a split second. Then he fled like a clumsy, howling wraith into the shadows with Butterstreet and Thomas hot on his heels. More terrified shouting and screaming followed as Red and his lunks ran off in the other direction as fast as they could, without even a thanks to Jim for setting them free.

Jim stared after them as they went when he suddenly felt four pairs of arms wrap tightly around him.

"Jim!" George, Peter, and Paul and Lacey cried out in unison as they pulled their friend close.

"Didn't doubt you for a second, mate!" George said with a smile as he clapped Jim on the back.

"Right!" Paul agreed. "Not for a minute!"

"I'm sorry," were the first words out of Jim's mouth. "I'm sorry I didn't tell you about the treasure."

"Don't worry, Jim," Peter said, smiling. "You came back for us."

"And you gave up your box for us," Lacey said, and as happy as her eyes were, there were tears at their edges. "It was the only thing you had left, Jim. And now it disappeared with the King of Thieves."

"Well," Jim said, a small smile forming on his own face. "Not exactly." And from within the folds of his jacket he withdrew his small wooden box.

"Jim!" George cried, eyes wide in amazement. "I didn't even see you snatch it! It was the fastest thing I've ever seen!"

"It's all about distraction remember?" Jim's smile widened across his face. "And I did have a pretty good teacher, didn't I?"

"But now that the Amulet is destroyed ..." Lacey patted Jim's shoulder softly.

"I thought about opening it for a second, I really did," Jim said, that lump in his throat forming just for a moment as he looked at his box that may never open. "But something happens when the magic starts to work. It's like you can see inside yourself. The same thing happened to me when I was in the Vault of Treasures. I looked inside, and I saw me, and then I saw you all with me, and I knew that I couldn't see any other life without you all as a part of it."

"You're our friend forever, Jim," Peter said.

"Yes," Lacey agreed and laughed. "We all are, forever!"

Once again, the five friends clasped together in the street. It was no matter to Jim that pirates and soldiers battled beside them, or that he had just nearly escaped death in the Vault of Treasures. His only care was that he had his friends and that they had him. And that's when Jim's hand felt suddenly quite hot.

261

"Ouch!" Jim cried as the heat grew more intense and with another yelp he dropped what he was holding and grabbed his hand.

"What's wrong?" Lacey cried.

"My hand —" Jim started to say, but George interrupted him.

"Jim!" he shouted. "Your box, look!"

The moment Jim's eyes found his box, he realized why his hand had grown so hot. His box rippled with blue flame, melting the snow around it. A voice whispered in Jim's ear, a rough, dry voice that crackled at its edges. "When the chains are removed from your heart, at the time appointed by fate." Then the voice cackled merrily in a laugh until a loud crack snapped in the night and the flames engulfing the box immediately snuffed out. Then Jim's box did something he never thought he would see it do again. It opened.

THIRTY–FOUR

ESCAPE TO THE SEA

Jim fell to his hands and knees in front of the box, his mouth and eyes wide open and his heart slamming in his chest. He reached out with one trembling hand and touched the corner of the box. It was still warm, but cool enough to hold. He picked it up and looked inside. It was all there: the unread letter from his father, written on a tattered and folded scrap of parchment, and resting atop the piece of paper - his father's shell necklace.

Without knowing exactly why, Jim reached inside the box and withdrew the chain with metal shell on the end. When he touched the charm, Jim had to capture a startled gasp. The necklace was also warm to the touch, but its heat seemed far from fading, as though the metal shell hummed with its own energy.

"Jim, it's beautiful," Lacey said from over his shoulder.

"It was my father's," Jim said, his eyes fixed on the necklace. A strange idea suddenly struck Jim, and without even knowing if it would work he reached up and opened the shell and found a flawless and beautiful pearl resting within.

"I'm glad that I at least have this left of your treasure," Jim said to himself, thinking about his father.

"The treasure?" George asked, wonder filling his voice. "What happened to the rest of it?"

Jim was about to explain further, when he looked up and found a pair of icy blue eyes set within a pale face staring at him from across the battle-strewn street. Bartholomew Cromier had seen the bright blue flame that had burned around Jim's box and the beautiful pearl resting on the metal, necklace shell in Jim's hand. And from the startled spark in Bartholomew's face, Jim knew that the deadly, black-haired captain wanted even what little remained of Lord Lindsay Morgan's treasure for his own.

"Jim Morgan!" Bartholomew cried over the din of fighting soldiers and pirates. "The Treasure will be mine!" Bartholomew ran straight for Jim and for a heart-pounding moment Jim thought the black haired captain would soon finish what he started in his father's study. But as a brave man had come to Jim's aid then, so another came now. Though Jim could still hardly believe who this one was: Dread Steele.

"You'll not lay a hand on the boy or anything left to him," Steele declared, throwing himself between Jim and Bartholomew. "You've taken enough."

"I've only just begun to take from him," Bartholomew seethed. "But the boy can wait for now. I shall first take from you, Steele – starting with your life!"

Bartholomew charged Steele and, man against man, they entered a private duel. Jim couldn't tear his eyes off them. They circled each other with slicing and arching steel between them. The piercing rhythm of their twisting and turning blades echoed in the cold night air. Bartholomew Cromier was faster than Jim believed a man could be. He made Jim's old fencing instructor look like an actor playing with toy swords. But even the wicked captain was unable to solve Steele's subtle movements. The pirate lord seemed to make only half the defenses and attacks Bartholomew did, and without a doubt, it was he who was in control of the battle. Steele was hardly winded, while the younger, dark-haired captain of the royal navy grew steadily more tired.

It was almost over now, Jim thought. Steele was moving in for the final blow when the sound of stomping feet rumbled nearby.

A throaty voice cawed from above their heads. "We have a bit of a problem here!" It was Cornelius, and he flapped down from the night sky and landed smartly on Jim's shoulder. "More soldiers are on their way. Too many for us to handle!"

"Jim!" George shouted, breaking Jim out of his trance. "We have to go now. They're after you, remember?"

"We all must go! We must flee!" Cornelius screamed, not just to Jim and his friends, but to Steele and the rest of the pirates as well.

The captain looked at the bird, then at his men and the children, then finally back at the nearly defeated Captain Cromier, breathing hard but still holding his sword forward to defend himself. Bartholomew smiled, though his lips trembled. "Come on, old man! Finish me off if you've got the guts! I'm not done yet!"

But the mysterious lord of the pirates only smiled at Bartholomew Cromier. "We'll meet again, captain," Steele vowed. "And I promise I will finish what I've started then." Then Dread Steele raised his voice so that all his men could hear. "Back to the sloop! To the sea, you dogs, for your lives depend on it!"

The pirates collected the defeated soldiers' muskets and swords and backed away for the first few steps before turning into a mad sprint down the cobblestone street.

"What do we do?" Lacey cried.

"Is that a talking bird?" George stared at Cornelius in amazement, but Jim didn't answer, because he was too caught up in events unfolding around them.

"Come on! Come on!" Cornelius urged, and without really thinking about where he was going or why, Jim, along with the Ratts and

Lacey, ran right along beside the fleeing buccaneers all the way back to the docks. As they ran, Jim heard the sound of Bartholomew Cromier raging at both the men there with him and those on their way.

"Pathetic! Pathetic! You don't deserve to call yourselves marines! Now get those other men here on the double. Regroup! Regroup and prepare to give pursuit!" Bartholomew screamed. Jim heard the pounding sound of the fast-marching soldiers behind them. It was loud and thunderous and frightening. It followed them all the way to the piers at the water's edge.

When the pirates and the children reached the sloop, they rushed straight away onto the gangplank and aboard the small vessel. Captain Steele came aboard last, slicing the mooring ropes away with his sword.

"Mister Gilly, get us out of here!" Steele growled.

"Aye aye, sir," said Mister Gilly, practically yawning the answer in his sleepy voice.

Just as the sloop floated out from the edge of the pier, the platoon of soldiers, led by the enraged Captain Bartholomew Cromier, burst from the streets and onto the docks. Cromier - Jim could still see his dark hair in stark contrast to the white snow covering the streets and the buildings - formed the marines up in a firing line.

"Form up and fire!" He screamed.

Bright yellow flashes sparkled at the end of the muskets, followed by two-dozen fierce cracks and puffs of white smoke. The children and the pirates ducked for cover, but the soldier's aim had been rushed and the musket balls pelted harmlessly off the hull of the sloop. And with the flowing waters of the river rushing toward the sea, the stout sloop slipped quickly out of range of a second volley.

The action on the deck was loud, filled with the salty curses of the pirates and the sounds of their labor, but Jim strained his ears to hear Bartholomew Cromier screaming from the pier. "This isn't over! I'll see you in irons or at the bottom of the sea, Steele. And you, Jim Morgan! I'll see you dead before this is all over. And the last thing you see will be your father's secrets in my hands! That treasure will be mine! Do you hear me, Morgan? Mine!"

Jim stared at the rapidly shrinking figure on the shore and a deeper chill than the winter wind made him shiver. Yet, just then, a comforting arm wrapped around his shoulder, and then another. It was George on his one hand and Lacey on his other. Peter and Paul leaned in close as well, and together, they kept warm on the deck of the ship.

As the sloop sailed down the river toward the sea to the sound of Dread Steele's orders and his men's replies, Jim slipped away from his friends for a moment and made his way to the prow of the ship. Leaning against the guardrail, the cold air pulling against Jim's unruly hair while he watched the ripples peel away from the sides of the ship as the sloop slid through the waters, he reached inside his pocket and withdrew his little box. Taking a deep breath, Jim finally pulled out the tattered parchment of his father's letter and unfolded the note – only to stare with stunned eyes at a completely blank page.

A bloom of despair panged in Jim's chest. Had Hudson picked up the wrong piece of paper? Had he gone through all of this just to find a blank piece of paper in the end? But slowly, as moonlight lingered on the yellowed page, swirls and curves of ink wound their way into visibility before Jim's eyes and a small smile cracked open on his face.

"More magic," Jim said, shaking his head and marveling at all he had never known about his father. Then Jim finally read the last words his father ever meant for him.

My Dearest James,

If you are reading this letter, I have finally fallen to one of my many enemies after all these years. The poison began its dishonorable duty the moment it touched my lips, thus I have no time to write all that I would wish to my son. Yet I hold onto some small hope, for this is an enchanted parchment, kissed by the light of a full moon, and it will empower these few words to say more than my weakening hand is able.

I will waste no time speaking of the dangers of your Aunt and her new friends – as you will undoubtedly learn that it was they who poisoned me. They seek a great treasure gathered from the depths of the sea, James – and, if you have any of strength in your blood from me, and, even more so I hope, from your mother – then the treasure will find a way of finding you, and you will be able to keep those wicked fiends from achieving their dastardly aims, for with such a treasure there would be little end to the miseries they would inflict on their fellow man.

But even more than that, I pray also that you will take this necklace from around my neck for your own. It belonged to your mother, James, and though she died long ago, when you were but a newborn babe, it was she that taught me of the greatest treasure of all. Of that treasure, I have no fear of your Aunt or the Cromiers looting, no matter what manner of magic or evil they dare to brandish.

For this treasure may not be stolen. No map leads the way to its location nor should it ever need to be hidden or buried beneath the sand. This treasure cannot be bought or sold – it may only be given from one to another. The greatest treasure on earth is love, James Morgan. Love between brothers, between the truest of friends, love between a father and a son. – love of a family, whether born or found. If you find this treasure within you, James – then you will be wealthier and happier than any King or Lord, no matter their rank or stature.

Whatever adventure befalls you after tonight will surely not be your last, my son. So be brave and be kind, and always, always remember – my greatest treasure was ever, and ever shall be, you, my son.

Love,

Your Father, Lord Lindsay Morgan

Wiping a tear from his eye, Jim looked up from the seal beneath his father's signature to where the Ratts and Lacey huddled around a little stove on deck, laughing as Peter and Paul imitated the pirate crew around them. This was his family now, Jim knew. And he was certainly glad to have them.

Jim came back down to join his friends, just as Dread Steele gave the order for the sloop to draw up sail and moor up at a small pier near a lighthouse, where the river opened up into the sea.

"This is where we must part ways, I'm afraid," Dread Steele said, Cornelius Darkfeather flapping down to a rest on the Captain's shoulder.

"Can't we come with you?" George said, looking crestfallen.

"Not this time, Master Ratt. It will be rough sailing for me and my men for some time, I'm afraid. But fear not, I will not leave you without help. Follow the little path from this pier to the cottage at the base of the lighthouse. The real MacGuffy, the one on whom I based my most current disguise, lives there, having retired from pirating some years ago. Jim, I'm assuming that the letter from your father displays his seal?"

"It does," replied Jim. "And it's even written on magic paper."

Dread Steele smiled. "The old rascal," he said, shaking his head. "He never could do anything less than magnificently."

"Is that why you came to our house in London, Captain Steele?" Jim asked. "Is that why you helped me? I thought you and my father were enemies."

"Even a pirate knows a good man when he sees one, Jim Morgan. Even when that good man is his adversary. And you're well on your way to becoming just such a good man yourself, like your father. But don't get the wrong idea completely about me, Jim," Steele added with a sly grin. "I am a pirate after all, and there was the small matter of a certain treasure."

"Right," Jim said, smiling back. "I'm afraid it disappeared, sir," he said, only a little sad now that he thought long and hard about the unfortunate fate of all that gold and wealth that had been piled up all around him. "Vanished like smoke when I took the Amulet." But Dread Steele just widened the toothy grin that glimmered in the moonlight.

"Lost treasures tend not to stay lost for long, young Morgan, especially not when Dread Steele goes looking for them. Even though it is disappeared for now, your father's treasure is still out there, some-where. But I imagine that if we let slip a small rumor that you already handed that treasure over to us, a certain Captain and his red-haired father would probably forget all about you and focus their attention on us, wouldn't you say Cornelius?"

"I would indeed, Captain," the raven cawed happily. "In fact, I've already been concocting a rather colorful version of the story that involves a small army of skeleton warriors and talking sharks - really quite brilliant if I do say so myself. I think a certain whisper of the tale into the ears of a few of the chaps at the Inn of the Wet Rock will do the trick."

"And as for you, Jim Morgan," Steele said, placing a firm hand on Jim's shoulder. "MacGuffy will take you and your sealed letter to the proper authorities to relieve your aunt of her current position as head of your house. Which would leave you, the true Lord Morgan."

"You know," Jim said, almost as much to himself as anyone else. "I thought so long about going back home and being the Lord Morgan myself, but now that I finally get to, I'm not sure that's what I really wanted after all."

"But Jim," Lacey said softly, taking him by his arm. "What else could you possibly want?"

Jim looked back into Lacey's blue eyes but then found his gaze drifting past her, out over the ocean to the moonlit white horses on the waves. The strong smell of the ocean salt and the scent of a sea breeze caught his nose and Jim's smile widened and spread over his face. Perhaps he knew what he wanted after all.

"Just like your father," Dread Steele said quietly, looking at Jim's smiling face. "Perhaps one of these days we shall meet again, Jim. And wouldn't that be something? The Lord Morgan and Dread Steele sail-ing off on some reckless adventure together?"

"It would be something, indeed," Jim replied.

But the time finally came for pirates and the children to say their goodbyes, which included a kiss from Lacey on the top of Cornelius's feathered head, which sent the pirate crew into a fit of coarse laughing and guffawing at the stalwart Raven, who ignored it all and bowed dashingly to the young lady.

And so it was that Jim, the Ratts, and Lacey stood on the little pier, watching the sloop sail out of the river and onto the ocean waves, heading off to who knew where.

"That was some adventure, Jim Morgan," George said, putting his arm around his friend. "You know, it may have been the best decision I ever made to let you join our gang."

"You?" Peter and Paul protested, hands on their hips. "It was our idea! You said he didn't stand a chance of becoming a proper thief, George," Peter added.

"Did not!"

The Ratts set in on each other, laughing and hollering as they wrestled each other down to the ground in a pile of kicking and punching limbs.

"I guess it's finally back to ordinary for us," Lacey added, shaking her head at the Brothers Ratt. But Jim was still smiling, and the mischief that once glimmered in his little boy eyes shined in them anew.

"No," he said, turning to lead his newfound family up to the lighthouse. "I don't think we're going to have another ordinary day for the rest of our lives. And knowing that, I can't wait to see what great deeds we happen upon the world tomorrow."

THE END

CPSIA information can be obtained at www.ICGtesting.com
Printed in the USA
BVOW08s0516121113

336072BV00001B/15/P